The Human Family

The Human Family

Menschenkinder

Lou Andreas-Salomé

TRANSLATED
AND WITH AN INTRODUCTION BY
RALEIGH WHITINGER

University of Nebraska Press
Lincoln and London

Originally published as
Menschenkinder
(Stuttgart: JG Cotta'sche Buchandlung Nachfolger, 1899).
Translation and introduction
© 2005 by the
Board of Regents
of the
University of Nebraska
All rights reserved
Manufactured in the
United States of America

Library of Congress Cataloging-in-Publication Data
Andreas-Salomé, Lou, 1861–1937.
[Menschenkinder. English]
The human family / Lou Andreas-Salomé;
translated and with an introduction
by Raleigh Whitinger.
p. cm.—(European women writers series)
ISBN 13: 978-0-8032-5952-2 (cloth: alk. paper)—
ISBN 13: 978-0-8032-1071-4 (pbk.: alk. paper)
I. Whitinger, Raleigh, 1944– II. Title. III. Series.
PT2601.N4M4613 2005
833'.8—dc22
2005043719

Set in Quadraat by Bob Reitz.
Designed by R. W. Boeche.
Printed by Edwards Brothers, Inc.

Contents

INTRODUCTION

The collection *The Human Family* is the first complete translation of *Menschenkinder*, the cycle of ten novellas that Lou Andreas-Salomé (1861–1937) wrote between 1895 and 1898 and published in 1899. It is intended to further recent criticism's rediscovery of Andreas-Salomé's significance as a thinker and writer, above all with regard to her literary contribution to modern feminism and the principles of women's emancipation. It will also enhance the recognition of Andreas-Salomé's enduring skill as a storyteller whose prose works augment her nonliterary writings on women's issues by couching her critical perspectives on conventional relationships in subtly variegated form in narratives that remain compellingly readable and relevant.

Lou Salomé was born in St. Petersburg, the youngest child and only daughter of a German career diplomat stationed in that city. She grew up in the German enclave there, in a family that encouraged her in the formal and autodidactic pursuit of her studies. At seventeen she began a relationship with the Dutch theologian Hendrik Gillot—the first of what was to become a pattern of relationships with an older male mentor with whom the stimulating intellectual exchange soon brought with it problematic sexual impulses. The relationship brought the young student to the brink of a nervous breakdown and proved fundamental in her decision, at age nineteen, to study theology and philosophy at the University of Zurich—German universities did not admit women until 1902.

In 1882, when overwork jeopardized her health, she journeyed to Italy, where she entered into a second tempestuous relationship. This time the man in question was none other than Friedrich Nietzsche, whom she came to know through his close friend Paul Rée. The relationship was brief, lasting barely a year, but intense. The captivated Nietzsche was moved to propose marriage, resolved to preside over the philosophical indoctrination of his brilliant new pupil/wife. Salomé's own misgivings about such submission combined with the machinations of Rée and Nietzsche's sister to end the affair. But the relationship had a stimulating effect on the writing of both. The contact with Salomé left its mark on Nietzsche's *Also sprach Zarathustra* (1882–1886; *Thus Spoke Zarathustra*)—and not merely in that work's notoriously misogynist passages. In addition, the interaction with Nietzsche and Rée provided the basic plot for her first novel, *Im Kampf um Gott* (1885; The Struggle for God), as well as the material for *Friedrich Nietzsche in seinen Werken* (1894; Friedrich Nietzsche as Revealed in His Works), the first major study of Nietzsche: an analysis of his life, work, and illness that contemporary reviews praised as a "psychological masterpiece" (Resch 10). In Berlin in 1887, she married Friedrich Carl Andreas, an orientalist and professor of Persian eighteen years her senior. Their union remained unconsummated throughout its forty-three years, having from the outset taken the form of a chaste child-father relationship. The marriage was not without its crises. In the early 1890s Lou, infatuated with social-democrat politician Georg Lebedour, asked for a divorce but bowed to her husband's demand that she terminate the relationship. At this time, while working on her analyses of Ibsen's social dramas, she also dramatized her own marital tensions to the point of pondering a suicide pact with Andreas. The frequent recurrences of her earlier ill health were likely also a result of Andreas's affair with Marie Stephan, the couple's housekeeper since 1901, who in 1904 bore and helped raise Andreas's illegitimate daughter, Marie. Yet the unusual marriage stabilized and endured until Andreas's death in 1930, enabling Lou to balance her intense artistic and intellectual activity with a tie to the everyday, bourgeois world of the domestic household.

Around the time of her marriage Andreas-Salomé began to establish herself as a theater critic, leading to ties with the German naturalist dramatists around Gerhart Hauptmann and also to another book, *Henrik Ibsens Frauengestalten* (1892; Ibsen's Female Figures), one of the first studies to grasp the emancipatory thrust of Ibsen's social dramas and an early document of Andreas-Salomé's own position against traditional women's roles. Starting in the mid-1890s Andreas-Salomé ventured outside her marriage into relationships that were both intellectually and sexually fulfilling, first with Friedrich Pineles, a physician, and then, from 1897 to 1901, with the considerably younger Rainer Maria Rilke.

These years were also her most productive in writing fiction and theoretical essays on women's issues of the day. The novels *Ruth* in 1885 and *Ma: Ein*

Portrait of 1901 bracket the publication both of "Fenitschka." "Eine Ausschweifung": Zwei Erzählungen (1898; "Fenitschka." "A Deviation": Two Novellas) and of the Menschenkinder cycle of 1899, the latter year seeing as well the publication of her essay "Der Mensch als Weib" (The Human Being as Woman): feminist critics still debate the degree to which the last-named work's essentialist starting point detracts from its feminist position against the confinements of conventionally constructed femininity.

Andreas-Salomé continued sporadically to write theoretical works and fiction through the first decade of the twentieth century—for example, Im Zwischenland: Fünf Geschichten aus dem Seelenleben halbwüchsiger Mädchen (1902; In the Land In-Between: Five Stories from the Spiritual Life of Adolescent Girls) and Die Erotik (1910; Eroticism)—until 1911, when she decided to devote herself to the study of psychotherapy. At the age of fifty she gained permission to attend Sigmund Freud's seminars and became his longtime colleague and friend. Though a dedicated psychotherapist for the rest of her life, she nevertheless found time to write and publish again, most notably the novel Das Haus: Familiengeschichte vom Ende des vorigen Jahrhunderts (The House: A Family Story from the End of the Previous Century) in 1919 (but written around 1900), the expressionistic drama Der Teufel und seine Großmutter (The Devil and His Grandmother) in 1922, Rodinka: Russische Erinnerung (Rodinka: A Russian Memoir) in 1923, and books on Rilke (1928) and Freud (1931).

Andreas-Salomé's sequence of relationships with prominent men ensured her a fame—and often notoriety—that could never be long obscured. But recognition of her significance as a thinker and writer in her own right has emerged primarily only in the last two decades. Her theoretical writings on women's issues struck even feminists of her own day (Hedwig Dohm, for example) as "antifeminist" and "essentialist," and critics long tended to read them as evidence of her privileged remove from social realities and of her subservient relationships to male masters. It was a common critical view that she merely followed or even exploited great thinkers she had known, or that she adhered to a view of women that held conservatively to their essential—and thus, by assumption, merely subjugated and supportive—difference to men. Her works of fiction, after an initial period of approval and interest, soon fell into neglect, considered to be merely fictionalized reworkings of her own experiences expressing the ideas in her essays through hackneyed plot and dialogue.

In the 1960s the enthusiasm and detective work of such critics as Heinz F. Peters and Rudolf Binion reawakened interest in Andreas-Salomé's life, although even the titles of those landmark studies reflected a tendency to reduce her to the object either of male desire (Peters, My Sister, My Spouse: A Biography of Lou Andreas-Salomé) or of schoolmasterly deprecation (Binion, Frau Lou: Nietzsche's Wayward Disciple; see Kreide 3–9). Analyses since the late 1970s, while pleading in biographical detail for the recuperation of Andreas-Salomé as a noteworthy thinker and writer, continued to focus on her significance in the lives of famous men, either discounting her fictional writings entirely or seeing her merely as a female exponent of themes well established in the male canon.

Only since the late 1980s have critics begun to move away from a perspective dictated by masters and master narratives and toward revealing Andreas-Salomé as a writer of theoretical works and fiction that developed a critical dialogue with the conventional modes of discourse and writing (e.g., Haines; Martin; Whitinger). These more recent studies view her relation to her great male mentors, for example, less as that of a disciple and more as an interacting and constructively critical colleague. Also, they link her to the feminist movement, arguing that her innovation and emancipatory concern have been overlooked as a result both of a simplistically rigid division between the theoretical and literary components of her oeuvre and of a narrow perspective on concepts such as female difference and essence.

Recent studies on her theoretical writings such as "The Human Being as Woman" have found in that 1899 essay an underlying feminist position that aligns her with such thinkers as Georg Simmel and suggests her significance as a forerunner of recent feminists who, by taking female difference as a point of departure for constructing woman, have arbitrarily been discounted as "essentialist" or assumed to be antifeminist. Other studies have focused on her works of fiction as narrative expressions of this feminist struggle, showing her involvement with fable and fiction to reveal a position on the status and image of women that is not at all consonant with a retreat into antifeminist essentialism. This latter direction in criticism has dealt primarily with the stories "Fenitschka" and "Eine Ausschweifung"—available in translation since 1990—with relatively few analyses of works such as Das Haus, the Menschenkinder cycle, and Der Teufel und seine Großmutter. However, Brigid Haines makes a compelling case for the significance and relevance of the Menschenkinder cycle for the feminist debate as it has evolved through the twentieth century, above all in the way the stories anticipate ideas of contemporary feminist writers such as

Julia Kristeva and Hélène Cixous and prefigure "many current debates about sexual difference" (Haines 82).

The *Menschenkinder* stories both explain and refute the tendency to fault Andreas-Salomé's works as too autobiographical and thematically repetitious— charges that do not stand up to objective comparison of these works to contemporary stories and novels by such writers as Thomas Mann, Robert Musil, and Franz Kafka. As well as remaining untranslated, the cycle—in contrast to the "Fenitschka" and "Eine Ausschweifung" duology—is not easily accessible even to German readers, who must hunt down copies of the original Gothic-script edition by Cotta of Stuttgart. This situation appears to have prevented the emergence of a fair and reliable consensus about the literary quality of the work. Yet such a consensus would have to acknowledge the subtle and complex variety with which the ten stories treat the recurring theme—reminiscent of the author's own experiences but certainly not tied closely to them—of young women, as they relate to men who represent various degrees of enlightenment and tolerance, struggling to express a complete and independent feminine identity in the face of the confining but often seductive roles that convention and tradition impose upon female essence and nature. While some of the stories expose and indict the domination that can confine, pervert, and waste women's potential—for example, "Abteilung: 'Innere Männer' " ("Unit for 'Men, Internal' ")—most show their female protagonists facing the challenges and sacrifices required to escape such enclosure into an independent, albeit uncertain, future. The entire cycle combines its socially critical perspective on the conventional perception of women with realistic visions of the necessity, possibility, and costs of liberating change.

No objective reading of the "Unit for 'Men, Internal,' " "Mädchenreigen" (translated here as "Maidens' Roundelay"), and "Eine Nacht" ("One Night"), for example, could see those stories simply as "fictionalized" versions of Andreas-Salomé's own encounter with Richard Beer-Hoffmann, any more than the complex "Fenitschka" story could be said to owe anything more than the essential action of one brief, early episode to Andreas-Salomé's encounter with Frank Wedekind. Each of the recurring accounts of a young woman's relationship to a somewhat older doctor departs from the author's personal experiences, and the three vary radically in their portrayal of the male protagonists— from the corrupt and selfish Doctor Griepenkerl of "Unit for 'Men, Internal' " to the anxious young medical student, Berthold, in "One Night" to the more insightful and sympathetic doctor Alex von Vresenhof in "Maidens' Roundelay"—with similar degrees of variation in the emerging maturity and independence of the young women involved. The other seven stories add a remarkable array of further colors and shades to this palette of woman-man interactions, with intricate variations on the degree to which the oppressive and seductive powers of patriarchal tradition complicate prospects of feminine emancipation.

Particularly impressive is the variety and complexity with which the ten stories develop one of the most prominent recurring themes of Andreas-Salomé's fiction: her sympathetic but unstintingly critical exploration, usually by favoring the perspective of her male protagonists, "of masculine projections of femininity" (Martin 176–77; see also Haines 86, 87). Some of the stories do indeed proceed from within the female protagonist. "Das Paradies" ("Paradise"), for example, opens with the heroine's dream of flight above the world of conventionally proper expectations, while "Ein Todesfall" ("A Death") focuses on the female foster child and foster sister of a father-son pair of complex artists. But even these stories ultimately emphasize the degree to which conventional outlooks and male perspectives articulate and control women. In most of the stories, readers come to the central women characters mainly from outside, and usually from the perspective of the male figures who attempt to define and control them. While for some of the male figures this involves an appealing attempt at openness and understanding, the tendency is more often either to adhere or to revert to conventional images and ideals—with even the relatively positive male figures, such as Alex von Vresenhof in "Maidens' Roundelay" or Cousin Dietrich in "Paradise," tending in decisive moments to attempt a dominating and, for all its nurturing and protective impulses, patently reductive control of the obedient little "princesses" of their desires. Often—for example, with the portrayal of Vitali Saitsev in "Ein Wiedersehen" ("A Reunion")—the perspective is such as to favor the men with their views and initially appealing good intentions in order to portray in an unfavorable light their readiness to impose simplistic roles and identities on complex women.

Although undertaken in the conviction that the Menschenkinder stories have appeal and relevance for today's readers, this translation has adhered closely to the original's style of narrative and dialogue and attempted to retain those elements evocative of German-speaking Europe in the 1890s. This was done on the principle that English-speaking readers, too, should encounter the stories as documents of another time and place and in the belief that the relevance of the stories becomes all the more compelling when they are shown to develop still-unresolved problems of women-men relationships subtly and complexly in a century-old and foreign context.

Several details reflect this effort to retain the foreignness of the text. For example, most place-names, with the exception of well-known metropolises such as Vienna and Munich, have been left in their original German: thus "Stephansplatz" and "Singerstraße" in "A Reunion" rather than "St. Stephan's Plaza" and "Singer Street," or "Schwarzensee" rather than "Black Lake" in "Unterwegs" ("On Their Way"). Similarly, German forms of address have been left untranslated, figures thus referring to each other with the terms "Herr," "Frau," and "Fräulein"—again to retain the foreign flavor as well as to avoid confusing or stilted English phrasings. Likewise, the proper names of individuals have not been anglicized, with even the name Marfa (in "A Reunion") retaining its Russian sound, although other Russian names have been respelled so that their English pronunciation matches that of the original German (the original's "Marfa Matwejewna" becoming Marfa Matveyevna, for example).

Preserved too, for the most part, was the original German's relatively greater propensity for lengthy sentences of sequential comma- and semicolon-spliced independent clauses as well as its preference for a frequent and often serial use of dashes—this to retain the original's emphasis on causal connection of the events described or the poetic flow of its descriptive passages. While on several occasions semicolons have been substituted for commas in order to avoid confusing English readers, shifts from semicolons to periods were held to a minimum of cases where excessive sentence length threatened to hinder comprehension. The original's idiosyncratically frequent use of dashes seemed intended to indicate uncertainty and self-reflection on the part of narrator or character, and thus all were retained in the translation, the only alteration being the elimination, in keeping with English convention, of the original's tendency to combine commas and dashes. Finally, German's differentiation between familiar and formal forms of address on occasion required clarifying expansion, namely when conversations between figures involved shifts from the formal "Sie" to the familiar "du," signals of important changes in the relationship between figures that would have been lost by unmarked translation of both forms to "you."

The only instances in which the translation differs intentionally from the 1899 original, therefore, occur with respect to paragraphing and to the orthographic symbols with which the original marked changes of scene within each story. Above all in cases involving dialogue, the original's tendency to use paragraph breaks to introduce both the new speaker and then his or her quoted speech was abandoned in order to produce a text that was less fragmented and more in keeping with present-day English reading and publishing conventions. As for the episode breaks within the stories, the translation has marked these divisions uniformly with sequences of asterisks rather than adhering to the original's mix of asterisk sequences and dash sequences.

The effort to avoid a translation that would elide complexities and subtleties of Andreas-Salomé's original was given a further urgency by the fact that the project itself is repeatedly mirrored in many of the stories in a way that invites critical reflection on how male representatives of the prevailing culture approach the female Other. As a male academic's attempt to understand, articulate, and communicate a foreign woman's writing, the translation itself is reflected in repeatedly varied forms within the narratives by encounters of educated male professionals with complex women whom they would grasp and define. Thus itself the product of a captivated male's attempt to capture and communicate the compelling female in the context, terms, and language of his culture, the translation contains subversively ironic reflections of itself, with men similarly representative of the prevailing Western culture intent on articulating the image and ideas of the exotic women they encounter—and doing so in a way that, for all its often enthusiastic good intentions, frequently embodies or lapses into an agenda of simplification, domination, and control. Aware of this parallel, the translator was at pains to avoid embarrassing comparisons to his male counterparts in the stories—or to earlier critics whose patronizing or proprietary approach to Andreas-Salomé was all too akin to the way many of her male protagonists are inclined to define and control women. This involved avoiding the omission of details and complexities essential to the original author's subversive or critical dialogue with conventional images of women or to her ironic treatment of her male figures' approach to women. Alerted to this parallel, readers of the translation are invited to weigh the translated text against the male discourse that it contains and to ponder in doing so the degree to which the translation has retained the original's concern with the gap between conventional male narratives and the entire female text that contains and transcends them.

A general example of this struggle was the resistance to any impulse to translate only a selection of the stories and in that way to limit the translation's appeal to a narrower, specific constituency. Thus the translation, like the original, begins with "Vor dem Erwachen" ("Before the Awakening"), with a female protagonist whose enigmatic behavior disabuses readers of their realistic expectations of female characterization. A more specific example was the decision not to alter and clarify the original's potentially confusing use of male pronouns and adjectives early in " Maidens' Roundelay," when Alex von Vresenhof learns of his "rival" that "his" name is "Hans," although there is no doubt that Hans is a young woman. Other instances are evident even in the way some of the titles have been translated. The translation of the cycle's title as "Children of Man" or "Children of Mankind," for example, is appealingly close to the original and would also coincide with a bygone convention in English to refer collectively to human beings as "man" and "mankind." Yet that choice seems less than felicitous in the case of a woman writer of the 1890s who is taking issue with conventional classifications of gender roles—in such works, for example, as "The Human Being as Woman," a title for which the translation of "Mensch" as "man" or "mankind" would be misleading. Accordingly, the phrase "human family" seemed the best way to convey without gender bias the original title's sense of community.

On the other hand, the translation of the story "Mädchenreigen" as "Maidens' Roundelay" might at first glance strike as an instance where a male translator has imposed a traditionally romantic reading on a woman writer's use of a female word. The story has in fact been referred to in English both as "Circle of Girls" (Resch) and as "Dance of Girls" (Livingstone), the latter coinciding with the primary translation of "Reigen" as a round dance, a roundelay. While either of those possibilities strikes one as a safe rendition of the original, the poetic turn of "Maidens' Roundelay"—it evokes a poem by Dante Gabriel Rossetti ("Heart's Haven" in his *House of Life*)—might initially encounter objections, since it awakens expectations of intense romantic union triumphing over girlish coyness that the narrative itself does not fulfill. Yet the resulting relationship of title and text mirrors the way the story, like other works by Andreas-Salomé, awakens but disappoints expectations about feminine identity and behavior. With its unfulfilled evocation of Rossetti, the translation chosen here recalls a passage in "Fenitschka" in which the male protagonist resorts to comparisons with pre-Raphaelite paintings in his ineffectual attempts to label and define the enigmatic title figure. Thus much as the earlier story shows the male protagonist refuted in his attempts to impose the images and dichotomies of a bygone art on the female title figure—this in a manner echoed by several male protagonists in the ten stories offered here—the story "Mädchenreigen," translated as "Maidens' Roundelay," repeatedly shows conventional notions of female behavior refuted by the complex and unorthodox female protagonist.

Works Cited

Andreas-Salomé, Lou. *Die Erotik*. Frankfurt: Rütten & Löning, 1910.

———. "*Fenitschka*." "*Eine Ausschweifung*": *Zwei Erzählungen*. Stuttgart: Cotta, 1898.

———. "*Fenitschka*." "*Eine Ausschweifung*." Ed. Ernst Pfeiffer. Frankfurt: Ullstein, 1993.

———. "*Fenitschka*" and "*Deviations*": *Two Novellas*. Trans. Dorothee Einstein Krahn. Lanham, Md.: UP of America, 1990.

———. *Friedrich Nietzsche in seinen Werken*. Vienna: Konegen, 1894.

———. *Das Haus: Familiengeschichte vom Ende des vorigen Jahrhunderts*. Berlin: Ullstein, 1919.

———. *Henrik Ibsens Frauengestalten nach seinen sechs Familiendramen*. Berlin: Bloch, 1892.

———. *Im Kampf um Gott*. As Henri Lou. Leipzig: Friedrich, 1885.

———. *Im Zwischenland: Fünf Geschichten aus dem Seelenleben halbwüchsiger Mädchen*. Stuttgart: Cotta, 1902.

———. *Ma: Ein Portrait*. Stuttgart: Cotta, 1901.

———. *Mein Dank an Freud: Offener Brief an Prof. Sigmund Freud zu seinem 75. Geburtstag*. Vienna: Internationaler psychoanalytischer Verlag, 1931.

———. "Der Mensch als Weib: Ein Bild im Umriß." *Neue deutsche Rundschau* (1899): 225–43.

———. *Menschenkinder: Novellencyklus*. Stuttgart: Cotta, 1899.

———. *Rainer Maria Rilke*. Leipzig: Insel, 1928.

———. *Rodinka: Russische Erinnerung*. Jena: Diederichs, 1923.

———. *Ruth*. Stuttgart: Cotta, 1885.

———. *Der Teufel und seine Großmutter*. Jena: Diederichs, 1922.

Binion, Rudolph. *Frau Lou: Nietzsche's Wayward Disciple*. Princeton: Princeton UP, 1968.

Haines, Brigid. " 'Ja, so würde ich es auch heutet noch sagen': Reading Lou Andreas-Salomé in the 1990s." *Publications of the English Goethe Society* 62 (1993): 77–95.

Kreide, Caroline. *Lou Andreas-Salomé: Feministin oder Anti-Feministin? Eine Stan-*

dortbestimmung zur Wilhelminischen Frauenbewegung. New York: Lang, 1996.

Livingstone, Angela. Lou Andreas-Salomé: Her Life (as Confidante of Freud, Nietzsche, and Rilke) and Writings (on Psychoanalysis, Religion, and Sex). London: Bedford, 1984.

Martin, Biddy. Woman and Modernity: The (Life)Styles of Lou Andreas-Salomé. Ithaca: Cornell UP, 1991.

Peters, Heinz F. My Sister, My Spouse: A Biography of Lou Andreas-Salomé. New York: Norton, 1962.

Resch, Margit. "Lou Andreas-Salomé (12 February 1861–2 February 1937)." German Fiction Writers, 1885–1913. Part 1: A–L. Ed. James Hardin. Dictionary of Literary Biography, vol. 66. Detroit: Gale Research, 1988. 3–17.

Whitinger, Raleigh, ed. Spec. issue on Lou Andreas-Salomé. Seminar 36.1 (2000).

BEFORE THE AWAKENING

The windows of the railroad car are so frosted over from the January cold that the passengers barely discern the dawn's light shining in. The ice figures on the windowpanes take on a bluish tint, and from the narrow gangway that runs the length of the passenger car of the composite train, past the separate compartments, the little serving boy can be heard as he hurries along from the dining car with his tray of clinking cups.

Of the three occupants of the first-class compartment only the old lady has already washed and dressed for the morning and is sitting there, freshly combed, brushed, and upright, while with ill-concealed interest she observes the pair across from her. The gentleman, who, like her, had lain stretched out on the seat and likewise found no sleep, is groping for the tie straps of the lap rug and fetching a crutch and a horsehair foot warmer out of the overhead netting, efforts in which he is visibly hampered by his stiff leg. He is half crippled, and they come from the south. That much the old lady had gleaned the previous evening from comments made by the daughter, who had rolled herself into a ball in the corner by the window and, in an almost impossible position that would have put anyone else's neck out of joint, appeared to have slept splendidly.

The father's intelligent face, pleasant and distinguished as it gazes out of the frame of his graying hair and beard, takes on a look of loving kindness as he wakes the sleeping girl: "Edith! We'll be arriving in Büchen soon!"

She lifts her sleep-reddened cheeks from the air pillow, stretches, shivers, yawns, and laughs up at him. "Did you get any rest?" she asks as she peels off the large, tiger-striped travel blanket, "—you, those things there, I'll pack them."

"You have to get yourself ready," he answers as he hands her a vanity case with toiletries, but still sits down and leaves the things lying, "the washroom is right at the other end of the gangway."

She shakes her head and, all slim and agile, moves about deftly in the narrow space to tie up their two large plaid bundles.

"I'm sure it's awful there; water spilled all over, messy, reeking of smoke," she responds with a questioning glance at the freshly brushed lady.

She nods. "In any case you're soon at the end of your trip for today. Lübeck, is it?" the old lady asks in response.

"That's where my trip ends, yes. But my husband is still traveling on to Hamburg today," Edith answers.

The old lady's eyes widen unnaturally and rest on the dissimilar pair with a look of startled astonishment. Good that no one has the time to notice. Even before Edith can throw on her winter coat the train stops, and outside the gangway door is pulled open.

Her hat in her hand, with only a blue traveling scarf fastened over her close-cropped, dark blond hair, she is about to step out.

Ice-cold, the sharp, misty morning air floods in from the gangway.

Then someone blocks the door. A tall man in a fur coat, his black eyes exuding cheer and good humor, reaches quickly for their hand luggage.

"Everyone out, ladies and gentlemen! Büchen!"

"Hans Ebling! Where in the world did you come from!"

"I've been traveling with you since back in Hanover—a bright good morning to you, Klaus Rönnies—Frau Edith, hurry along!"

The old lady must remain seated. She is traveling through to Hamburg. But her eyes are staring out of her head as if she were trying to look around the corner. "Good heavens! He's her husband! The cripple she has to look after! How is that possible? This child—how old can she be? Eighteen? Even that other fellow is too old for her."

In the meantime the three are crossing over the tracks and looking for seats on the local train to Lübeck, the other two helping Klaus climb in.

"Whom are you visiting in Lübeck, dear friend?" asks Klaus Rönnies, who looks happy and excited. "I never heard of you having any contacts here."

"—Whom— — —?" Hans Ebling tosses his felt hat into the overhead netting and runs his hand nervously through his thick hair, whose brown is already mixed with single strands of gray— "—oh well, yes—an old friend— fellow student from the old days—fellow artist. —Yes, you know, so one day in Stuttgart I met your business manager and confidant in the Neckarstraße, and he had just received a long letter from you. That's how I learned what route you were traveling."

"How nice for you, Edith! My wife wanted to rest a night in Lübeck before coming to Hadersleben to face the tumult of the family circle. Our luggage is going on there directly, while I have business in Hamburg."

"Where you don't want to go?" says Hans Ebling, looking happily at Edith.

"If she came along we would have to stay longer for the sake of our friends and acquaintances there, and we're weary of traveling," Klaus Rönnies answers for her.

"How is your wife doing in Stuttgart?" asks Edith, yawning one last time.

Hans Ebling furrows his brow. "Fine, thank you."

Klaus Rönnies does not ask; he knows that his friend, after youthful years of romantic adventure, still "got caught" after all.

"The two of us have a longing to be 'back home,' " Rönnies says, changing the subject, "with me yearning for my cozy corner by the fireside, where a whole stack of newly arrived journals, pictures, and books must await us—and with Edith likely yearning even more for her dear creatures, her dogs and horses, calves and cows, her birds and her plants as well. She likes to think nothing will work without her."

"And it doesn't work, either," assures Hans Ebling, who has no yearning to be back home, "it's bad enough. The whole winter I would miss not being able to walk out past Göppingen every day to your small estate. And surely that's the only reason I knock about for half the year in Vienna and Paris and Rome and Munich. Who's to blame for that?—That's why I love the summer so."

Edith, silent, looks out the window; the landscape lies flat in the peacefully blowing snow, and deep in the background is a stretch of snow-covered forest. The train makes a few stops at stations along the way to take on noisy schoolchildren; at last the pointed spires of Lübeck come into view.

"What shall we do now?" asks Hans Ebling as the three of them stand on the platform.

"I'll disappear and belatedly make myself beautiful, and the two of you can wait for me in the station restaurant," says Edith.

"Ghastly! Does it absolutely have to be at a railway place?"

"I really can hardly make it into the city, my train is leaving soon," says Klaus Rönnies.

Hans Ebling takes out his watch. "Soon? — — How soon? —Very well, as horribly lacking in atmosphere as it is," he declares in resignation, as his face beams and his teeth sparkle brightly out of his dark beard.

When Edith returns she finds the two of them sitting at the table, the coffee already served, in animated conversation, as Hans Ebling studies the railway schedule. "It's crazy, really. If you wanted to go to Hamburg, you could have gone there right from Büchen."

"Yes. But I wanted to get Edith into a good hotel right away. That's what you can do now."

"Certainly. And then we'll take a great huge walk. And afterward we'll dine at the Schifferhaus."

A minute passes as they drink their coffee in silence. Hans Ebling stands up for no reason, then sits down again.

"You've grown nervous. People have no idea what a frightening effect the prose of a railway café can have on an artist's nerves," Klaus Rönnies comments ironically.

"No. I've just painted too much in the last while . . . And missed out on all sorts of things . . . But now you must be on your way," asserts Hans Ebling, his gaze fixed on the large round station clock.

They walk slowly out to the platform and pace back and forth. By then it is still more than ten minutes until the train leaves.

"A heartbreaking parting for two days," Hans Ebling adds ironically to himself.

Still eight minutes to go—still five. And then still five. Sometimes time simply stands still.

Klaus Rönnies looks uncomfortable and embarrassed. He has almost become nervous himself. "I think I would really rather climb aboard," he says somewhat hastily, shakes his friend's hand and kisses his wife.

"Until we meet in Hadersleben! Have a good time, Edith!"

She seems restless, she follows him with her eyes while Hans Ebling helps him aboard. And suddenly she pulls open the compartment door and is standing beside him.

"Klaus, dear, what is it? . . . Something's wrong! . . . Should I come along?"

"But child, what a notion! Nothing's bothering me." He takes her head and whispers into her ear: " . . . It's just nonsense, mouse. I just didn't feel right bidding you adieu in front of him. — — I thank you."

She puts her arms around his neck and gives him several good-bye kisses.

"No . . . don't . . . don't . . . Edith!" he fends her off, " . . . I beg you, hop out . . . The train could start up . . ."

The signal sounds. Hans Ebling has turned away discreetly, thinking to himself: "I know what's going on behind my back. They're playing husband

and wife. And really aren't man and wife. He can't have become any more lively than he was long before he married. But for just that reason he shouldn't be kissing her either."

Not until the train pulls away does he turn around. Edith is standing beside him.

He looks into her eyes, his own gaze an inscrutable mix of fun and seriousness. "Well, so now you're mine for twenty-four hours. —Frau Edith, assuming for a moment I were your husband now, I'd lay my head on the railway track."

She looks at him, her eyes shining with high spirits. "No need, dearest husband. Hans Ebling is quite harmless."

They both laugh.

"Very well, a servant and a good hotel! You'll just let me take care of everything, dearest wife? For, you see, they cannot but take us for man and wife."

The hotel is right nearby. A servant leads the way. A hotel like any other.

Hans Ebling accompanies the porter up one flight of stairs. He orders the rooms and arranges to have them heated. In a few minutes he is back downstairs where Edith is waiting for him.

Outside the snow flurries have stopped. A heavy, lightless sky arches over the city and blends in the distance with the surrounding white plains.

They make their way out through the streets to get to the higher, tree-planted paths in the parks. The snow sings under their feet. Not a bird to be heard, except over the field that spreads out beside them when a pair of jackdaws flies up, cawing. With their wings spread, etched so sharply against the dull, lead-grey sky, floating along slowly, they call to mind a Japanese bird print, black on white.

Hans Ebling has fallen silent, captivated by the landscape all around him, where the light birch trunks with their snow-laden branches look as if they were delicately etched in pencil against the background sky. A symphony of white colors. And yet, playing in the treetops, barely visible, a gentle mix of reddish, greenish, brown shades.

"This year there's even deep snow down in Swabia; we hoped for it for the fields, which froze so the year before," says Edith, "the snow is good for them. But it's good for something else: for the children, so that they can go sliding down the hilly streets of Stuttgart with their little sleds. When I see that, I would like to be little forever and have a sled."

He laughs. "I think nature must affect you only physically . . . or at least so strongly that its significance as an image recedes . . . Anyway, how did the south appeal to you this time? Compared to the previous winter in Rome, I do hope Meran fell short? I say I hope so because I had the good fortune to be with you in Rome."

"No, it wasn't that bad. In Rome I could hardly catch my breath. In part because of you. I forgot that I was on holiday. In Meran, on the other hand, I went about and visited sick people and had all kinds of pangs of conscience. I was ashamed of being so healthy and strong."

"So healthy and strong? . . . Of course, you must feel that way often anyway when you're with . . ." he almost said: with Klaus. But he went on: "with us others. You're actually much too healthy . . . too unchallenged . . . well, too pretty and lovely as well."

"What a shame," says Edith, "usually you're not at all so boring."

"Ah, it wasn't meant to be a compliment. You're getting me wrong again. People who make us look bad we should avoid. At least it takes an awful lot of courage to keep company with you, the way . . . I, for example, wouldn't have had as much courage in Klaus's place . . ."

She blushes vividly, but smiles. "In his place you wouldn't have needed any. I had the courage for him. The courage and everything else as well . . . He didn't marry me at all; I married him," she responds in a defiant yet cheerful tone, giving the feeling that she wanted to defend him with her comments.

"But that's only words. It all comes down to the same thing."

"No, it's not just words. A real fact. And so natural. We were together anyway, inseparable. Klaus was always Mama's favorite brother, and since he settled down there in Swabia for his health's sake and we went to be with him, I came to like it better there than anywhere else. Neither Copenhagen nor Holstein did I like as much. And in addition I detest the empty life in the cities. And when Mama died, then I found it should remain as it was. And I married him. Then it did stay as it was."

"Hmm!"

"Yes!" she says emphatically, angry at his expression; "and it couldn't be more beautiful. We've always agreed in our interests and inclinations."

He does not answer, but his one unarticulated syllable has spoiled her mood. Or she has spoiled it herself with all that she has said that afterward displeases her. Or by speaking about it at all.

Hans Ebling has the choice of these three possibilities. He tries to calm Edith again. But she remains irritated. She rejects his arm when they come to a slick icy stretch, even though she starts to slip and stumble. And finally she walks on a pace ahead of him.

He observes her with slow deliberation and great thoroughness, taking deep pleasure in how she goes along before him on the snow-blown path, catching up her skirts so that her slender ankles are visible.

Her gait has always struck him as especially charming. Walking, she grows. Although she is of medium height and not gaunt, all her limbs—her every line—are so slim and long and fine that she strikes one as tall. Her shoulders are still too slender—not fully grown out.

"Flowing grace," thinks Hans Ebling and calls out: "Kitten."

She does not look back. "Oh, rubbish! I'm not a cat."

"By the softness of your movements you could just be one. And I've heard you purr before when someone stroked you—and I just now heard you hiss. But I wasn't thinking of a cat at all."

"But rather?"

" . . . So, you really want to know? . . . I was thinking of the catkins that hang from the willow trees and shake as soon as a breeze blows. Delicate, downy, pale yellow. If you touch them, the aroma and color stay on your hands, like touching a butterfly's wing . . . a harbinger of spring."

She stops and turns toward him.

"I forgot: I have to send a telegram. In Hadersleben they have to know exactly when I'm arriving. We should have done it earlier."

"Do we have to do it right away?"

She nods.

"Very well. So, to the main post office. It stands in all its grand new splendor next to the railway station."

They set a rapid pace back to town. As they walk, the monotone lead gray of the sky breaks up a little, and the sun makes an appearance for the first time. Glowing red, like an immense moon, it stands in the opening of the clouds, giving off both above and below a dazzling trail of rays.

At the telegraph office, Hans Ebling leans by the window and watches as Edith, leaning over the desk beside him, takes a form and, in large but by no means delicate letters, writes: "To Herr Professor Theodor Rönnies. Hadersleben. —Arriving tomorrow morning. Edith."

He reaches for her hand, making the pen squirt out a long line of ink. " . . . You wrote it wrong. It should read: tomorrow evening. And we don't know what time. I'll check the schedule."

"I'm leaving this evening," says Edith.

He looks at her in silence. Then, after a pause: " . . . You're serious? . . . You don't want to stay overnight?"

She shakes her head.

" . . . And why not? . . . What's happened . . . ?"

"Nothing. I've lost interest in staying."

"Edith! . . . And if I beg you, really, seriously beg you! . . . not then, either?"

She shakes her head.

"That's unkind of you. Almost as unkind as if you had terminated your friendship with me."

She shrugs her shoulders and takes the form.

"Tear it up! . . . Do say something! . . . Have you lost your tongue, child?"

She does not answer, turns to the wicket and pays.

"There's still time . . . Don't leave. Let's send another telegram."

"I'm going," Edith says.

They leave the post office and head into the city. Hans Ebling looks at her from the side. "Did she have to telegraph in order to stay true to her resolve; did she have to commit herself to it? . . . Was that why it was so urgent?" he asks himself, and bright joy mixes into his deep displeasure.

In the meantime it has become brighter outside. In truly royal splendor the white landscape lies there under the radiant winter sun, its radiance reflected in every ice crystal and every wisp of snow. And in this sea of light, pale blue and rose colors shimmer in the sky and find a delicate, barely discernible reflection on the gold-white ground. Blue rose shines from the depths of the half-frozen Trave, and blue rose hovers over the snow alight with life.

Hans Ebling comes to a stop. "Isn't winter a colorful painter, then, in spite of spring!" he calls out in delight, and before his eyes hover Madonna faces by Botticelli and angel heads from the early Renaissance.

Edith gazes straight ahead at the city's skyline rising beyond the Trave. The many-angled roofs and houses line the street along the bank until it bends sharply in toward the center of the city. And above, the greenish shimmer of the church steeples, their slate-gray hue colored with age. Wondrously picturesque and sunk in dreams, Lübeck lies between its two waterways, stretching long and slender and forgotten.

"And there—there's the surging sea!" she cries out spontaneously.

Something powerful, rushing toward her with irresistible force, she adds in her fantasy to the scene she beholds—sees how it comes surging from afar to envelop this small bit of landscape and death and winter.

And precisely this, this something that is not there, that is not visibly present, seems to her the most beautiful aspect of the picture—its most necessary and most moving part.

They walk on in silence.

"Now we want to look for the Schifferhaus, it must be close by," says Hans Ebling cheerfully, and the joy that until now has only slightly sweetened his annoyance suddenly fills him to the brim: "Lübeck is a wondrous and wonderfully dear city, full of fairy tales and the most lovely children of the human family."

"How so?"

"Because we are walking about here," he responds jokingly, "and because today all things are telling me their secrets."

"Why?"

"Good question! Probably because the sun is luring the secrets out of them . . . But seriously, nothing in the world brings joy like the things around us, the 'lifeless' things, as we call them, the forms and colors and I don't know what. Nothing speaks so clearly and so unassumingly brings such good feeling. That is the 'Joy of Things,' and you don't really know it yet. At least not this way . . . And perhaps you are not supposed to become well acquainted with it, for it may be that for natures like yours such acquaintance comes only through pain: through knowing silence and weariness—something in the way of resignation—of disappointments in the living relations of life."

She gazes attentively into his face. He looks so good and earnest in this moment. "And you?"

"I?" he takes off his hat and nervously runs his hand through his hair again; "I know no better joy. All else is common—in comparison. What a wondrous good fortune that things in their inexhaustible wealth always remain, always new, always pure, always consoling and cheering, no matter what impoverishment and ruin we ourselves might come to know—no matter what life might do to impoverish and ruin us."

Edith does not answer. She feels something like shame at his being so filled with what she knows so little about. He is an important artist, but what is she? She is used to seeing him as something that to a certain extent belongs to her and is in a small way dependent upon her moods. In this moment she feels that she fears and loves his superiority.

At the famous Schifferhaus they are practically the only guests. The rustically carved and colorfully painted seaman at the door directs them with his inviting gesture into an empty room; only in the farthest corner sit two Lübeck gentlemen over a glass of grog, their pointed beards and rigid faces making them look as if they were carved in wood themselves.

Edith and Hans sit down near the window, order their dinner, and let their gazes wander about the quaint hall, with model ships hanging from its low ceiling. Edith is quiet and introspective, but during dinner the cozy warmth and the good Rhine wine loosen her tongue. Her mood changes. She gets to chatting and grows congenial.

Hans Ebling does not contribute much to the conversation, but he has a finely thinking, finely perceptive way that draws her out, encouraging her to tell, as does the wine that he pours her. And that is just what he wants to do. For now he feels as if they were wandering together through the fields as they did so often back in Swabia in the mild summer evenings, when Edith would let the quaking blades of grass glide through her fingers and so trustingly let him partake of all her life and living. And in her chatting words he sees so clearly the whole of daily life there again, this calm and healthy mix of practical and spiritual interests—and the lovely, fresh, even-tempered cheerfulness that Edith's whole being exudes to impart character to everything, everything.

"Do you know what a blissful human fate is, my child? Shall I tell you?"

She nods and sips from her glass.

"The way that you come from the north, from the powerful north of the Holsteins and from the refined, all too refined north of the Danes, and in early youth are transplanted in the most blessed piece of German soil and the German south, to take root there until all the seeds blossom forth, unfolding carefree and unhampered . . ."

She nods again and says: "That is Klaus's achievement. Being in the country is good only in the company of such an intelligent, earnest man. Since the time that he could no longer be an actual farmer he has become almost a scholar. Without him I would have turned rustic. I have that tendency."

"No, not for turning rustic. But it's true that you are able to assimilate everything spiritual only in a peculiarly close proximity to real life itself. You can surely become a university-trained zoologist or botanist if all the while you're allowed to raise animals and plants, look after the field dung, and supervise the milking."

She laughs and looks satisfied.

"But something is still missing," he goes on.

She looks up, surprised. "Well?—and that would be?"

"I don't know yet. I only tell myself: All this is beautiful, because it is rich, blessed ground for the loveliest growth. But what will it bring forth? What blossoms? You still haven't bloomed yet, Edith."

"What sort of blossoms, then?" She asks, uncertain and naive. She is almost a little hurt, without really knowing whether she should be.

Hans Ebling looks at her and feels something like true emotion as she sits there and ponders what he might think can still be lacking about her "blissful human fate."

They finish their meal, the conversation slows. Hans Ebling has the feeling that a touch of melancholy has descended upon Edith. But perhaps it is only weariness. The night's travel and the long walk in the snow are taking their toll. Her cheeks bright red, her eyes tired, she begins to yawn.

"Your large eyes are becoming quite small," he comments with a laugh, "I'm afraid you need to sleep."

"Ah, yes," she admits meekly, "if I could just go to sleep here."

"We're just about there," he consoles her and hails a passing carriage while the waiter helps Edith with her coat. He is seized by an uncontrollable desire to take Edith in his arms, just as she is, and carry her—just cradle her, rock her in his arms until she is asleep, nothing more.

He sits beside her in the carriage, sweltering hot, and looks out from the window onto the roadway with snow piled high on both sides.

In a few minutes they arrive at the hotel, and Edith is shown to her room.

Number twenty-one? Number twenty-three?" asks the porter and opens two doors one after the other, a third door situated between them.

Edith stays in number twenty-one, where she finds her lap rug. She casts off her hat and coat and looks around. The bed stands, freshly made, along one side wall, opposite which a door leads into number twenty-two. A fire is crackling in the tiled stove, it smells of fresh linen and closed air.

Then someone opens the door to the next room, and there stands Hans Ebling on the threshold.

"You're not actually asleep on your feet, then, are you? I wanted to suggest that you do that in here."

"Where? . . . What kind of room is that, then?" she asks, astonished.

"It's between our two bedrooms. It's our salon. We have to have some place to be together. We can't keep taking walks forever."

Edith looks into a small salon with its front wall extended by an arch of windows, its floor covered in soft, thick carpet, a comfortable settee at an angle in front of the fireplace and illuminated by a fire of large logs. Hans Ebling carries in the lap rug and the foot warmer and closes the connecting door.

"I shan't bother you any more. Good night. When by all human standards you've slept enough, I'll come knocking softly." With that he takes her hand, kisses it, and departs without a sound.

Edith stretches out with a feeling of utmost comfort on the broad, soft settee. She is so tired that she is barely aware of anything. At one point the maid comes in to check on the fireplace. Then all is completely still, with only the fire crackling quietly.

"There are surely only a few other people besides us in the hotel," she is still able to think, and then her thoughts become confused.

Whether she has slept and how long, she does not know. She feels as if the day's events had just finished and she was still trying to sleep. But she hears a gentle knocking at the door. Is it the maid come to look after the fire? Had she not just been there? Half awake, she calls out: "Come in."

It is Hans Ebling. "Well, are you awake? Did you sleep well?" he asks and sits on the foot end of the settee.

Edith lifts herself up slightly.

The lighting in the room seems changed. Is it really so late already? Or are the many windows so thickly frosted that they block most of the light? The room seems as if enclosed by a pale, shimmering wall of crystal that no one can see through.

"Just like in a fairy-tale palace," she thinks dreamily and has a longing to go on sleeping that way, but instead of being completely asleep, with open eyes and with that sweet weariness in her limbs.

In the fireplace the burning logs have collapsed, the embers below them glimmering red.

She tries to rise but cannot. "I must have slept in my boots still damp from the snow from our walk. Now they're pinching and hurting me and I didn't bring any other footwear," she murmurs and lies back down.

Hans Ebling touches cautiously at her boot and unbuttons it. "You don't need other shoes, what do you think my hands are for, then," he answers and pulls her boot off. The warm little foot in its dark stocking rests in his hand like a rescued animal. Edith makes a feeble show of resistance but he holds fast, and with a few quick, gentle moves he undoes the second boot as well.

"Hold still—just lie there quietly and keep still," he says; he reaches for the foot warmer and pushes Edith's feet into it, "or else the two little birds will fall out of their nest."

"Thank you!" she responds instinctively, and then, with a deep sigh: "It smells like springtime."

He stands up, goes around to her at the head of the settee, and leans over her. In his hands he is holding a bundle of roses—roses in all colors and in full bloom—loose, unbound, on long stems.

"Oh, how magnificent," she exclaims with delight, "you must put them in water . . ."

And then it pours down upon her, a gentle, precious rain of hundreds of fragrant rose petals.

"These must die," says Hans Ebling, as he plucks off the last ones. Single petals fall into her short coiffure, onto her face; he brushes them away carefully, his hand brushing as he does so against her hair and cheeks with a gentle caress that she can scarcely feel, scarcely distinguish from the touch of the roses. Edith closes her eyes and breathes in the fine aroma that rises up around her. Doing so, she looks so childlike and at peace that Hans Ebling feels himself overcome by a sudden, powerful delight.

"My child—my dear, dear — — you lovely, sweet girl."

These words, now with the familiar "you," he says not audibly, but merely moving his lips, and kneels down beside her by the settee so that she cannot see him.

She remains lying, motionless.

And he gazes at her for several minutes and thinks: "This too is pleasure. It takes a long time to learn. Ten years ago I couldn't have done this. It requires growing older, without the impetuous clumsiness and impatience of youth. Older? Or only more depraved, more knowing, more aware, enjoying the details instead of being consumed by the whole . . . For example, something like this, kneeling here and brooding."

As he is thinking this, he repeats with his hand the gentle touch of before that Edith allowed to happen so naturally, and then he brushes the hair from her brow the way one does for a child.

"This she knows: that's how Klaus does it, too," he thinks and feels angry, "I seem to be behaving quite paternally—already able to play the father. And she feels childlike while I do so—still able to play the child. Thus do the two extremes meet and seduce each other."

He glides his hand down, caressing, along her cheek, toward her throat, and slips it under her neck. Far from letting that waken or startle her, Edith seems to have slipped back into the earlier half slumber, from which she had barely awakened. She rests as if in thrall to dreams, and into the pure creature comfort of lying like that, free of will, her limbs relaxed, there comes a strange, unusual sense of well-being that she has never known but that she now feels she has always longed for — — weak, dreamy, like the fragrance of roses that envelops her.

Without knowing it, Edith yields to Hans Ebling's touch and, unconsciously, almost imperceptibly, she nestles into his caressing hands.

He feels it distinctly and is filled with joy and gratitude as though someone had unexpectedly dropped flowers into his lap. Every stirring, however gentle, however faint, that trembles through her nerves, he perceives and yields to her and follows her with such wondrously fine surety, as though his sensitive artist's hands were possessed of their own spirit and consciousness. And with all the gentleness of his touch he feels as if with all his fine senses he were seeing Edith naked before him, as if he were seeing before his closed eyes the slender outline of her supple shoulders, her too slim hips with still that boyish something about them, the gentle curve of her limbs, whose grace he knows so well from their each and every move.

Like a musician who lets sound on his strings the first tones of a melody, he imagines he hears music about him, playing a gentle prelude, sweet and soulful, soulful like the golden hues that run across the snowfields to awaken the snow to life.

His face transforms as he harkens, and it takes on a strange beauty; it bears a new expression, listening, attentive, enraptured — — an artist's devotion.

Time passes, it grows dark. The frozen windowpanes shine pale white through the deepening dusk, and here and there they glitter, a small spark of light as the street lanterns are lit. Everything in the room lies wrapped in soft shadow. The glow of the fireplace has died out; only single sparks still play under the ashes.

★ ★ ★

Hans Ebling is lying on the floor and kissing Edith. He kisses her hands, her shoulders, her lips. Once he gives her lips a long, intense kiss, without her making a move. He does not know whether she is asleep, whether she is awake, whether she is dreaming. He feels under his hands the calm, measured beats of her heart and how gently her breath heaves her youthful breast.

Then an electric bell rings shrilly out in the corridor.

Edith opens her eyes. A shudder goes through her entire body, but she says not a word. Her eyes, wide open, stare straight ahead into the twilit room, on past the man beside her. All within her is as if under the spell of a profound amazement, of an astonishment with which one sometimes awakens in a dream, in a totally foreign, totally improbable reality. Into this reality not even her fantasy has ventured before, nor has she toyed with it in dreams. Well might she too have once dreamed darkly of a grand love and of almighty passions, of a mysterious storm of madness that can inspire ecstasy and also destroy with a crushing force because a single person inwardly feels the rise and fall of life in its entirety.

But here, in this new reality, there exists no such beloved person — — she finds only herself. There is no storming madness that would draw her to him, her powers at the peak of arousal — — there is only the profound rest in a state of gentle delight, as with drawing a deep breath or drinking silently to still one's thirst.

She feels in as serious a mood as she has ever known before in her life, but seriousness without burden and full of trust. Perhaps it was the same then, when she was still a very small child, going on unsteady feet from father to mother and making with a child's astonished and unchecked seriousness her first discoveries in a world that still spoke to her in strange, fairy-tale voices.

Hans Ebling holds her in his arms, his face against hers. "Who are you?" he whispers, his voice muted, addressing her again in the familiar form, " . . . what are you dreaming of? why do I not understand you? why do you not know longing? — — I did not wake her with my kisses. — She is asleep. — — Are you capable of love? — Whom? — — Never? — — But of course, it will come. — One longing will come over you, pure and powerful — and you will cast yourself at the feet of the man who arouses it. — — Do you not sense it? — — The longing—for the child."

She parts her lips slightly, a tremble runs through her limbs, and suddenly her eyes fill with large, warm tears.

Hans Ebling cries out briefly. He drinks the tear that glides down her cheek; he covers her face with wild, unthinking kisses. Forgotten is all that he had planned, cast aside the wise moderation and the tentative caution of the experienced man inured to pleasure; hot and unchecked his passion breaks through—carrying him and all his thoughts away as the wind does the chaff. He pleads, raves, trembles, begs, and, beside himself, he lifts her in his arms and clasps her to him.

Edith has slowly straightened up in his arms. Without a word, without a sign of being startled. But like a lightning flash of disillusionment a sudden awakening and understanding shoots through her eyes.

It is almost totally dark, they can barely discern each other. And yet, just as quickly, at just such lightning speed, he understands her, feeling that she is lost to him—that she has gone cold—awake—strange—in an instant a thousand miles from him, as if she had said: "Ah, so you're here? I thought I was alone. Why are you giving me such a start?"

He is still holding her fast, but touching only her clothes, his hands going lame. "Edith! My child! My beloved! Beloved! My everything!"

She has stood up, the wilted rose petals gliding off her. Slowly she walks, in stocking feet, across the carpet to the corner window, where she stops.

She does not ring for service; she does not call for light. She just stands there and, lost in thought, breathes on the windowpane until there is a small round peephole in the frost that lets the world outside look in on her.

Outside, the streets are lit, and a sleigh drives by with jingling bells. It brings a sound so bright and cheery and innocent into the room, and somehow she thinks with urgent clarity of the Stuttgart street children with their little sleds, and it makes her smile . . .

A quarter hour later Edith orders tea and a lamp. When the porter appears with the lamp and a full serving tray, she is all alone in the parlor. She sits by the fireplace, her feet propped against the grill, and reads the train schedule. Only when dinner is ready does Hans Ebling come in and sit at the table.

Edith rises, pours two cups of tea, and behaves just like a housewife, just as she usually did at the tea table back in Göppingen. Exactly as she is standing there in her dark blue traveling suit, the colors of her face as fresh as ever, is how Hans Ebling thinks he has seen her so often, as the riddle of a woman that has charmed and tormented and enchanted him.

Except for the serious, inward expression of her eyes nothing about her has changed, not even her friendliness toward him. But it is a distracted friendliness, as though she were thinking about something else at the same time. He sees that she is most deeply concerned about something—concerned with herself, not with him. Without her knowing it, her riddle is charming and tormenting her today, and with that she forgets almost entirely that he is there too and intimately involved in the situation.

And surely for that reason he can detect no trace of excitement or anger or embarrassment about her, because for her he has disappeared, and only her own experience looms large and strange before her.

Hans Ebling is unable to eat; he pushes his cup away, stands up, and paces back and forth in the dark background of the room, beyond the lamp's circle of light.

He knows quite well: it is only his injured pride, and that will pass, but he cannot control himself—he is moved and shaken to know so suddenly and clearly, to grasp so completely, how little he means to her.

Until then, of course, it was no different, but uncertainty leaves the thoughts room to play with unlimited possibilities. And in such a play of thoughts he enjoyed her trusting openness. Now he has felt the boundary between them.

To himself he calls her unfeminine, egotistical, cold, cruel to the extreme for sitting there so immersed in herself. And it hurts him, not to be able to see into her, not to know what she is feeling inside. All this she is experiencing totally alone. Had he inspired her to love, then her being would reveal itself to him. But instead he has even now reached the limits of trust.

When it is time to go to the station Edith gathers up her things, rings for the porter, orders the carriage, and makes ready to travel. She looks up in surprise when Hans Ebling too reaches for his coat.

"What are you so surprised at?" he asks, his address formal again, "that I still exist? I only retreated to the shadows, but I was always here. — — I was hoping I might accompany you to the station."

They ride the short way through thick snow flurries that have begun again. When they arrive, the train is already there, but no one is allowed to board.

Edith stands at the farthest edge of the platform and watches, unthinking, as a mechanic turns on a tap over one of the wheels of the last car. A hissing rush of steaming water gushes out and pours down beside the track where it begins to freeze even as it is enveloped in its own steam.

The minutes crawl by just as slowly as they did that morning when they were waiting in the same station for Klaus's train to leave.

The comparison must occur to both of them.

Finally it is time.

Edith climbs into the compartment as Hans Ebling holds the door open. He jumps in after her and closes the door. For a moment they stand facing each other in silence, in the pale light of the ceiling lamp.

"So, you're traveling along," is all she says, her address, as always, formal.

"Yes. I have to. I shan't disturb you. I just can't part with you that way, Edith."

She does not answer, but sits down in the window corner and takes out her watch. It is an hour and a quarter to Kiel. There she must transfer to the Hamburg express to Hadersleben.

Hans Ebling really does not disturb her. He sits on the same side of the compartment in the other window corner and stares out. He is at odds with himself and feels ridiculous and stupid as well. Now, of course, she is not thinking of him, but when she does later, unpleasant memory will be bound up with it. Then it will always occur to her that this last evening was not to be. And it was not to be because Hans Ebling was not able to carry it off. He had misplayed his role and lost his mask. He had been stupid and in love— too much in love. The sincere, unaffected man in him had put the cautious, pleasure-seeking seducer to flight.

"And her whole life long she'll consider that to have been a misdeed on my part," he thinks bitterly, " . . . the fact that I held you too dear to be intentionally bad . . . dear God, I do love you, I do love you!"

Edith feels sorry that he is sitting there so silently. His words from before did touch her. As serious as her heart now feels, she is still far from any ill feelings toward him. For through all her seriousness and introspection she still feels full of freshness, health, and inner well-being, without understanding why. Just as after deep sleep or when recovering from an illness the nerves tend to feel well. She feels herself in a warm-hearted mood and thankful, but knowing neither to whom nor for what.

As the train pulls into Kiel she turns to Hans Ebling and says: "I have to change trains here, and I'd like to ride in a ladies' compartment."

"Which means you find my company hard to bear. Did I really disturb you?"

"No. But that's what I want."

"As you command."

He reaches for her luggage and stands up to open the door.

Then she is all at once at his side, raises both arms and lays them around his neck.

"Adieu!" she says quietly.

And fervently, calmly, without any sign of feminine love but with the open warmth of a grateful child, she kisses him on the lips.

Surprised, he still feels her warm, fresh lips on his when the door is pulled opened from outside, the two of them are on the platform, the other train pulls up, the doors open and close, and strangers hurry past, separating them.

Edith looks around in her compartment. No one else has boarded, she will be alone. She stretches out her arms and takes a deep breath. Before, she had imagined this with longing: a solitary, quiet night journey, all quiet, and she alone with herself. That will let her sort everything out—yes, and she will take herself to task, too.

She is so accustomed to take on everything quickly and independently that she simply plans to do these two things, as matters to be taken care of.

Hans Ebling is still standing by the car and, filled with the most contradictory feelings, gazing up at the window behind which Edith has disappeared.

Then she lowers the window. Just in the moment when the whistle blows. A crazy desire seizes him to see her face gaze upon him, if only for a moment, and greet him.

But she does not look out. Only her slender hand in its gray suede glove reaches over the window ledge, and, as the train pulls out of the station, a blue travel scarf comes fluttering toward Hans Ebling.

A breeze pulls it out of the hand that was holding it. It flies up, flutters down again, and is caught on the shiny metal door handle of the compartment. Like a little blue cloud it hovers there, waving in the wind.

Hans Ebling runs a few strides along beside the train; then he swings, with a jump that would have done him proud back in the days of his most daring gymnastics—and could have cost him his neck—onto the step, his foot touching it for only a second, and snatches away the scarf.

On the platform, the other people have gone their way, but the conductor aboard the train calls out to him with a flood of threats.

The scarf clutched in his hand, Hans Ebling makes his way back to the station hall.

"When does the next train leave for Lübeck?" he inquires of the first official he meets.

"Five in the morning," is the answer.

So he will be waiting in the station until five in the morning. He does not want to go back into the city—alone.

In the station restaurant, just like the one that awakened his impatience early that morning, he sits shivering patiently in front of a glass of flat beer.

His hurt, cross mood has passed, his thoughts hang, full of wakeful, warm interest, on Edith, following her on her night's journey, running once more, hour by hour, over the events of the past day from morning to evening. What happened this day in the depths of her soul? He cannot say. What will occur in her life, perhaps, sometime, as a result of this day? Did she kiss him because she loved him? No. Does someone kiss that way to return a caress that has left one cold? No. Whatever he might think, whatever he might worry about, or hope, or fear, that is all empty fantasy. He has not lifted the veil from her being.

But while picture upon picture rises up in his artist's mind he does not tire of pondering in his enraptured fantasy that old, eternally young riddle to which he has devoted the years of his youth and that has captivated him once again.

* * *

In the meantime, Edith is lying stretched out on the cushioned seat of her compartment. At the next station another lady boards, but it does not disturb Edith, and she takes no notice. All the resolutions she has made for this night, all the deep thoughts that she wanted to fathom, now elude her, and the fact that she had intended to take herself to task she has entirely forgotten as well.

With the foot warmer under her head as a pillow she sleeps sweetly and soundly, dreaming of a broad, sparkling white surface of snow on which a little sled with brightly jingling bells is sliding downward — — — downward —

UNIT FOR "MEN, INTERNAL"

"Look here, Otto, an official note of gratitude from the von Brinken family: 'For the widespread show of sympathy at the death and burial of our unforgettable sister and niece Christiane von Brinken, nurse at the House of St. Michael.' "

Doctor Otto Griepenkerl is standing at the window of his study and looking out in silence as an east wind drives a fine, cold November rain against the windowpanes. Behind him across the room, in the bright light of his green desk lamp, his wife is sitting, leaning over to read the evening paper spread out on the table.

"Christiane?" he repeats distractedly after a while, as if astonished, and in his thoughts he involuntarily corrects himself: "Christel!"

"And the sympathy was widespread indeed," comments his wife; "it's always the wrong people who die, Otto. Even you doctors can't change that. And she was so healthy, Sister Christa. Not a gray hair on her head. But perhaps that's because she was blond. Don't you think so, too? In my hair, for example, it's easier to see the gray earlier."

Doctor Griepenkerl does not answer. He is still looking out on the street scene right outside his window, on the busy activity of the big city, the hustle and bustle, and the people, their umbrellas held high, hurrying along.

"How comfortable it must look in here, from the street outside," he thinks, apropos of nothing—"this nice room on the ground floor in the greenish light of the lamp." And he thinks to himself: "Christel had no home."

"Pneumonia of that kind snatches many a person away so quickly," his wife comments. She folds up the newspaper, her ample hands with their many rings. "The pastor said so beautifully: 'This was a soul who might await death in peace, whenever it might choose to call her, for her entire life; from tender youth onward, she stood in the service of Christian charity and self-sacrifice— let us follow her example.' — Yes, I too had great respect for her. But to follow her — — not everyone can live that way. For so many people, and for the ill and suffering, I mean. We can do no more than our duty. Is it not so, Otto?"

"No, of course we can't," he answers somewhat impatiently. She is such a faultless spouse and mother, his wife—she does have a right to hear a small compliment at this point. But he is annoyed by her tone; he is in no mood to praise.

"I'd rather not disturb you any longer. You surely have much to do. Tomorrow you have your lecture again early in the morning. I'll go and see now how Ernst and Martha are doing with their schoolwork."

He merely nods without turning around, while she leaves. But from the doorway she looks back to cast a friendly look at the imposing figure of her husband, with his slight tendency to portliness and with his wise, stolid face. Perhaps in this moment he is not in a good mood—but all in all his outer appearance makes the impression of indestructible contentedness.

He himself comes, amid his annoyance, to think with conviction: not only from outside might it look cozy and comfortable in here—it is in truth full of peace and happiness. An exemplary wife, well-raised children, a solid career, respect and reputation, and a nice fortune. The value of all earthly goods of this sort, moreover, Doctor Griepenkerl knows full well how to appreciate. Except that today, on this cold November evening, melancholy comes creeping in through every little crack of the door. Deep down, in the depths of his soul, deep and subdued, there he feels even today an inviolable contentment. But he has no desire to admit it to himself, no desire to praise either his wife or his life.

He turns away from the window, goes to his desk, and rummages around there for a while. He has to pull the lamp over to help him find what he is looking for. At last it falls out of a yellowed envelope: a small photograph, somewhat faded, of a very young girl in the uniform of the merciful sisters of the House of St. Michael. A white apron over a small-patterned, close-fitting linen dress, a white nurse's cap on her thick blond hair. Under that a very dear face, from which roguish brown eyes gaze out. He immediately recalls verses of poetry as soon as he sees these eyes again. Not his own verses, of course—for Doctor Griepenkerl is without doubt one of those people who have never let themselves be moved to write verses. He turns for his purposes to recognized models, and most preferably to the classics, just to make sure.

But these verses, how well he came to know them, as if he himself had composed them—known them right down to the small alteration that he had to make so that they fit perfectly:

My senses ofttimes are oppress'd,
    Oft stagnant is my blood;
But when by Christel's sight I'm blest,
    I feel my strength renew'd.
I see her here, I see her there,
    And really cannot tell
The manner how, the when, the where,
    The why I love her well.

If with the merest glance I view
    Her dark and roguish eyes,
And gaze on her dark eyebrows too,
    My spirit upward flies.
Has anyone a mouth so sweet,
    Such love-round cheeks as she?
Ah, when the eye her beauties meet,
    It ne'er content can be. [1]

To the rest of the verses—written by Goethe in love with the unknown Christiane R.—there is a tone that should not have suited the image of Fräulein von Brinken. It was precisely her refined upbringing, precisely the fact that she had grown up knowing the advantages and prejudices of the nobility, that made her seem so absolutely attractive to the son of a petit-bourgeois household, the student from a simple family. And yet, when he really thought about it, there was nevertheless a fresh, almost robust earthiness about her. Not a trace of reserve or affectation. Noble bearing came as naturally to her as did her most audacious roguishness, and it all radiated an effervescent joy of living. This harmony of form and freshness, of refinement and earthiness, he found completely enchanting. For, after all, he himself bore two souls within his breast, of which the well-known one clung with all its senses to the earth in a sensuous joy of living, while the other took great pleasure from the array of

---

[1]The poem is Goethe's "An Christel," which the young poet, then twenty-five, wrote to an unknown sweetheart in 1774. It was originally titled "Auf Christianen R." but later "Christel" and "An Christel." The translation used here is the 1882 rendition "Christel" by E. A. Bowring, chosen because of its relative contemporaneity to young Griepenkerl's poetic moment. In the original and in Bowring's translation, the second line of the second stanza describes the beloved girl's eyes as "black" (schwarz), which Griepenkerl has altered to "dark" (dunkel).

noble ancestors from whom Christel had sprung—and in essence had a strong inclination in favor of all that led upward in the world and in society and would confer there a respectable reputation.

Right on the very first day he became acquainted with Christel in her parents' home she struck him as wondrously beautiful. And then, too, she reminded him of an image from Goethe, although the points of comparison were actually quite few, namely that of the formally dressed Lotte cutting bread—although the main feature of that picture was totally missing, the circle of little brothers and sisters gathered around her[2] — Christel was just standing there and seeing to the setting of the table, a stack of damask serviettes over one ample arm that peeked out of its silk, lace-trimmed sleeve, while in the other hand she held a crust of bread from which she herself was taking healthy bites.

Among the guests who frequented her parents' home Doctor Griepenkerl was one of the most modest, and no matter how serious his intentions soon became, he had for the time being to admire Christel only from afar and with greatest reserve. Indeed, he did so for some time with the greatest respect and solicitousness. But it was quite strange: no matter with how much deference and formality of bearing he might approach Christel—it always came off between them like a comedy that they were staging for the benefit of others. He himself had such a vague grasp of the various social formalities so new to him that he was often afraid they could all at once, under the influence of some kind of crisis, desert him completely; and so in this case as well he clung to them with a certain exaggerated dignity. Yet even in the course of the most correct and formal conversation that he conducted with Christiane von Brinken, he could hear the most audacious words and allusions ringing through, and he enjoyed the appealing ambiguity of the situation.

But his future spouse—as he constantly thought of her to himself—was not to suspect or know of such godless impulses. That was just so specially appealing: to anticipate possessing her, so to speak, as the girl of his frivolous

---

[2]The reference here is to an episode in Goethe's first novel, *The Sorrows of Young Werther* (*Die Leiden des jungen Werthers*), in which the title hero is enraptured by the sight of his beloved Lotte as she cuts bread for a brood of her little brothers and sisters. That scene was popularized as an illustration by Wilhelm von Kaulbach (1805–1874), *Lotte, Brot schneidend* (Lotte, Cutting Bread). Kaulbach's illustration was subsequently the basis for a painting by Ferdinand Raab (ca. 1865), and its lithographic version also became a popular item of interior decor in bourgeois households of the Wilhelmine era, an expression both of the domestic values that that class professed to hold dear and of their cherished role as lovers and propagators of traditional German art and culture.

dreams, whom he would hug and kiss—and at the same time to know her as the distinguished Fräulein von Brinken, who she was for all the world and for him as well. And as she was supposed to be for him, too! He would have had it no other way!

He was still able to think back on his behavior during that time with great satisfaction, and back then he felt quite clearly how he was becoming more and more welcome in that house. There was another young man who was a frequent visitor there with him—Hans Ebling, a very talented, respected artist—and he got the better of that fellow by far. Hans Ebling was ardently courting Christel's older sister Liselotte, but he had no thoughts of marrying. And every time he fell in love—and he did that often—he made himself impossible, compromising the object of this love right and left. Doctor Griepenkerl would not have compromised his Christel for all the world. "Look, don't touch!" was his motto on this point.

For touching there are other women in the world, with whom a fellow can get by as well as he can until he makes it into the respectable feeding grounds of marriage. — — Hans Ebling of course did not admit that either—he claimed those were precisely the only women who should not be considered for that purpose—but he was always talking in paradoxes.

Later, Hans Ebling had almost disappeared from the von Brinken house because the parents did not welcome him there; but he turned up again unexpectedly when both parents died only a short time apart from each other, leaving the daughters virtually without means. Liselotte, Ebling's old flame, who had already turned down two proposals for her hand—an assessor and an officer—decided to take her senior teacher's examinations and devote her life to teaching. Christel, on the other hand, was dispatched, by decision of the gathered members of the von Brinken family, to nurse's training. Special inclinations or wishes of her own she seemed not to have, and she was accustomed to obeying the advice and will of her family. They chose the House of St. Michael—the "public hospital" as it was also known—because it had no expressly religious character, which Christel would have resisted, and to a small degree also because Doctor Griepenkerl, who just a short time before had been hired there as an assistant physician, approved of the move. — —

Doctor Griepenkerl holds the small faded photograph up to the light again. Beside the attractive face framed by the white nurse's cap, the hand firmly holding the photograph looks unpleasantly sensual and ungainly—the carefully tended hand of the doctor with its somewhat too short fingers.

He casts the photograph back into the desk drawer and begins to pace the room. Not for a long, long time has he revisited this old memory—death had to come to stir and waken it again. But he truly had no reason to shy away from such recollection. Just that he had better and more necessary things to think of in his busy life than old love stories.

Poor Christel had suffered much during her first time at the hospital. She was able only slowly and with difficulty to accustom herself to her Cinderella role. For two whole weeks she would look forward to her free afternoon, which she was wont to spend with Liselotte—once every fourteen days. Doctor Griepenkerl was very pleased that in this way she was cut off from any contacts of which he was not aware, that there was an end to the parties and balls, which always made him fear that she would end up on the arm of another man—and that her current hard life made her sufficiently undemanding to one day find life at his side lavish enough. On the free afternoons he too went over to Liselotte's, whose apartment was close by the women's academy at which she was studying then, and there he often encountered Hans Ebling. The small rented room with the narrow bed alcove, with which she had to make do, she decorated so beautifully and elegantly with ancestral furnishings that Christel could imagine she was back home again. Then she would huddle so happily in the old armchair, whose high carved back bore the family crest of the von Brinkens, stretch her tired little feet out on the grandmother ottoman with its old-fashioned beadwork, and nibble on the candied fruits that Liselotte always had ready for her. For hours then she would happily forget that there, in this rented room, among strangers, she was sitting as deserted as on some tiny island in the middle of the ocean. Liselotte never forgot that; but in the midst of her family's old furnishing and portraits of her ancestors she looked like queen of the castle.

One day, as the two young men were heading home from visiting the two sisters, Hans Ebling commented: "You're really a dreadful philistine, Doctor. You like this charming creature, this Christel; you fill yourself up with wedding projects and the most honorable intentions and look on calmly as she troubles and toils, losing her freshness and cheerfulness, without it striking you as a pity. And then when you're finally at the point when you dare at last to smother her with kisses as her officially betrothed, she will have long ceased to be the old Christel with the laughing red lips."

"About that you really don't understand a thing," Doctor Griepenkerl had answered indignantly; "what I love about her no period of trial can destroy. You, of course, see her as merely a pretty picture. I insist that she prove herself to be more than that, namely the feminine ideal that each of us has shaped one way or another in his mind, as long as he is not as jaded and blanched as you are."

Hans Ebling laughed. "And that's something you're really proud of? Our own weaknesses and faults play no small role when we give shape to our ideals, my dear fellow. Especially our ideals about women. It would be interesting to detail this a bit in your special case. —In any case it's rather unpleasant for those concerned 'to be idealized,' as I see it. —Those who tax women less highly are more sympathetic toward them."

So Hans Ebling spoke then in all harmlessness. But events saw to it that this discussion remained in Doctor Griepenkerl's memory. He was subsequently unable to forget or get over the fact that he had spoken with such reverence of Christel as his feminine ideal.

Shortly thereafter he encountered her quite often in the hospital, for she had been transferred from the ward for the wounded, for men suffering from physical injuries—referred to in the nurses' jargon as the "unit for men, external"—into a ward for internal illnesses, where Doctor Griepenkerl worked as one of the young assistant physicians. How often did they find themselves at the bedside of one of the patients, how often did their eyes and hands meet, how difficult it often became to keep the mask in place, to adhere to formal behavior—and this doubly difficult in the face of the excited, uncertain, and nervous mode of behavior that Christel was exhibiting of late.

And then—then she was put on night shift. Too clearly, too repulsively clearly did this scene still haunt his gaze.

Adjacent to the large ward, with its twenty beds occupied mostly by typhus patients, was, as in every ward, a small reserve room containing a single bed, where on occasion one of the patients was isolated if, with loud groaning or some other ailment, he was disrupting the others too much.

One night Doctor Griepenkerl had opened the door to this side room to check on its occupant, a young laborer with heart disease who was to die soon after.

Sister Christa was busy with him.

Indeed, so busy that she did not hear the door being opened.

She was standing there, bending low over the bed, her eyes closed, her arms hanging down motionless, letting herself be embraced.

It was only an instant. The two started up when they became aware of the doctor entering.

But were it not for this instant, this saving, insight-bringing instant, Sister Christa would be his wife today. That is not a pleasant thought! Whenever it occurs to him he does not think, as he did before, in a spontaneous feeling of sympathy: "Christel had no home!" but instead he just thinks with a feeling of belated fear: "If it hadn't been for that, I would have taken her into my home!"

But he does not care to think back to that ugly picture. Christiane von Brinken is dead and buried, and, as everyone testifies and claims: after a life of strict, selfless dedication to her duty, filled with sacrifice and worthy of reverence. One had to believe, in people's eulogies, in the good that lived after them. And yet — — and yet! — — Behind that? Behind all the world sees with its shortsighted eyes? Behind her whole outer life in the hospital—in the quiet hours that no one knows anything about? Is it thinkable then that the moment he had witnessed remained the only one of its kind? Is it probable, is it even possible at all, that such a way of behaving was an expression of her hidden nature and that she was yielding to it even then?

On the other hand—the Brinkens were good stock. Liselotte had remained as serious and excellent a girl as one could wish, worthy of the highest degree of respect. For that very reason, when a few years ago she had taken over a private school for "young ladies of good families," Doctor Griepenkerl had sent his own little daughter to be educated there. Whenever he saw Liselotte— her dark hair now white as if powdered, her face still bearing the same Brinken family features that in her youth had been a bit too pronounced but now suited her exquisitely—then he always felt as though he had only dreamed of that moment with Christel. Such is the power of Liselotte's reserved dignity. She has done well, she has bearing. He feels they had mutual respect for each other— he and she. But he is not sure of that, for there is something so impenetrable about her. — — —

Doctor Griepenkerl has interrupted his walk about the room and sat down at his writing desk in order to look through his lecture notes for tomorrow. His most cherished wish of embarking upon an academic career was fulfilled as a result of his wife's fortune. For when he did in fact marry, he did not look to the nobility, where in any case he also lacked further connections. Instead of the south German noblewoman he chose a north German bourgeois from a rich merchant family. And his choice was excellent—the finest goods. But that does not mean it was a marriage of convenience. For him things simply always turned out so fortunately that reason and affection joined most felicitously.

Thus the nasty experience with Christel turned out the best for him. He is simply always the man who knows in any situation what he wants, and gets it too. With such people providence is in league. At least that is how his wife puts it. He himself has nothing to do with providence and the like. And so he ascribes it to his own ability.

But having arrived at this point in his thoughts, Doctor Griepenkerl sighs and pushes his notes away. After his whole long promenade down memory lane his mood has not improved one bit, and he almost feels a gentle regret and loss when he thinks of Christel.

There is simply nothing perfect under the sun, and it would be foolish to insist on it. His own perfect wife is missing one small thing—or one could also say: she possesses an excess of virtues. But along with that her senses have come up short. In a word, she is lacking what flashed so alluringly at him out of Christel's roguish eyes. Even her redoubtable beauty was of a certain nerve-easing sort. Never did he think of verses when she was around. That was amply compensated for by her good qualities. But that meant that her husband lost in virtuousness in precise proportion to her surplus of it. — —

Well, ultimately that is something no one can know. And it does not concern anyone else. He is beyond even the slightest reproach. There is not a living soul who would not have to admit that he is a perfect husband, father, citizen, and professional man. He is always seen to be on the right path and on duty—and that alone is how they must judge him. The other things—the fact that a fellow has occasional need of a small fling, of an occasional bit of private rest and relaxation on the side—that is ultimately really only a question of temperament. That really is beside the point—so totally beside the point that a fellow barely takes note of it himself—nothing but a very small, a very decorous devil's tail, which can crop up even in the most faultless life. — —

Out in the forecourt the bell rings. Doctor Griepenkerl pays no attention: he is sitting now and making notes on his papers.

"Is the doctor in?" inquires a familiar voice out in the reception room.

"Fräulein von Brinken! Take off your coat! Please, come in. How nice of you to come!" calls his wife in a tone especially muted for his sake, as if a man who was ill or sleeping were lying next door in the study.

Liselotte has stepped into their living room and is being helped out of her coat. Her long black mourning veil hangs down over her dress, and with an expression of profound gravity she gazes out from under her prematurely gray hair, which wreathes her face like a white cloud. Anyone who meets Liselotte finds it hard to believe that she has remained unmarried and never had her own children: children's hearts fly to her and likewise too the trust of parents.

"My husband is very busy right now, dear Fräulein—won't you stay with us a while—he'll be coming over later. Or is it something I can pass on to him?"

Liselotte shakes her head. "Thank you, no, it's a personal matter. And I cannot wait for him. You simply must allow me to disturb him. It will take only a few minutes," she answers, and Frau Griepenkerl accompanies her, hesitant and uncertain, to the door of her husband's sanctum.

When she knocks there is a rather reluctant "Come in!" But when she obeys that command, the chair flies back from the desk and she is welcomed by the most gracious bow and the most charming face.

"I had to speak to you for a moment," says Liselotte, "there could be no delay, for I have something to give you."

"There is nothing given from this hand that would not also bring me joy," he quips gallantly.

She takes from her black velvet purse a closed and sealed letter.

"No—not joy," she responds, her voice muted, "but something great and precious. Push aside your work or whatever it was you were doing, cast aside what you're working on, and don't for a second time call out 'Come in' when there's a knock at the door. —— It is the legacy of my sister Christiane to you."

He is holding the letter in his hand, in surprise his face as expressionless as possible, and searching for words.

She stands in front of him in her deep mourning, her head slightly bowed, not looking at him. "Now it is in your hands," she says coldly, almost with hostility, "I wish I had burned it."

A slight bow of her head to him, and before he can step forward and open the door for her, she has left the room.

Outside, his wife receives her with some anxiety and concern, also some curiosity, in her eyes.

"My dear Fräulein von Brinken, you're leaving so soon? He must be very busy."

Liselotte nods. "Very busy. We don't want to disturb him now." —— ——

But Doctor Griepenkerl is standing beside the chair he has just left at his desk. Resting his hands on the desk top, bent over the loose letter pages that lie before him, he is reading what Christiane von Brinken wrote down for him six years ago.

"House of St. Michael.

"I am writing these lines in the event that I predecease you. In fact, I am hale and hearty now, and I've a long time to work yet. But no one can know how soon they will succumb. And at that time I want to have done what the dying criminal does when he summons the priest in his last hour: I want to have made my confession. But not to the priest, but to my guilty accomplice.

"No, that is likely too harsh a word and an unjust one as well. In any case you are the only person on earth who is to learn that I have the death of a human being on my conscience.

"Let me start at the beginning. Everything is so closely connected. It often seems to me as though the most portentous events of our lives, as a small segment taken out of our everyday events, would have turned out differently.

"When I came to know you, when I was nineteen, I was still a child. Good and ignorant and happy like a child. Never had I truly liked anyone so seriously, except for Liselotte, my parents, and, when she was still alive, my grandmother. And at the same time they were all absolutely superior beings and persons of respect for me then. For even Liselotte, even though she was only three years older than I, was almost more like a mother to me than a sister. And you, too, at first became a person of respect for me. You made a so much more sober and serious impression than all our young lieutenants and junior civil servants. That would surely have appealed to my cheerful nature very little if it weren't for your attention to me. With that I do not mean to say that I came to like you out of flattered vanity. I mean to say only that the first step, the decisive step, came from you, you took me, you woke me, you woke my self-awareness, you made me feel special and chosen. And then there was still something else as well that I cannot define. I cannot describe it exactly. It was the way you looked at me and touched me. Of course, we behaved formally toward each other— more formally than with all those young men, some of them our relatives, with whom Liselotte and I joked and laughed in our parents' home. But with none of them was I, as I was with you, overcome by the wondrous feeling that the external forms of behavior were nothing more than surface and appearance, while our real thoughts, our real behavior, went in a different direction. I always felt, without really understanding why, that we interacted with each other in a close and secret manner. Feelings, all manner of yearning impulses as I had never known them and that I did not understand, awoke in me. I tried to find out whether Liselotte was having similar experiences and what she thought of it. Yet as soon as I began such a conversation, Liselotte fell to warning me about you. Naturally I took that amiss of her, for I could see that everyone in our household respected you and spoke only well of you and your future. I usually got back at her for that by blackening the name of Hans Ebling, of whom she thought highly though he was nevertheless said to lead a scandalous life. She once responded by saying: 'There are people in whom others see all that is ugly, and their reputation adds to that. Of such people it is easy to be wary. Then there are others of whose inner life we see nothing, and their reputation is good. That is very exemplary, but it is not endearing. People hold their belief in Hans Ebling's shocking way of life as the result of a single, reliably verified story: only because it took place in society.'

"When our parents died, Liselotte was the only person who advised against sticking me in the hospital. They didn't listen to her, and that came to be a great misfortune for me. The nurse's profession, as I have come to know, is suitable as a longtime endeavor for only two types of people: for those with a pronounced special interest and talent for nursing, which is not for everyone, and then for all those who experienced some kind of ruin with their hopes and their life's fortune, in a word, for those resigned people who feel good by alleviating the suffering of strangers in order to forget their own sorrow. There remains yet a third possibility, namely that the lot of the merciful sisters is so favorably molded, eased, and improved that no unusual mercifulness is needed in order to bear it, that it stands up to comparison with other bourgeois professions that do indeed place demands on a person's ability and competence but not on a purely abstract selflessness. Then the profession would also lose the unpleasant distinction that results in the destitute orphans of our social class falling in thrall to it as the profession most befitting our rank and station.

"From a young, twenty-year-old, life-loving thing such as I once was one cannot demand too much. My heart was full of expectations and excitement, I would have had to pull myself together for any activity in order to do a satisfactory job. And on top of that there was the vigorous resistance of my refined habits and nerves. I was not at all afraid of blood and surgical operations, but I had a nameless revulsion at any contact with infection and soiled bandages, with the coarseness of the daily chores and tasks. I began to suffer physically from the fact that I was working too long and too reluctantly. Did you not see all that, you, under whose very eyes it was all taking place? Your approval of this choice of profession for me was one of the strongest reasons that I bore up and carried on. In my excited imagination I tried to look at my work as something imposed by you as though it were a test that I had to pass in order to win you. I knew very well that only a strong sense of honor held you back from courting me openly, and that you would do so when the day came when you would have at hand the material means to do so. But those means were a long time in coming, and I was faring no better. When I was transferred away from the women and children and into the unit for men, things became worse still. More often than before I saw you at the sickbed in moments of unsought, unwanted intimacy, and stronger than before you exerted that strange attraction that I did not know how to define. And all the while I would repeatedly experience a strange confusion when, now as before, I encountered that formal bearing in your outward behavior, bouncing off it helplessly as if it were a smooth wall.

"Let no one think that the senseless overburdening with work, the much too difficult assignment with these ailing men would have been a remedy against that, because it wore me out and exhausted me! On the contrary, it was the best ally in the project of ruining me; to it I gave all my strength, all my power to endure, and I was left there insecure, overworked, and weak.

"Perhaps you still have the little picture that you asked for right after my convocation: 'All for the charming contrast,' you said, 'in which this uniform stands to your countenance.' I was flattered then; I did not yet grasp the lack of sympathy and cold-heartedness in the way you wanted to see me dressed up just that way.

"Among my fellow sisters I had good comrades but no true friends. We von Brinkens do not make friends easily, and I really could not have revealed my dearest secret. So Liselotte remained my only confidante. But she wasn't doing well herself. She presided over her books almost as unwillingly as I did at the bedside of my patients. Sometimes I found her deeply depressed, once in tears—Liselotte in tears!—working on an old Anglo-Saxon grammar. Or perhaps it was not the grammar at all that she was weeping about. I did not know. Another time she struck me again, in just as unmotivated a way, as if radiant with life and happiness. For a while I thought she had given her heart to someone, but who could that be? Hans Ebling could not make her look that happy, there was no relying on him.

"At this time, about a year and a half after I had entered the House of St. Michael, a young, deaf-mute laborer was admitted as a patient. He had been suffering from rheumatic fever, and this had revealed an older, severe heart condition. Sometimes he would be bedridden with exhaustion, and then he would be as lively as could be. He stood out with his youthful handsomeness, his head full of soft curls of brown hair, his deep-blue eyes so remarkably clear and shining—the eyes of the heart patient. And he was a deaf mute. Now, as I write this down like any other fact, it strikes even me as something incomprehensible that for years I have been able to think about it only with horror and dread. As if his being a deaf mute possessed a ghostly, supernatural power, yes, as if he had been not a common mortal but rather a being more than human.

"At the outset, his silence only made him beautiful in my eyes. You have to know what a rough and sobering effect the words of the laborers had upon me in order to understand that. This man did not speak, he made no jokes, he didn't go ranting on about his impatience, he did not take his pleasure lying in his bed like a master with the sisters like servants at his beck and call. This man lay there quietly, more helpless than the others, calling me to his bed only from time to time and with a slight, touching gesture. What disturbed me about his comrades was their outward way, and it made me unjust toward them; what I liked about him was also only his exterior, but that made me inclined to invent for him all that was missing. With that our upbringing took its revenge upon me, with its tendency to put more value on outward form than it merits and to becloud our gaze for the inner life.

"Because he was restless at night and often groaned loudly in his sleep, his bed was moved after a while into the side room. Here he was very ill for some days and made constant demands upon my care. Then, after his attack had passed, his eyes followed me incessantly with an expression of persistent tenderness. With the grateful tenderness of a child who has been helped and now longs to see its nurse. And as if he were a child dependent on me I had become fond of him as I propped him up in bed, fed him, and watched over him. Then upon the state of total exhaustion there would follow again his excited phase. Often he would reach for my hand or my arm and hold fast; often he would gaze at me as if demanding something from me, staring into my eyes with an expression of irresistible will. I complied with his wishes as well as I could and as far as I understood him; I took the lively gestures with which he called me near or tried to keep me close for his only way of speaking, and without it worrying me I felt in his hand, in his gaze, a beneficial force.

"Then I was assigned the night shift.

"You will think that I needn't go on to tell what happened now. But you cannot know, no, you can never have any idea of how exclusively during this whole time my thoughts centered upon you. I held only to you, and only you alone did I love! I yearned for you with all my soul, and this yearning—unstilled, kept in constant uncertainty, at once aroused by your presence and confused by your behavior—precisely this yearning became my ruin. I cannot explain it, I can describe only how I felt—was I ill, was I confused?—I do not know. I know only that I was aware of no disloyalty to you—yes, that this same intensity of passion that you awakened in me made me powerless toward him, that laborer. I felt weak in my arms and knees when I was near him, and I wept in my dreams for you when I slept. —If we could see down into the nocturnal dreams of a human soul, then perhaps we would often understand it in its contradictions and secret fears. In my dreams, the two figures were so inextricably mixed that I saw only the one man whom I loved, but that was you. It was you whom I gave his body, and I prayed to you to speak to me of your love, to give me certainty and assurance—to cast away what made you so distant and formal toward me out of concern for appearances—and it was you who could not speak to me because he was deaf and mute.

"Then I would have poured out my heart to Liselotte, and perhaps she would have saved me. But Liselotte had deserted me. For a month she had been in Paris in order to learn to speak French, and for months by then her thoughts had no longer been concerned with me. I felt that she was keeping something secret from me, and that made me fall silent myself. We were no longer completely candid with each other, and when we were together we often spoke of spring, which was beginning outside, rather than of ourselves. And she would venture out into the spring—'The flowers have been in bloom for some time now!' she said, her eyes aglow—and I remained behind, sad and alone, staring from my nurse's quarters down into the hospital courtyard, where the bushes were covered with new green buds.

"On the night when you so unexpectedly entered the side room of the large typhus ward he embraced and kissed me. Only those kisses did I ever in my entire life receive from a man, only those hands ever touched and caressed me—and yet their effect was as great, as horrible, as only shame, disgrace, and depravity can bring.

"For a second it struck me as something impossible, something insane that he and you could stand there before my eyes as two separate beings and figures. What I had felt without any inner conflict to be an indivisible, mysterious unity, now suddenly, with hideous vividness, split into two unnatural masks that I supposedly had been carrying within me. I saw everything as it was with glaring, unpitying clarity. I saw myself as a whore, exposed and branded by the man I loved. I do not believe that there is any crime for which such a moment of hell and eternity would not atone. I do not believe that there is any man who could empathize with what a woman goes through in such a moment.

"But it would be of no use to go on speaking of that. I would like only to add that my torment and humiliation merely chained me more inseparably to you. The sudden loss of what constituted my life's hopes enhanced your worth yet a thousandfold and absolutely glorified you in my eyes. The more despicable I became in my own eyes, the greater and nobler did I hold to be the reserve with which you treated me, the calm self-control with which you waited for your time. I yearned now to be near you in a different way than I had been before, I yearned for you as for the presence of the pure and exalted, of which I had shown myself unworthy.

"With dull despair in my heart, apathetic and broken, I attended to my accustomed duties during the next night. The deaf mute had suffered a severe attack during the day and was to be given a dose of digitalis every two hours to raise his sunken pulse rate. Until the moment when I had to enter his room to give him the medication he had been as if banished from my thoughts. Now that my gaze fell upon him as he slept, I felt a feeling of wild hatred well up in me. And as wild and untamed as this feeling was, there was something about it that helped me: I ceased at least for a moment to berate and disparage myself—I became indignant and outraged at another person. Perhaps my first reaction was more moral, but this second reaction was the more natural for me, for basically I was in fact lacking the proper sense of guilt. But in my hate there was at the same time too a strange and cold horror: that must be the hate toward him to whom one is hopelessly in thrall, with no hope of salvation, as if one were consigned to the devil himself. For that is what is so terrible and incomprehensible: the fact that I was at the same time afraid of him. I feared his awakening, his gaze, the nearness of his hand, which had gone so thin and white. I was afraid like someone lying paralyzed and destroyed on the ground unable to make even the slightest move to help herself. The more monstrous and atrocious I imagined what had happened to me, all the more superhuman did the power he exerted have to be in order for me to explain it.

"I stood rigid at his bedside as if in a trance, holding my breath and feeling, as intense as a burning desire, the sole wish: 'Do not be here! Do not be here! Do not wake up! Do not wake up!'

"Time went by slowly; all around was deathly quiet, only now and then a labored groaning breath or a cough came from the large ward next door.

"My fingers held tight the small bottle with the life-giving drops, clasping it until they went cold and stiff.

"Then he stirred.

"I gave a start, and with ice-cold terror in my heart, with lips dry and eyes wide open, I looked down on him.

"But he merely moved his arm a little, as if searching for something. And then he sank back again.

"My heart began to beat wildly, my pulse was racing. My feet trembling, as if I now needed my every effort to save myself from lethal danger, I stole from the room. The hours went by, one after the other.

"Oh, this night! How I recall it, burned into my memory with each of its endless hours! I stole past his door; more than once my hand was on the door handle, but I did not open it again. Strangely and as if mentally deranged I was horrified and tortured by two conflicting thoughts. The one kept whispering to me: 'He is dying! He is lying there, helpless and suffering. He is struggling for breath, he will suffocate! Don't you see his fingernails digging into the bedsheet? And the medicine in your hand means life for him!' —But the other thought, it was like insanity, it was like a mocking laughter: 'He cannot die at all, never, ever can he die! Does he not have power over himself and over you? While you are tormenting yourself he is lying there smiling.'

"I do not know which of these thoughts triumphed.

"When morning dawned, they found me lying by his door, unconscious, the little bottle in my hand.

"He was dead. — — —

"Did I go in to him, did I see him dying? Did I see him when he was already a corpse, as he was lying there, stiff? Are those only images and fever visions that frightened and startled me while I hovered for weeks between life and death with a severe brain fever?

"I do not know.

"When I awoke once again to clear consciousness, Liselotte was sitting at my bedside. She looked pale and gaunt, as though she too had been through struggle and illness, but her dear eyes gazed with such deep understanding, looking with so much sympathy and goodness into my eyes that I regained my first feeling of happiness as I wept my eyes out, my arms around her neck.

"Not only had she hurried to me at the first news of my illness, she also accompanied me to the small estate of our old uncle, where I was to recover in the summer months. Surely her way of surrounding me with unspoken love contributed the most to my becoming healthy again. But my yearning to tell her all, this she did not encourage. One evening in the garden as we were sitting together and my hand slipped into hers, she suddenly embraced me and said very quietly, tenderly, and urgently: 'Christa! Don't think me strange and cold! I understand everything, I know everything! But you must remain silent! We all must. Later you will understand and be happy that no spoken word torments your soul. You hope that it will ease your pain to speak, but speaking will burden you. Do not torment yourself with past thoughts and actions, grant yourself your own right to what you may have done, but think that the world too lives by its own laws and must do so. Into the depths of our hearts the world cannot look. And as to our deepest and most hidden feelings, even the person most dear to us also belongs to that "world." You are not obliged to live to please the world, but you are obliged to preserve your peace of mind. And when you are tormented and when peace of mind comes hard for you, then take it as the price you choose to pay for what you accuse yourself of.'

"That's the gist of what Liselotte said. Whether from my fever fantasies or from her own assumptions, she had pieced the situation together wrongly, she misunderstood me on the main point. But nevertheless I clung to her words as a drowning person clings to the plank thrown out to save her. That was less because of the content of what she said than because her words simply contained advice that could instruct and guide me. From the fear and total confusion of my feelings there grew a strong need to be dictated and guided in what I did. For to do the one thing that I had apprehensively resolved to do—namely to confess, and not simply confess in confidence to Liselotte, but to confess to that very 'world' of which she spoke—I did not have the courage.

"And so out of all she said I heard only that I might remain silent where I found speaking so inexpressibly difficult—even though doing that meant I also had to keep silent toward her to whom I had so ardently longed to confess. The greater the self-control that the secret between us demanded, the more proper, the more just did it seem to me to exert such control. I seized eagerly upon what could resemble a voluntary atonement.

"Liselotte worked quietly to move my uncle to suggest that I leave the hospital completely and stay with him. When I informed Liselotte that it was my firm resolve to devote my entire life to nursing, she wept. She merely said sadly: 'If that is how you feel, then that is how you must act, Christa.'

"I dreaded my resolve as I dreaded being buried alive. Yet precisely for that reason I thought that I had to take it upon me. How could it be otherwise?

I was able to see and judge what had happened only with the eyes that my upbringing had given me. And from that came the inner need to impose upon myself a penance for what I had done and to seek out the most difficult of all sacrifices. In this way—the way of Christian asceticism, whose articles of faith are already wavering in many of us but whose moral ideas have become part of our flesh and blood—I became, in the quiet, hard struggle of the soul, the selfless, dutiful Sister Christa whom people praise me as today. To raise myself up to the level of Liselotte's private morality I lacked the character and at that time also the independent mind. From this morality—which is also purely the result of certain circles of life and prejudices of class—I adopted one small piece, retreating to it on occasion from my everyday conscience as if into a hiding place. This small piece contained the words: 'The world does not need to gaze into our most private hearts, and what happens there is not to be made profane before the multitude. Nothing belongs to us so exclusively as our penance and longing.'

"Today I am much, much older than I was then. In the gray monotony of my life I have learned to ponder many things in silence. I have given up the painful work of condemning myself and glorifying you. I have regained the lost calm of my soul, even though it is a dead calm. I was allowed—I was supposed— to forget myself in the service of others, with all that may have lived in me in the way of regret or longing, of sorrow or happiness, and I did that with such dedication that basically I no longer possessed a real self of my own— yes, until I had become the perfectly mechanical care machine that they only have to rewind daily.

"And now I ask myself why I let slip at the beginning of this letter the word 'accomplice.' There must be words and angers that are able to steal into our dreams without our acknowledging them when we are awake. I take back this word and place my confession as the lone guilty one in your hands as if in the hands of a person who clearly knew better than I did how to keep himself pure and resolved amid the confusions and temptations that surround us.

"I do not want to cast doubts on the reverence of my youth.

"You rose and I fell in the struggle of life.

"I suppose it had to be that way. —

"Christel von Brinken"

MAIDENS' ROUNDELAY

The decorator had already been working for hours on the upper main floor of the old family hotel. The roller blinds in the rooms that opened out onto the shaded garden were undergoing some repairs—that sort of thing was often necessary here in this rather old-fashioned building. But despite that it was so comfortably situated, more like a quiet garden house than a hotel in the middle of Munich. Those who lived here tended to like to stay for a long time, as could be seen from the rooms. These were not rooms for tourists just passing through.

Especially this one room where the ladder was leaning by the window: even the way the broad, comfortable writing desk stood, with a pelt rug under it. And then the felicitous notion of taking the bookshelf, for which there had been no real wall space, and having it extend out into the middle of the room from the narrow wall between the two windows—that arrangement resulted in two well-lit niches and was not so bad at all: say, for a gentleman's room making do in close quarters with what furnishings were provided.

Opposite the writing desk, by the window, was a large armchair of well-worn woven straw, and on the low little table in front of it lay, beside the simple smoking paraphernalia, a riding crop. Above it, held fast with bright shiny thumbtacks, hung several photographs: faces of pretty young girls.

The decorator climbed down off his ladder and gathered the tools he had scattered about on the dressing table by the bed screen. There was room enough for him to do that, since just a single comb, carelessly pushed into one corner, gave the only indication that this was meant as a dressing table. It could hardly be a vain man who did his hair here every morning.

Diagonally across the hall, the door to the last room where there was work to be done stood open—it was a magnificent corner salon. It seemed to have just been occupied: a calfskin bag was lying on the carpet and only the vanity kit had been taken out and opened on the table. The evening light of the sun, its reddish glow falling in through the crown of the blooming chestnut tree outside, flashed and shimmered on the silver trim of the numerous boxes, crystal bottles, brushes, and hand mirror that were scattered about.

Among them lay a handful of long-stemmed, richly aromatic red roses.

At this moment a light but firm tread came down the hall, stopped not far from the door, and a young girl cast a fleeting glance at the still-life arrangement on the table. Yes, it was clearly a young girl, quite young even, and the fact that she did not appear so was likely a result of the cycling costume with knickerbockers she was wearing.

She took the small cap from her dark, close-cropped hair, drew a key out of her pocket, and, when she found the door to the room unlocked, said in a half-questioning tone to the decorator, giving him a friendly nod: "I suppose you're already finished in my room, then?"

But the man, who was just setting up his ladder there, forgot from sheer surprise to answer in the affirmative; for the room that she occupied was clearly the "gentleman's room" across the hall!

In the meantime the house porter had entered the corner room with a suitcase on his shoulder and right behind him a tall young man who immediately had the suitcase opened and then busied himself with the vials and bottles on the table. The decorator up on his ladder, whose presence was excused with many words of explanation to the new arrival, had to laugh to himself: he would now really be quite in favor of having these two hotel guests exchange rooms and their belongings as well! If things kept on this way, then in this topsy-turvy world they would soon be doing the women's rooms like those of the men, and vice versa.

From the alcove attached to the small salon came a fine, faint aroma of very costly soap and subtly perfumed cologne, which mixed with the breath of the roses on the table. The gentleman stepped back from the dressing table, changed his coat, and pushed open the glass door that led from there out onto the broad veranda that ran along past several other rooms.

A few stone steps led from there to the garden. Beneath the large chestnut trees hung glowing lanterns; at some of the tables, guests had already settled down to a pleasant evening meal. Others were sitting farther away on the comfortable wicker benches hidden among the blooming hedges, chatting in the light May twilight.

At one of the brightly lit tables, the one nearest the veranda at which two young people were dining, one of them arose with some difficulty and walked, slightly limping, up the stone steps.

"Are you ready, Alex? Why are you taking so long, then, everything's growing cold and losing its taste," he commented, taking the new arrival by the arm. "I think Knut really likes it here, and you?"

"Yes, I like it too," the other nodded. "The place appears to include an entire bathhouse with every possible sanitary facility; perhaps the longer stay here will do you good, Ferdinand," he added, as he guided him back to the table.

"Ah, me! I'll not hold out here much longer without you two. I'd like it best if I didn't need any other doctor in the whole wide world but you, Alex."

The third young man at the table raised his blond head and laughed with good-natured mockery. "That's a fine doctor!" he said. "You're at least seeing to it that one person in the world reminds you of that fact."

"Spiritually is how I meant it," murmured Ferdinand.

But Alex responded cheerfully: "Don't make fun of what I've done, I beg you. I've passed the main state medical exams—so there you have it! And I have to keep on reminding myself: if someone has had to go to such lengths as I did to conquer his laziness and, harder still, his sensitivity, to complete studies in that field—"

"And ultimately still to remain, what I, unfortunately, can only temporarily be: A Free Man," interjected Knut. "You're still, after all, to your good fortune, the wealthy son of a wealthy father. And so I ask: why? You're crazy, I'd say!"

"Not so very crazy. A person can just suddenly—as a result of upbringing, habit, what do I know—come to feel so soft and effeminate that he gets a rage to toughen himself up. Prejudice, for all I know."

"So that in the end he becomes a useful member of human society," Knut commented dubiously, as he set on his pince-nez and peered intently toward the far end of the garden.

"No, but so that afterward a person feels a pleasant inner sense of being allowed to let himself go with undiluted pleasure," Alex answered, pushed back his plate, poured some wine, and lit a cigarette.

Ferdinand laughed. The other fellow had not really been listening. He seemed totally absorbed by what he was looking at in the far end of the garden.

"What, if I may ask, are you looking at that's so special?" Alex asked after a pause.

"I see your widow," Knut responded quietly.

Ferdinand laughed all the more, in the manner of very nervous people, as if he could not stop. "So, you've taken on a widow," he commented and almost choked from laughing.

Alex shrugged his shoulders. "No idea. How do you suppose she came here?" he asked.

"Quite simple—extremely simple: she came traveling after you. Only I just cannot grasp this secrecy," Knut burst out, quite excitedly—"after all, you're among friends here."

"I don't know about any widow," Alex asserted phlegmatically, "of course, there was a widow in the hotel in Florence, but how is she supposed to have been my widow?"

"You must know," said Knut, turning to Ferdinand, "he sat the whole day with that widow and demonstrated to her with his damned philosophy how, since her marriage had left her with no taste for marrying again, she should at least take a lover. Wasn't it so?"

"Well, not quite, actually." Alex was now looking into the garden too, and went on: "It's really her. Perhaps some kind of coincidence. I feel it's my fault. For even if you're not exaggerating horribly, dear Knut, then that would prove my selflessness, wouldn't it?"

Knut suddenly reached his hand out to him: "You're serious? Please, do be serious for half a minute! You have no interest in this beautiful widow?"

Alex laughed quietly, wide-eyed. "Interest—the way you mean it: not a trace," he said, and shook Knut's hand.

Knut looked embarrassed. "But that's really crazy! plain crazy!" he murmured, "and I— —well, yes, why were you sitting with her then? —"

Alex did not answer. He smoked, thinking to himself. Knut poked around nervously in the gravel at his feet with his cane. Then he stood up and looked around. And all at once he had disappeared into the far end of the garden in the direction of his persistent gazes.

After a while Ferdinand asked: "Did you really have nothing going with the widow, then?"

Alex shook his head. "Not my taste at all. But she was not uninteresting as a human being. Does a fellow have to behave like a bird of prey each and every time? All greed has something ugly about it. In that way Knut is so — — well, I'm no better."

"But you are. I think you would be in any case, if you didn't happen to be Baltic. I mean, if a non-Russian with a Baltic estate had better, more pleasant prospects. And that's just why you became a wanderer—but really, you do wander much more pleasantly and with more enjoyment than the rest of us do, Alex," said Ferdinand.

"Yes, it has its charm. The roaming about, that is: from life to life—always roaming: but, if possible, not without leaving some trace. This widow, for example—who leaves me, speaking as a man, cold—will in some way be guided by me, by our conversations, in her future acts and thoughts."

Alex lowered his head as he said that. He had folded one corner of the tablecloth back from the marble tabletop and was drawing a delicate Madonna face with a pocket pencil.

Ferdinand leaned forward. "The widow?" he asked.

"But dear fellow! Where are your eyes? The dear little maid at the table to our right. She's sitting between two gray-bearded papas, looking like a small wood-carved Madonna between two saints."

Ferdinand moved his chair inconspicuously a bit to one side and looked over attentively. "She has a delightful little profile," he confirmed, "but how perfectly you've captured it! And the tightly plaited braids around her head give her something touchingly primitive. Really not bad at all between the two graybeards."

From the table at which the three persons just mentioned were sitting there came the sound of loud, broad Hamburg German. Only the little Madonna, who might have been at most sixteen, was keeping completely still.

Alex, who had kept on sketching, but repeatedly looked over with dark eyes that could see so exceptionally finely and sharply, suddenly said: "I have a rival. She looks so innocent and charmingly naive, yet she's flirting already. And how! I even think there's some agreement there."

"With whom, then?" asked Ferdinand, straining his myopic eyes. He saw clearly how the young thing, as if by chance, had once turned her head to one side and then blushed vividly. But perhaps she had felt them looking at her. On the other side, over a bench in the near-dark bushes they glimpsed a bright glimmer of light, very small, as if from a cigarette.

The waiter approached and began to clear the table. A cool evening wind blew through the crowns of the chestnut trees, causing a shower of blossoms. When Ferdinand shivered slightly and looked around for his coat, Alex took out his watch and said: "Better go to your room now. We really haven't come here to put your health to the test. Tomorrow's another day."

"I go unwillingly," the other man responded but stood up right away, "I'd most like to stay up the whole night with you. But you are going to stay on, aren't you? For sure?"

Alex nodded. "For several days, for certain. I am, at least. Knut perhaps not—I don't know," he answered and shook the pale, sickly hand that grasped his own warm, slender fingers, "good night!"

While Ferdinand left with his somewhat limping gait, the three people at the other table involuntarily watched him go. The two old gentlemen indifferently, the little Madonna face with a mild curiosity that suddenly put Alex off.

Nevertheless he stood up and found a place to sit outside of the bright circle of light cast by the lanterns, positioning himself so that he could keep his eye on the table and also come closer to the flickering cigarette in the dusk-dark bush.

Quite clearly he now saw how the gazes from the table were always darting in that direction. The upper body of the person at whom they likely were directed could not be made out through the lilac branches, but at one point a hand reached far out and picked something up—a quite strangely small hand—and now it was making a signal toward the table.

And the little Madonna face looked down, covered with the red blush of shame, but all the while smiling, shy, and furtive. Suddenly a faint sound of amazement escaped Alex's lips.

The two graybeards were preparing to leave, which made it possible for the lanterns to cast their light across the gravel pathway unobstructed all the way to the bench. And there he clearly saw two long girl's legs in black stockings by the lilac bush. So that was his "rival"!

Nevertheless the play just witnessed retained for Alex's feelings something strange and coquettish. Even now, as his little Madonna cast a fleeting glance of farewell back toward the flickering cigarette, she had a look of feminine bashfulness and at the same time of cunning. In her confusion she had lost one of her gloves, left lying there beside her chair.

At the same time, still more guests were leaving. Some of the lanterns were extinguished. It became quite quiet in the garden. When the last departing steps had died away and the waiter had gone around the corner with his clattering tray of dishes, the beginning song of the nightingale could be heard, sweet and soft.

Alex did not move. His "rival" remained motionless where she sat.

They sensed each other more than they could actually see each other. But still there was something unstated between them that linked them to each other. Alex had the feeling that each of them was waiting for the other to move first.

A rather strong gust of wind blew aroma and blossoms down onto the garden paths. The nightingale stopped singing. It fell silent just as suddenly as its love call had begun.

Alex rose to his feet and walked slowly to the table, still illuminated by the lamp, with the little glove lying beside it. Then, just as he was about to bend over to pick up the glove, with lightning speed, as if shot up out of the ground, someone was standing beside him. A slender, dark girl in a boyish ensemble; a pair of wonderful brown eyes, filled with expectation, gazed into his face.

She quietly let him pick up the glove, but then she reached out her hand for it. "Please, give me that!"

They stood face-to-face and stared at each other in silence for a moment. Then Alex asked with a slight bow: "You know the lady?"

Impatiently she shook her head. "No. But that's just why I want it. I would like to become acquainted with her."

He gave a fleeting smile. "Perhaps I am in the same situation—?"

She crushed her cigarette and threw it away in a wide arc. Then she gave him a searching look, with eyes like an examining magistrate: "Who are you, then?"

"Excuse me ——" he bowed again and introduced himself— "Baron Alexander Vresenhof. Here is the glove you desire, gracious Fräulein. I am happily consoled by the fact that with its help I have had the good fortune to make your acquaintance."

She reached hastily for the glove and shrugged her shoulders derisively. "She has good taste!" she tossed off, and she was gone.

★ ★ ★

Alex was sitting the next day in the open doorway leading out to the veranda. He was holding a book in his lap, but he was not reading. His gaze would repeatedly wander down to the garden, where his "rival" of the evening before sat surrounded by several young girls—the little Madonna, by the way, not among them ——.

His rival's name was "Hans"—so he heard him called, and even in the guest book he was entered as "Hans Holtema." And so there he sat, formally holding court—or more correctly: he was courting, for the young girls were treating him totally as a suitor.

The problem "Hans" aroused Alex's lively interest; he was not quite convinced that there was really only something harmless about it. Then, when the young girls allowed themselves to be accompanied to the exit, he laid his book aside, cast yet another glance behind him into the corner salon where Ferdinand was lying asleep on the divan, and then stepped down into the warm, bright garden.

When "Hans" returned, he timed it to encounter her on her way. He greeted her very obsequiously and ventured to ask: "Well, gracious Fräulein, did the glove do its duty?"

She returned his greeting but answered his question only indirectly by remarking in a very direct manner: "Please do not think that I might out of gratitude now serve you for my part as your glove and set you up with an introduction to her. For young girls that's not in the least appropriate."

Her tone and the amusingly wrong interpretation of his overture took him aback. He did not know how much of it he could take to be genuine. All the same he merely commented in a conversational tone: "That is certainly quite an outrageously bad opinion that we've caused you to have of us. You make us out to be so totally inappropriate, without any mercy?"

"What young girls need, they receive best and most profoundly from their own kind," she remarked with sudden seriousness, but then quickly changed her tone and said: "There were actually three of you at dinner yesterday? Are you together?"

"Not as fellow countrymen, but as friends. We often get together and meet in our various homelands: a Dane, a Belgian, and a Balt."

"Oh, a Belgian—as I am!" she said.

"You're a Belgian, gracious Fräulein?"

"Half. My mother was from southern Germany. In any case I wasn't in Belgium for long. My parents are no longer alive."

Her voice became very soft as she said these words. Alex feared that at any moment she would swing away and leave him standing when they came to the hotel entrance. He commented as cautiously as possible: "It's so seldom that one encounters such independent young ladies—don't you feel lonely?"

"Lonely? I have things to do. And in any case in our times that is no longer so unusual. —But I have so much to do that—" she broke off and added with almost childlike pride: "I'm preparing to write my matriculation exams in the autumn. Yes, my God, it's late to be doing that," she commented quickly, not understanding his astonished gaze, "I'll soon turn twenty-one. But one doesn't always immediately accomplish everything that one strives to do."

"Do you intend to go to university? And study what?" asked Alex, who suddenly found her so different from yesterday, almost like a child.

She nodded. "Jurisprudence. To establish a law practice for the protection of women's rights," she asserted at once, without hesitation.

He stifled a smile. But he did not answer. It was impossible that she really was merely a dear, naive child. No, definitely not that! He recalled her comment from before, and after a short pause he asked slowly: "I would really like to know what you meant when you claimed earlier that what young girls need they get best from their own kind—? Aren't you going to let me know what you meant?"

She had just been about to say good-bye and enter the hotel; but now she stopped and replied uncertainly, hesitating: "That—? Oh, that is so important and so strange—a secret."

"A secret—?"

She looked at him as if mentally taking measure of his capacity to understand. She parted her lips slightly, as if about to speak, then she suddenly shook her head with a deep dark gaze. "One doesn't tell that to a stranger. — I couldn't, anyway." And with that she went into the hotel.

Alex stood watching her go. Opportunities to encounter her now and then he could easily find here in the garden, but that all depended purely on chance. In any case, he wanted to find an opportunity to talk to her in greater detail, to come to know her better, without all the phrasing and compliments. Slowly he walked up to the veranda. Tomorrow he would try to pay her a visit.

The next afternoon, when he was scribbling a few words on his card in order to have it brought to Miss Holtema by the house porter, Ferdinand looked over his shoulder.

"So, it's not the Madonna any more!" was his only comment, "you *are* fickle."

"Maybe it's nothing feminine at all," Alex said with a smile, "perhaps nothing but a statement she made—or supposition I've made—what do I know? But I think that this very young girl has something remarkable to tell about."

"Something that you wouldn't already know—?"

Alex stood up and put the card in his pocket.

"Ah, dear fellow," he said, "just don't share Knut's typical view that we know everything about women. We don't know anything. We know only a little about all those things that we see only from our personal perspective—and isn't that what we do with them?"

Ferdinand fell silent. Knut was always full of interesting stories about women, and that cheered Ferdinand, a man who was ailing and cut off from contact with women. But the little that Alex revealed usually counted for as much as all Knut's stories.

Alex had thought Hans would receive his visit in one of the lounge rooms for general use downstairs. But to his surprise it turned out differently. She was working in her room and simply invited him to come in.

And so he got into the "gentleman's room," the one that the decorator had thought to be such an unsuitable room for a girl. Hans was sitting behind a large inkwell and a pile of books, wearing a somewhat longer skirt than yesterday and a soft, loose-fitting blouse. She greeted him just as if they were equals, offered him a chair and cigarettes, but remained seated at the desk.

As they were exchanging their first words, Alex turned his gaze to the beautiful young girls' faces in the pictures on the wall by the straw armchair, looking at them with interest. "Relatives or friends of yours, gracious Fräulein?"

She shook her head. "No. Girls and women I don't know, but whose photographs, owing to their beauty, I was able to acquire. And sometimes, to my great pleasure, their company."

"In order to save them from the company of men, right?" he joked, struggling to keep the conversation moving in the direction he intended.

Hans looked at him indifferently with her dark eyes. "Are you coming back to that again?" she asked, her tone slightly mocking, "it really is simple enough, I should think: we know how between young girls and young men love affairs are always starting up. That does not lead to anything beautiful— that's all I wanted to say yesterday."

"In the first place, they don't always start up at all, and in the second place it sometimes does lead to something beautiful," he interjected, "or shouldn't the love of which poets sing count among the things of beauty?"

Hans gave him a very superior-looking smile. "Poets sing about what they dream about, not about what is," she commented, "and girls fall in love with what they dream about, not with what is: for that reason there's nothing to the much lauded beauty of love."

"But doesn't many a man make many a woman's dream come true, and vice versa?"

"No!" she countered, her answer so loud and emphatic that her voice resounded harshly. Then she added, shrugging her shoulders: "You don't need much experience at all to know that. You could counter me by saying that I would have to know many more men than I have seen, for example, during three years with my family leading a very active social life—but that's not true. Your feeling tells you so indisputably: the girls who learn to love the man don't know him at all, they make their own image of him out of one of their own wonderful dreams."

Alex did not answer immediately. When she spoke, she struck him as so remarkably mature and at the same time so childish. There was about her an almost masculinely logical way of expressing herself, for all her naivete, that had such an effect.

"So for that reason you simply claim that women can give each other what they need so much better and more deeply. But how do they do that, then? Do you tell each other your dreams? That must become boring in the long run."

This reproach irritated her. She shook her head vigorously, so that her short brown hair fell over her brow. "By no means do they tell each other their dreams, but rather they live for each other. You see, one woman can give another woman precisely the very same ideal support and protection that she expects from the allegedly superior man."

Alex became very attentive; he said quite slowly: "That's not totally clear to me. But no matter. In any case, that way only one of the two women would receive what she wishes and dreams for, but the other would still go away empty-handed, for she would have to develop only masculine qualities for the other woman, and where would that leave her dream of happiness?"

Hans leaned forward and crossed her arms around her knees. She smiled imperceptibly. "You are quite sly!" she said appreciatively.

"What you mean to say is: you consider us in general to be quite dull witted?"

"Well—for the most part you don't have much going for you. If it's anything more than a matter of two times two equals four. But nevertheless I can hardly explain to you what you want to know—it's complex."

"I can imagine. It's probably things that hover only half clear in your feelings — — actual matters of feminine feeling."

"Oh, no!" Hans suddenly rose to her feet. "It's a very cohesive theory that I've worked out about it."

She leaned with her back against the desk, and turning her pale, slender face right to him, she said, like a teacher: "Do you know what love is? I mean: the most profound thing about it? I will tell you: it is a mystery of completely sharing the experience of what is happening in the other person. As if hypnotized, as if replaced or exchanged with that other person, you follow the most subtle stirrings of that other person's soul, enjoying them, experiencing them, in that person. For that reason they call love a kind of insanity or possession by the other. What is the result? The result is that both persons experience the same thing—that they become identical, so to speak—or in the special case you're talking about: that woman who, for the other woman's sake, must develop masculine strength and ability also shares in enjoying the happiness of the other, who for her part is allowed to feel tender and femininely yielding. She enjoys it as if it were happening to her, as if she herself were the one enjoying it."

"Of course, the application of this theory seems very mysterious to me," Alex commented hesitantly and suppressed a wish to pose more probing questions, "but you have tested it, in any case?" he added, and also stood up.

Hans nodded and stared ahead. "Yes. It's like a daily incentive to me that makes me more competent and forceful for everything," she added simply, "without it I might not work as ambitiously as I do. I would like women to see how much they can do."

"But aren't you working too hard, as well? You actually look a bit gaunt," he asked as he made ready to leave.

She extended her hand in a friendly way. "I'm supposed to go to the country for a few weeks, my doctor says. Unfortunately, it turns out that the professor with whom I have most of my sessions is going to be traveling for two weeks," she said.

"But I hope not beginning today or tomorrow. I very much hope to see you again," Alex responded on his way out.

He thought that Ferdinand was already waiting for him, and for that reason he went back to his corner room. When he arrived, Ferdinand was sitting at the table, surrounded by loose pages of writing, and looked up distractedly when he came in.

"I'm disturbing everyone else in the world at their work, and I'm the only one being lazy," said Alex and sat down with him. "Lucky man, you, who with poetic talent can create any world you choose."

Ferdinand threw down his pen. "Yes, since you've been around—only thanks to you, Alex. Then I can put something together. It's not much in any case. With my shaky health and this old leg injury—yes, if I could live, if I could have experiences like you fellows!"

"Then you would surely achieve nothing—like us. Life is the great temptation. Not only in the usual common sense. But a person can really squander a huge amount of mental and even poetic energy on it—for example, just in enjoying a more pleasant life."

Ferdinand leaned back wearily on the divan he was sitting on. "At least you know how to console a person," he said with a smile, "but now: this amazon of yours? How was she now? Frightfully androphobic, distant, defiant, a snapping turtle—I suppose? That's how those types always are."

"She's not that way—not even that," Alex said slowly. He went on: "That always involves at least a trace of feminine self-assertiveness; a part of all that defiant amazon feeling involves some of that defiance of the man. But she's simply quite open, as though she were one of us. Up to this point that has much charm, no doubt about it. But later!"

He snatched a piece of paper out of the pile that was lying about and, with rapid strokes, so vigorously that the pen splattered, drew a face that looked somewhat like Hans: an aged, more masculine Hans with a sharp mocking line running from the side of her nose down to her mouth.

"Phew, no thank you!" exclaimed Ferdinand, "that would be a shame! Does she really have to turn out looking like that? Is there no remedy, O you doctor and philosopher?"

"Unfortunately I'm only a dilettante and amateur," Alex muttered and with nervous hand deepened all the shadows until the ink ran together on the paper, "she'd have to develop some taste. Acquire taste for the likes of us. No matter, in the end, how and with whom: simply as a cure."

Ferdinand blinked at him through half-closed eyelids. He calculated in this moment that Alex now supposedly could be kept here for several more days—and he was not wrong.

There followed summery warm, humid, storm-laden days, and nevertheless Alex still stayed on. Of course, he wasn't always with Ferdinand. He immediately left his place at his side as soon as he spied Hans in the garden, and on one occasion he even went out with her.

Late one afternoon they both saw the little Hamburg Madonna, who in any case in daylight and in her modish hat lost much of her early Renaissance attraction; she was sneaking out of the seclusion of an arbor in the garden, showing all the signs of fearful secrecy. Right after that she was walking arm in arm and chatting harmlessly with one of the old gentlemen who, apparently looking for her, had just come by.

Alex went over to the arbor; Hans was sitting there, reading and smoking. "Hans, what was all that?" he asked with a voice whose suppressed excitement in its tone surprised even him, "is perchance the little Madonna secretly keeping company with you?"

Hans nodded. "Silly people," she commented indifferently, "since they take me for an emancipated student, they're afraid that I'll bite."

Alex came up close to the arbor bench. "Well isn't it a kind of seduction that you're engaged in there? Luring her into being secretive?"

"Ah, yes. Seduction to all that's good. Bad enough that she has to be secretive." Hans took a deep breath and looked at him with shining eyes. "If you knew how it makes this little thing happy—she actually looks up to me as if to an ideal."

"And that pleases you quite well, I think?" Alex had sat down with her and looked excited and impatient.

Hans shook her head and lowered it way down. "Is that a question of mere pleasing, then?!" she responded seriously. "It is the grandest and most beautiful thing that such a young thing can ever know, it is what we all yearn for so immeasurably! that only appears to have anything to do with me personally— I am not that vain and childish—but I guide it in some direction that gives new life to such a poor human existence, that inspires, perhaps giving it a greater security that lasts. —There is nothing more a person can do for another person."

Her voice sounded deep and sad. Alex fell into an embarrassed silence. He had the feeling that in such moments she stood high above him. But also that he would have liked to take her in his arms and kiss her, this strange child, almost priestlike in her thoughts.

After a while she said wearily: "Tomorrow I'm leaving."

"Tomorrow already? Why so soon?"

"First I want to go out and see whether I can find myself a nice place to stay. I want to go up the Isar Valley. The things I'll need for a few weeks can come later, of course."

"Of course you'll be accompanied by a whole horde of girls?" he said unhappily.

"No. I'm too tired and worn out for that. Why are you asking about that anyway?"

"Because otherwise I would like to go with you, help you."

"You? Ah, why? I'm so accustomed to helping myself in all matters."

"Perhaps you could become unaccustomed to it for a single day—?"

After a pause she said: "Good. For one day. Although it is strange. Why do you want to do that, really?"

Alex was silent. Then he asked quietly: "You don't know—?"

To that there was no answer.

★ ★ ★

It was still early evening, but where the coach and pair was entering the gently climbing mountains between Breuerberg and the Kochelsee, twilight was starting to spread. The carriage was coming up this way for the second time today. The first time was when Hans and Alex had gotten off the train and then, after a good walk, had ridden out into the blossoming spring in order to find before evening a suitable place to stay for a few weeks. All the way up and all the way back nothing seemed good enough for Alex, until at last, in the small mountain village they were approaching now, with farmers that had taken him in a year ago, he found something fairly nice.

There was really no reason for them to part if he was still intent on catching the train back to Munich. But then he had come to think that it was urgently necessary for him, with the help of the two rested carriage horses, to convince himself that the neighboring villages were not, after all, really better situated.

The early summer in all its first gentle freshness wafted and sang about them. Their conversation had died out some time ago. Only Alex now and then tossed out a word, for the sake of the coachman, who had climbed down and was plodding along beside the horses, their little harness bells jingling their monotone into the silence.

Alex beheld in his memory a slow procession of all manner of pictures—not unlike the present one—the frame of their external circumstances and figures ever changing, and he recalled how often, after such a blissfully beautiful day, he had wandered on with a glad heart. Today, too, had been a no less than beautiful day. Yet pulsing through him he felt the awareness that there at his side, right next to him, her slim, slender arm nestled instinctively against his own, was Hans, with her dark eyes—dark as his own, as if they were brother and sister—gazing out into the landscape, completely lost in thought.

He felt as though the jingling of the little bells was calling to him: "Don't go on! Don't go on!" Yes, as if it called him to find rest and peace and, finally, happiness, without moving on.

"Now we're almost there!" he said half aloud, as the coachman climbed back up onto the box of the carriage, "and now I must leave right away," he added and inclined his head down more to the little face looking up to him as if transformed, whose features he could no longer make out clearly. But as he did this his right arm, which lay stretched out behind Hans along the back cushion of the carriage, made a slight—slight motion that caused her to sink toward his shoulder.

It happened almost without either of them willing it. The hour had come. Their hands and lips met—never before had a hand, never before had lips come to meet his own with such trembling emotion.

Alex was sure not to be so vain as to overestimate the stammering euphoria with which Hans lay in his arms. Yesterday and in recent days she had still been so easily familiar with him. If now the close proximity, the nearness of the man whom she trusted, had made her blood surge—this hot southern blood behind all her girlish whims—that did not mean serious love. But could not come to be what not yet was?

The wagon stopped at the sloping path that led up to the farm. There was no one in sight, far and wide. In the peaceful twilight the farmyard lay there with its adjoining fields; they could clearly hear the fine, eager chirping of the crickets in the tall meadow grass.

The farmer's wife, who had likely gone back to her fields one more time, had taken care to set out a candle in the shiny metal holder on the railing of the wooden veranda, in case it grew late. Crossing this wooden balcony, which climbed up along the low incline of the hill and which was part of the place Hans had rented, they entered the two small parlors of the farmhouse.

She almost stumbled as Alex accompanied her across the lawn moist with dew; she wrapped her hands around his arm, clinging to it as if her knees were trembling.

When she reached the veranda, she slipped into a chair and burst into tears.

Alex knelt down beside her and wanted to cover her small pale face with kisses, but she pulled away from him quickly, dried her eyes, and, addressing him with the familiar "you," said: "Stand up! You must not kneel. Not to me, ever. I will serve you in all ways. I love you."

He embraced her intensely and felt in this moment only gratitude and happiness. "Just when did that come over you, Hans?"

"I don't know," she answered innocently, "it came while we were in the carriage."

"In the carriage?! Not earlier?"

"I didn't know before. But now it seems to me as if I had always—always been waiting for you. To follow you alone, to look up to you alone. "

"Ah, dear, foolish Hans! Didn't you demand just that of the others? Weren't they supposed to look up to you?"

She had to laugh between her tears and went quite red. "Yes, of course I'm foolish! That was arrogant and childish. That was just because I didn't have you. Then at least I had to see it in others, how sweet—how sweet that is. Oh, you! You alone can do everything, know everything, will teach me everything. You looked that way, too. Everything about you looked so complete—different than they do with the usual people—so dear and so handsome."

Her cheeks were burning now, her eyes shining as if in ecstasy. Alex had sat down beside her and drew her to him. "Does she really mean me with this great love?" it flashed through his mind in the midst of his excitement, "is she, in her innocence, confusing her own momentary surge of feelings with great love—and mistaking my outer being, which might please her, for my inner self, which she hardly knows?"

"There is much I want to teach you!" he said out loud as he pondered these questions and kissed her cold hands, "all the many things that are part of being a woman and about which you still know little—things you've likely never thought about, you scholarly fellow. Like a beautiful butterfly you shall emerge to me from your cocoon. Your hair we shall let grow long again. Shall we? Oh, see what a shame that you've made your hair look so boyish, and I can't play with it. Why have you been wearing it so short? And since when?"

She nestled against him shyly. "I love women's hair long!" she admitted, "but for myself— it takes so much time to care for it. I used to pull at it frightfully, worse every morning—and finally—"

"Your patience ran out and took your hair with it?"

"Yes!" she admitted and laughed quietly.

"But now you'll have time to care for your hair. And do other similar things as well. You will care for yourself and make yourself beautiful for me. Won't you? Shall I tell you what is so beautiful about you? Do you want to know? About all your apparent boyishness? The fact that you still don't know anything about feminine coquetry and that you conceive and unfold everything only through love."

"But no coquetry?" she asked, astonished, and looked at him.

"No—that is only a word for it—for unfolding your beauty. You'll see! And

I—I will surround you with all things lovely that I can think of. My wife shall feel like a little queen."

She listened attentively, as if expecting that he would continue to enumerate the splendors of their future married life. When he didn't, she did it for him: "And then we shall both work. That is: I only as your pupil. You must tell me everything that you do and pursue and how I can participate. You mustn't think, for example, that I am ambitious for myself! No! As far as I'm concerned, I can burn all my books. I shall be proud only of you—but boundlessly proud. Wouldn't you say that's the only way I'll feel like a real queen? Only because I am caught up in your striving!"

Alex stroked her short, soft brown hair. Then he was silent. A strange, unpleasant feeling mixed coldly with his honest infatuation. At the moment he did not rightly know what it was, but he found no answer.

Hans noticed that he had fallen silent. "What's wrong?" she asked quietly and very lovingly.

"Nothing, nothing. —I think the farmer's wife is shuffling around there next door. Don't you hear? She'll have served a light evening meal in the side room. She'll notice if we don't go in—what do you think?"

Hans nodded obediently. She stood up and peered through the door into the room. There the table was neatly decked with a coarse linen cloth and on it a frugal evening meal of cheese, butter, ham, bread, and a hefty pitcher of beer. A small lamp on a glass base shed only meager light into the deep parlor with its giant bed and the window niche full of blooming, pungent-smelling geraniums.

The farmer's wife had greeted them as she departed and asked whether they had everything they needed and what the coachman should have for the night. Hans sat down at the table and stared into the flame, not thinking of eating.

Alex paced the room a few times, yet, as he did so, looked at her with delight: did she not look ecstatic, transformed? But how would it be after they knew each other better, when they were married? No, perhaps even tomorrow—the day after—when they really became clear about their future?

Hans would always measure him against an ideal, incredible standard, which he would have to meet if her euphoria of this evening were ever to become more than only a fleeting enthusiasm—if she was to love him. She knew exactly what she wanted, and expected everything of him. In her humility there was something hidden that he dreaded.

Now Hans raised her head and, distracted, noted: "Neither of us can eat."

"The farmer's wife doesn't have to know that," Alex remarked, went to the table, poured beer into the stone mugs, and cut bread and cheese.

Then he lowered the knife, gazed into Hans's eyes, and asked suddenly: "Tell me, what would you do now, Hans, if I wasn't at all the man you just decided to think I am? Not at all such a paragon of ideals and strength and diligence and I don't know what all—would you love me then, too?"

At first she did not understand him at all. As she sat there that way she had just been immersed in the still, inward effort of attributing all manner of the most secret and beautiful dreams of longing that she had ever possessed to one specific name and one specific image—Alex's image and name.

So when she had grasped his question she had to smile. She answered trustingly only: "How else are you supposed to be?"

"What? Well, I could have a completely different view of life and ultimately too a different view of the woman and her role. I could be one of those men I'm sure you know who do not at all fulfill your often very demanding and unworldly dream of life. Then would you show, instead of all your great humility, some tolerance? Would you also love such a man—?"

Hans looked at him, silent and wide-eyed. Then she slowly shook her head.

For some moments it was quiet. Alex thought to himself: "She would immediately be disappointed—at the first cause." And as he imagined that to himself, his vanity rose up in him; this, her disappointment, he did not want to experience. No, in no way—.

The farmer's wife knocked at the door and then came in to clear the table. When she noticed that practically nothing had been eaten, she left without a word.

Alex said somewhat hoarsely: "You see, I must go. And it's time. I can still make it to Breuerberg."

"— And: when?" Hans asked, almost only by moving her lips.

"First I have to go back to Munich. But then I'll come—I'll write. Or you can come. — We'll arrange something."

She stood up slowly, went past the table, and brought him his hat herself; it was lying on the windowsill.

Through the open door they stepped out onto the wooden balcony. Hans leaned with her back against the railing. The lamplight cast a bright strip across the two of them. Her face looked serious; it looked tormented and astonished.

And suddenly her arms were around his neck: "— Why did you say that— why did you ask—that before—?"

Alex remained silent. They gazed into each other's eyes, deeply and honestly, as if their eyes alone would have to reveal everything to them, enlighten them about everything, better than words can tell.

In her eyes was love. But in addition to love something else, something strange, a something that, frightened and hesitant, seemed to be asking itself: "Are you really the one I love—?"

Perhaps a few seconds passed, but he felt as if it were minutes, hours, eternities.

Alex felt as though they were parting from each other, as though, stealthy and quiet, the bonds they had made were coming undone.

He caught himself half wishing that it might be so.

"Farewell!" he said, his voice tense, and then quickly added: "Until we meet again."

Hans gave a shudder. Slowly she let go of him and stood there, pale, quiet, as if an incomprehensible coolness were enveloping her. She wanted to say something, but instead only made a gesture with her hand that sent him away or waved good-bye, and then she stepped back into the room.

Alex climbed down the stairs with hesitant tread. He walked over the meadow grass toward the roadway, which shimmered bright gray in the gathering dusk. Then he stopped, turned, and went back toward the wooden balcony. "Hans!" he called softly.

But she no longer answered.

He stood for a long time in the high, moist grass and gazed toward her windows. He really wanted to spend the night near her. Across the road there were other farms where he would find lodgings for the night.

Then early tomorrow morning he could still see her once more—.

★ ★ ★

The next evening was a happy one in the old hotel garden in Munich. There were even colored lanterns hanging between some of the chestnut tree crowns. A cheerful party was seated beneath them at one of the large dinner tables. Knut had returned from a short excursion; he had taken up along the way with a family with three very pretty daughters, and they had unexpectedly encountered acquaintances at the Munich hotel, and most of them women, too. The champagne corks were popping. Even Ferdinand was there, deep in animated conversation with a young Englishwoman; he did not even find time to ask Alex about the success of his outing.

Alex had not dined with them. He stood nearby, leaning against the trunk of a chestnut tree, making the most perfunctory responses to those sitting closest to him, and gazing into the fresh, smiling girls' faces as if under a spell.

He felt he had seen such faces today for the first time with waking eyes, with all the thoughts that, unclear and unusual, might be moving about behind those white foreheads. And he imagined Hans among them, thinking he could hear and understand what they were dreaming and longing with each other, so naive and assured. A whole gentle, loving roundelay of girls he saw before him, into whose circle, in truth, a man could never intrude.

Then came the husband, real life, the struggle, and resignation.

Yes, today he understood everything, and he had written it all to Hans today. No other man on earth could understand her better; on earth there were no ideals; he loved her, and with him she would have as good a life as she could anywhere else.

Early this morning he had wanted to see her again. He had walked out to the meadow's edge as soon as he saw signs of life at the farm. There—to one side of the wooden balcony—he had stopped and waited —

Hans was standing there, leaning against the wall, her head sunk low upon her breast, her eyes closed, and her slender cheeks moist. Her arms she had stretched out behind her in a peculiar way along the wall, like someone steadying herself while sleepwalking.

That is all he saw. There was no more to see. And yet something like shame rose up in him about approaching her.

Suddenly he felt unassailably certain that Hans too, despite all his love and care, would live in loneliness her whole life long.

ONE NIGHT

A young, simply dressed girl steps into the main entrance of the Municipal General Hospital.

The long, yellow main building, when seen from the street, looks quite gloomy, but inside, in the large main courtyard, the grand old chestnut trees are in full Maytime bloom, and on the benches under the low-hanging branches convalescents can be seen sitting in the twilight, wearing their bright hospital clothes and conversing peaceably with each other. In the warm breeze the blossoms fall listlessly from the trees. After several days of rain they mix their aroma doubly sweet with the odor of iodoform and carbolic acid that now and then wafts out from one of the wide-open windows.

The young girl passes the porter's office and then cuts across the treed grounds toward the administration building without the fat porter addressing to her, in all his dignified seriousness, his customary question as to whom she wants to see. For he knows her; not long ago she was a patient here with scarlet fever, and since then she has repeatedly come to consult with one of the doctors in the unit. Only the gas flames, which are already lit in the stairways of the administration building, shed their bright and intrusive light into her small, fine-featured face with its smile at once roguish and fearful—made fearful with her every light step echoing with such strange clarity in this almost solemn stillness.

Then from the upper floors comes an older nurse in her white apron and cap and with her serious, businesslike expression; she does not ask any questions either; she too finds it natural that no one can come and go here who does not belong here—who, either as a suffering patient or as an active worker, belongs in this cloisterlike peacefulness of a hospital.

Two flights up, the girl stops in front of one of the thickly padded double doors leading into the single rooms of the young assistant physicians, looks shyly to all sides, quietly turns her key in the lock, pulls it out again, and cautiously opens the doors.

In the small, square room with its high, wide bay windows a lamp is burning on the desk opposite the bed. No one is in the room. But as she takes off her dark straw hat there is a knock on the door from outside. Startled, she pauses and, hat in hand, holds her breath. Then someone knocks again and again, now more loudly. And then once more. A female voice, from close to the gap between door and frame, implores: "Doctor, I beg you, for God's sake and by all the saints—come to us. We are waiting anxiously for you! Doctor, sir, I beg you!" Then a pause. A heavy sigh. Someone scratches something with the bit of chalk on the slate that hangs by the door. At last comes the sound of steps receding down the hall—hesitant, reluctant.

After a few minutes she hears the sound of different steps coming up the stairs—they are bounding up—two steps at a time. A quiet, special knock at the door, and the girl opens it.

A young person enters, a tall, blond fellow with a sinewy neck and a still narrow chest, both arms filled with small bags and beer bottles wrapped in paper. He scatters it all, on the table, on the leather sofa—letting it fall where it may—and, reaching for the girl with both arms, hugs her close, close to him. "At last! at last!" he murmurs, still out of breath from his rapid climb, "—you dearest! My dearest one, you! Like a piece of good fortune here she stands in my room. A hundred—a hundred thousand times I've missed you."

He looks so fresh and good and full of life with his young, almost beardless face.

But she gazes confused into his happy eyes—somewhat anxiously. "—Berthold, someone came knocking. Someone came for you."

"Well?—and?—did anyone see you, notice you here?"

"Me, no. But it was so urgent—Didn't you meet her outside?"

"No, see whom? who was it?"

"A woman. She knocked again and again. She begged that you might come. She said: for God's sake and by all the saints—"

He lets go of her. His features are tense and pained. All joy has left them. "Marie!" he murmurs; "their maid. Number 21 Querstraße."

"She wrote something on the slate outside, Berthold. Don't you want to check, so that you'll know whom you're supposed to—"

"Whom I'm supposed to visit? Well, yes, do you think I have a private practice here or something? I, who have just completed my studies and begun my practical training? No, my dear. It's always the same person who comes."

"But what is it then, Berthold?"

"Nothing that I can help. They have the best doctor—everything. All they want is to have a person they know and trust, a friend, friendly support, to help them deal with—the most horrible. —They've known me since I was a child. We're even distantly related. But it's not just that—they're fond of me, and I— I'm fond of them, too."

"And someone there is very ill?"

"Very, seriously ill. He is—the husband. And how devoted his wife is to him! No one could expect that it would end so quickly—right now, today or tomorrow. It could have gone on for weeks. That's why we convinced her it wasn't so serious—she could never have endured knowing it for weeks. She just recently had a baby—their first child." He is still standing in the middle of the room as he speaks, as though he were listening for something.

She nestles against him. "—Berthold! Wouldn't you really have to go to them? shouldn't you go right away—"

Slowly he pulls a chair up to the table. His face is dark and resolved. "No. I was really waiting for you, Elly. —And now that you're here—and as hard as it is for you to get away—and as long as we've waited for this—don't you have to admit? It's not purely a matter of pleasure that we finally had to see each other alone again, that we had to discuss what's most important to us. Isn't our future the most important thing—? And during the day, when I'm on duty, I can't do it then."

And he takes her face quietly and gently between his two hands and kisses her on the mouth and kisses her lightly waved blond hair, still cropped short since her illness.

She returns his kisses, and everything about her laughs and glows with happiness. "Sit down here!" she says then, "let me see what you've brought. Don't you have your usual huge appetite?— it's a wonder you had enough patience for kisses?!"

And singing to herself she opens the narrow cupboard where she digs out a table napkin from among the collars, neckties, and handkerchiefs, and hidden behind it two plates and cutlery, in order to lay out the evening meal on one end of the desk.

Then she notices that he has propped his head on his hand and is sitting staring. She cannot catch his eye, the lamp lights only his long, slender, well-groomed hand, which he is holding over his brow.

"You!" she says suddenly, dropping the fork she was using to take the cold cuts out of their paper wrappings and lay them out on one of the two plates, "— I beg you, go to them! You wouldn't have any rest if you didn't. And if it's on my account—then I would rather you go."

Almost brusquely he shakes off the hand that she has laid imploringly on his arm. "— If I tell you anyway that I'm not going! Can you really want me to do it if I tell you after all that I don't want to?—No?—Well then, that's all I want!"

He draws her to him, taking her on his knee and running his caressing fingers through her wavy hair. "So come, then. Stay here and be so kind as to not keep talking about it, be so kind. And why talk about just that?!—You haven't told me anything yet—tell me, how was it, then? Was your aunt really willing to let you stay overnight with your girlfriend?"

She nods. "Yes, she was. My aunt is nice—really nice and sweet. If only she weren't so anxious about everything—especially about how men aren't really honest—how much I would rather tell her everything! Everything, just as it is. Do you know what I mean? But I can't do that, she wouldn't allow two young people like us to get together, two people who aren't anything yet and don't have anything. — — Maybe she's so strict just because she's such an old spinster, don't you think?"

He tosses down a glass of the foaming beer and shakes his head. "Your aunt is basically right, Elly, quite right, when she shelters you for all she's worth. There are so many flashy types and idlers loose on the streets here—and on top of that you're not from here, not from this area, not used to living in the city—wouldn't know how to deal with them."

She laughs, while letting him feed her with cold meats and bits of bread as if she were a small bird. "No flashy type would have anything on me," she says; "I've already been here a year now, and on my daily walk to the kindergarten I've been talked to often enough. I haven't found one of them appealing—not a one— except just you. You alone."

He hugs her close. "And me you trusted right away, didn't you? And you appealed to me right away, too, the way you lay there in the hospital bed. Right away I liked you. — — And then: the fact that neither of us is from here, both of us provincial children from the same little town, and the two of us without parents, too, especially that. A bit of misery draws people together as well, don't you think?"

She merely nods. A warm wind is wafting in through the open bay window above them and from time to time blows a strand of Elly's hair across the man's cheek. They cease talking and eating. Their favorite conversation, about the origins of their love and its supposedly eternal duration, ultimately comes to a natural end in intense kisses and tender vows.

The bags and papers before them are lying about empty on the plate they were both eating off; only a few roast almonds and chocolate candies remain. He did not forget to bring along some sweets, for he himself is fond of them. But today he does not have the feeling for it, and he drains glass after glass.

A moth wanders into the room and is fluttering about the lamp, whose porcelain holder already has several tiny moth corpses stuck to it. Outside it has become completely quiet, dead silent. And more strongly, more intoxicatingly than before, the aroma of the tree blossoms pervades the night.

Elly is still sitting on his lap. Her hand has slipped into his hands, her head nestles on his shoulder. Now and then he whispers something, quietly, as if dreaming—like the fluttering of the moth around the quietly burning light— some word or other, some empty word, an involuntary overflow of what fills their souls for the moment. Or she murmurs a half-coherent sound, which, only a longing sigh, is smothered by the warm lips that press longingly to hers.

Even now they still want to use the few hours granted them to discuss clearly all the important things for the future—but later—just a little, a very little bit later—for in these minutes they do not have the strength for that. It is their first, totally safe, totally unthreatened moment of solitude together that they find so intoxicating. For the first time, the intruding world around them is extinguished, wiped away; for the first time they are alone in the world. — — —

Then there is a knock.

He gives a start, and then he hugs her closer. He bows his head low, deep down to her, as if he wanted her to hide him.

There is another knock, more impetuous, more urgent. The knocking so heedlessly disrupts the preceding silence that it is like a physical force tearing the two apart.

Elly tries to free herself from his embracing arms and stares helplessly toward the door. "Can you act as if you're not here—if someone knows that you're inside?" she asks, barely audibly.

"Only the nurse from my unit knows that," he answers in the same tone, standing up without a sound.

Both stand motionless. The knocking stops, but someone presses up close to the door.

"She can tell that the lamp is burning in here," he murmurs and, as if in fear, takes a few steps forward on the carpet, not to open the door, but instead going to one side and totally away from the door, all the way to the closet—just as though the door were of glass and transparent and he had to hide in a corner.

Elly, her eyes wide and uncomprehending, watches his foolish behavior. Then comes the woman's voice from before, urgently, begging for help: "Come, Doctor, please come! Don't leave us alone in such misery! The man of our house lies dying and cannot die, and my mistress is seized by a fit of hysteria and cannot believe it, just won't believe it, and insists on hearing from you whether it is true. Have mercy, Doctor, and come."

The horrible words echo through the whole room, to the farthest corner, so that there is no hiding from them—they fill the whole room, as if echoing a thousandfold from the walls, dying out only when, from inside, the key is inserted in the lock and turned.

With one swift pull Berthold throws open the door. He steps out into the hallway. Elly is unable to hear the brief exchange that occurs outside in low voices.

Then he comes back into the room. "I must go there!" he says and looks disturbed and anxious, "I must go, Elly."

And as she gazes into his face, she suddenly grasps that it is not only being with her that held him back from going. — Something else as well, something stronger—what, she does not know.

In silence she watches as he puts on his coat, how he puts various things in his pockets. "— It's surely much better that you do go," she finally says quietly, "you might not have been able to bring yourself to go—later."

He is not listening to what she is saying. "Stay here!" he says hastily, "lock the door from inside. Don't open the door for anyone, do you hear? Not for anyone."

"— Here?!—you want me to stay here—?" she asks, startled, "— but just think how late it might become, and—"

"No, no," he interrupts her quickly, "it will take only a short time—I've told her that today I have the night shift and can't stay away. So it will be just a short hop away—only a few houses from here—so you'll stay?"

"I don't know,"—she murmurs, uncertain.

"I beg you to stay! Don't leave me missing you when I come back; don't make me return to an empty room! I couldn't bear to lose it, this evening with you. And now in such a hurry that we cannot arrange a single thing—are we to part this way and not see each other in such a long, long time? Look, that's impossible. So you'll stay—won't you?" And he seizes her hands and holds them tight. His gaze, anxious and intense, fixes on hers.

"Yes!" she says, convinced.

"Thank you! — — And forgive me, my dearest, for leaving you." Quickly and intensely he kisses her hands and her face. Now it is she who pushes him to the door as he hesitates.

At last he is out of the room. She hears his footsteps down the hall. Now he is hurrying, almost running. —

Elly leans her back against the door and feels like crying. So much pain, longing, love, and a sweet, hot excitement constrict her breast. What does she care about leaving at the right time to go to her girlfriend's! But these precious, irretrievable minutes that they have fought for only after so many obstacles and unsuccessful struggles—is it not unbearable to spend them now alone and without him—without him, who just now had his arm around her—without him, to whom every nerve in her body cries out?—

Elly gives a quick stamp of her foot and, her gaze full of angry, yearning impatience, takes in the whole brightly lit little room. On the desk she sees the grease-flecked paper bags, the apple peelings and almond husks. With a sigh she starts gathering up the dishes with a housewife's instinct, shakes out the napkins at the oven, puts the empty beer bottles behind the sofa. As she does so, she casts an almost reverent eye on the individual everyday objects in the room, the books, the instruments that Berthold works with. He strikes her as so knowledgeable and important compared to the men in the simple, practical professions whom she used to know back home as a tenant child! And his appearance is part of all that for her—his appearance, surely not handsome, but well-groomed, that of a son from a good family who, even with the greatest scarcity of financial means and the hardest striving to get ahead, does not neglect himself. —

Elly climbs the one step up to the high bay window, sits on the ledge and looks out over the dark treetops into the sky so thick with stars. From off at an angle across the way the large, round clock of the hospital chapel shines her way, just like a giant moon. And the seductive early summer surges and wafts into the room and all around her and fills her completely, to the very brim of her heart, with her young, exulting, intense love. — — What exactly this love really loves she does not know herself, whether she loves what is good and able about the man who has better clothes and manners or what in the first honest glow of youth is drawn, longing and awakening the glow of desire, to the woman— she loves without judging and without differentiating, but she loves with full devotion in these hours of waiting and yearning.

She presses her forehead against the window frame and blinks, tired and dreamy.

When she listens that way to the monotone, soft rustling of the blossoming treetops it sounds like a lulling cradlesong. And she likes to listen to it, for she knows well the trees and their rustling, the wind and the blossoms that lead her off to the dreamland of childhood memories—and to the little tenant farm on the Bavarian border that her father still had then, and to the path she took to school, alone through the stands of birch, to the teacher in the next village who taught her so many good things, and to the large servants' hall downstairs at the manor house where, after work, the tired people would sit listening to the harmonica.

★ ★ ★

The hands on the round hospital clock move on from one quarter hour to the next. When it strikes one, Elly suddenly starts up out of her half sleep as though a hand had touched her shoulder. She is sitting, leaning forward on the window ledge; one wrong move and she could have slid off, in the middle of her dream, and now be lying on the rain-wet flagstones in front of the administration building, a mass smashed beyond recognition.

It makes her shudder. She jumps down off the sill, and, amazed and incredulous, her eyes fix on the shining clock face across the way. One o'clock! It was not a dream that she heard it chime like an alarm call, it really is one o'clock!

Now it is much too late to think of going to her girlfriend's. She has no excuse to go there. It would still be better to stay here and wait until activity begins on the hospital grounds early in the morning; for then, with patients arriving early and the hospital personnel having to deal with them, she can slip away without being noticed. She was once here herself so early in the morning when her aunt became unexpectedly ill during the night.

She is still standing there, startled, indecisive, pondering, when a key is turned in the lock from outside. She dashes over and unlocks the door, ready with a cry of joy to run to the arms of him who at last is rescuing her from the eerie loneliness of the room. But he gazes at her distracted, as if only just now, upon seeing her, he had forced his way back to her. He looks pale and exhausted.

"— Yes, it is late, it turned out to be a late, horribly late night, didn't it, poor Elly? It's almost impossible to let you out and take you home now—if someone sees you — — ! And the porter would have to open the door for us."

"If only it were later, much later!" she says dejectedly, "—morning bright would be best. People are already coming and going here so early. I think it would still be best if I wait until the sun comes up."

"— The sun—?—yes—" He says this without really having listened. He is about to hang up his coat, but stops in mid-move. Then he throws it carelessly onto the corner of the sofa and purses his lips as though he were getting ready to whistle. But he does not whistle. He only makes as if he were about to, and then, nervously, he runs his hand again and again through his close-cropped hair.

Elly stares at him with eyes that still show signs of their disrupted sleep. "— — Is he dead?" she asks cautiously.

"— Dead? — — Yes, now he is. —At last he's dead. In the end we all must die; no one can get past it. What is it all about, in the end?" he comments in a light, careless tone. Then suddenly: "— Such nonsense! Such a senseless disease! Senseless, I tell you! And such a man in the prime of life—didn't he have a right then to live, to be living right now?—He never expected much from life—no, no one can claim he did. He mostly had a bad time of it, often a miserable time, had to support his parents as well—had to struggle all the time; life dealt him blow after blow, you might say. —Then he finally marries this dear little wife, finds this modest little job, a bit of happiness—and he was happy!! For now things had to go better for a little while. Not long ago he said to me one more time: 'Don't think I expect anything special; I want nothing, not success, not good fortune—just let all kinds of luck leave me in peace, just leave me aside, let me be—just as long as I keep what I have.'—Dear God, it still rings in my ears, the way he said that!"

"And what did he say then, when he became so fatally ill?" she asks, her face crestfallen, sympathetic.

"— About that—? What he said about that?" murmurs Berthold, looking at her but hardly seeing that she is standing there; there is suppressed anger in his voice and in his eyes, and she hears how he is gnashing his teeth. "— — He didn't say anything about it, nothing, not a dying word did he say. He lay there silent, silent and enraged—yes, enraged, in inner turmoil about his death. There was rage in his gaze—often a dull hate when he looked at his doctors and at me as well—and he let himself be tormented by all the rules of our arts, right to the death throes, long and gruesome and not wanting to end until at last they strangled him and with him his anger, too, that helpless, ferocious anger."

He speaks with his voice lowered, muted; she sees how he clenches his right hand, his fingernails pressing into his palm. —Perhaps to keep back the tears. —Then he walks slowly over to the sofa and sits down on the end of it—looks up and reaches his arm out to her. He draws her to him and bows his head; he does not kiss her, but she does feel that only now is he with her again.

"Look, I was afraid," he admits with a fleeting smile at being so distraught and exhausted, "— quite simply afraid to go there, to be there. —Of course, I had to tell his wife the truth as she lay there, seized with paroxysms of hysterical laughter, while he was groaning away in pain in the next room. —It's gruesome, that sort of thing. A person is so helpless, so miserably helpless."

She runs her hand, gently and timidly, over his short-cropped hair, now moist with sweat. "— Aren't you all a little used to it by now—from working in the hospital?" she asks meekly.

"From working in the hospital? That's really something quite different. Usually it's a stranger, just a case—medical interest predominates by far, numbs any inclination to softness. —Only when they are here for longer, when you come to know them well, then it's harder, but it's still bearable—. Only when it happens this way—outside of the hospital where, so to speak, illness and death belong—and when all you can do is make the sacrifice of watching, unable to take any action—and in addition it's good people and friends and a life that you know about—. And then this wrenching death taking such a modest life—"

"You poor man!" she says, shaken, as she feels the tears that he has been holding back, "— perhaps you all go through this at the start—or perhaps you're better, more compassionate than the others."

"More compassionate?!" he asks derisively.

He has let go of her again and stood up. He begins to pace the narrow little room.

"No, you see! That's not compassion! It's anything but compassion! What makes you think it's compassion? For death—we too must surely face it. Yes, that's true, sooner or later but for certain—absolutely for certain. Do you understand that?! — — No, don't tell me you understand it, for that's just it, the most horrifying thing, that we understand it suddenly and totally only in such moments or hours, as though we were touching and feeling death while otherwise it just keeps far off at such a distance—an unclear something. But it's not far away at all, not at all; it just looks that way, it just turns its back on us, as it were, until—until it turns around to face us—"

"Dear God, how much he's talking and how quickly," she thinks to herself. She doesn't respond. A fine feeling keeps her from injecting some banal comment into his dark mood.

Then suddenly he draws her to him—wildly, passionately. "Elly, don't listen to what I'm saying—it's so useless of me to be burdening you with this! But you see, child—I am thinking of you and of myself when I talk this way. I really would like to hold you, protect you—wasn't that our future, our dream? — — and still I am powerless—powerless against death's presence in the world, the death that will take you and me."

The last part he merely murmurs, drawing her ever closer to him and kissing her with rising passion. Then just as suddenly he lets her go. His eyes go dark. "Forget it, be together and forget about it, yes, we can do that for a while, and that's what we'd like to do. But we are supposed to come to terms with it and fight through it and confront it—we must! Then we have to gather all our vital strength and curse and pray—and—and I can't come to terms with it."—

She looks up to him helplessly; he sees that she is weeping.

Exhausted, he sets her down. "Come here!" he says in a different, friendly tone, "sit down beside me. I had to keep watch all last night in the unit, and the previous night I was on journal duty—I think my raging weariness is causing all this."

He makes room for her to sit and lies down far back on the sofa, almost stretching out, and takes her hand in his two. But then right away he stops looking at her and stares up at the ceiling instead, and his gaze wanders unsteadily back and forth without finding anything to come to rest on.

"If you could just rest!" she says and looks down compassionately on his tense, nervous features.

It makes him impatient that she keeps looking at him so persistently. "What do you mean: rest? what help can that be, then, I'm not a horse, you know!" he answers irritably.

Hurt, she falls silent. How differently she had imagined the evening would be. She looked forward to it with too much longing and joy! And now he is not paying any attention to her at all, it is almost as if she were still sitting here alone. Her reason has followed his excited comments, but her feelings are not able to follow him all the way to these unfortunate people, not all the way to the horror of death — —.

Her feelings are absorbed by longing and dashed hopes and injured love, and these feelings are stronger than that pale, incomprehensible death that "keeps its back turned" to her, as Berthold said—. But then, too, he spent the night at someone's deathbed, while she just sat at the window, nestled in the aroma of the blossoms and the rustle of the treetops, dreaming.

The lamp on the desk burns dimly. From time to time its little flame crackles as if it were about to go out at any moment. From the other side of the room the narrow bed shimmers white in its iron frame. A big, fat fly is humming and buzzing between table and lamp and alights greedily on a forgotten piece of apple peel.

How lonely, how deathly lonely it is in the little room! Elly stares at the fly as it nibbles, and she feels more deserted than she has ever been in her life. Large tears well up in her eyes and fall on her dress—different, heavier tears than before. — —

She is awakened from her dismal thoughts by a strange sound. It is coming from Berthold. He is lying stretched out uncomfortably on his back and snoring. He has actually closed his eyes and he is sleeping and snoring.

Her tears cease as she stares in amazement. So why did he insist he wasn't a horse? He's sleeping off his emotional exhaustion just as he would a physical weariness.

His right hand hangs limply over the edge of the sofa, his left, which is still holding Elly's fingers, is cold and damp. His face looks pale; his boots, which stick out over the end of the sofa, are stiff with dirt from the street. In this moment he lacks any aesthetic appeal, any personal charm that in Elly's eyes would set him apart from any socially lesser men. And in this moment the emotional distance that his apparent disregard and benumbed insensitivity have momentarily created between them is compounded by that sudden physical alienation most often caused by the most minor things. In this moment it is as if Elly has completely lost him from her heart and from her senses. Or is it merely that from his previous dark words nothing but black shadows are rising up to darken everything and take the glow from her love? Is she merely freezing from exhaustion and hurt and boredom, or are dark, incomprehensible shadows creeping out of every corner to make her shudder? And what is it then with all love and joy, if even the merest breath from the realm of death can pale them—what is it then with all love and joy if in fact so soon and so surely everything must die and decay? —

She thinks this thought at first only in defiant bitterness, with the desperate longing to immerse herself totally in that thought and be really unhappy with it—but then she thinks it with horror and tries in vain to free herself from it. She imagines she is hearing again the conversation from before, only this time not only her reason is following the words—for this time the whole mood of death overtakes her and holds her fast. She feels as though she were being cast from her rose garden out upon a bare rock cliff in the wild churning sea. But not just she alone, but with her all people—all humanity—every single person who has ever lived and loved and died. She feels herself inextricably and miserably bound up in the great universal suffering of life, her small, isolated sorrow of love absorbed by it and submerged in it. In this moment she could not have kissed or slept. She sits, her hands clasped around her knee, staring into the night with burning, wide-open eyes.

The wick is smoldering in the lamp. She rises quietly and puts it out. The sky above the hospital courtyard begins to take on a delicate red. Hazy white morning clouds draw across the horizon. From the tops of the chestnut trees that rise like a black compact mass against the sky she can hear a small sleepy birdsong. Here and there the light from a window in one of the side buildings shines into the dark tangle of leaves, outlining a branch that sways heavy with blossoms.

Berthold is still asleep. Leaning his head far back, he is lying there sleeping so soundly, so deeply, so in thrall to his great, dream-filled weariness.

Elly kneels down beside him, and in the tentatively dawning morning light she bends over his pale face with its silent features now so soft and the deep peace upon his brow, which before had twitched and furrowed in nervous anguish.

He lies there like one sleeping, or like one dying. Someday he too will lie that way in death—he will be snatched from her or she from him. —And warmly her love for him wells up again in her heart—love without bounds, without reservation, as though she herself had only now escaped death simply to love him. But new love, love become new—not for the lover alone but for the human being, whom suffering and death, whom life itself in all its mystery and power, in its becoming and its passing, bound to her in its most mysterious depths. And a new, newborn desire— not only to kiss, but to live life with him until the hour of death.

Until the hour of death. —Would the love and joy of their tender hours help them through until then, would they remain alive and strong through all that— until then?

Elly draws a deep breath, and, with the hint of a smile on her lips, she bends deeper still over the slumbering man.

No—tenderness alone might not suffice.

Perhaps life's earnestness might often come to destroy the lovers' play as it had today, perhaps the little song of love might often die out unheard amid the painful, confused tones that assail his heart, as it had today. —But with a happy face she will from this day forward raise up her arms to him, in gratitude that he does not merely caress her and forget life's seriousness when he is with her, but that he struggles with life for himself and for her. And in her lap he shall rest his head when he is suffering. Perhaps then a tender dream will always rise up anew— in a night like this one—and, ever again, secretly weave, in the dark, new love around their life. — — —

Elly stands up without a sound and quietly prepares to leave. One more gaze, of almost motherly concern, she casts upon him. Gladly would she pull off his heavy, dirty boots so that he could rest better. But that would surely wake him. So instead she merely pulls a blanket from the corner of the sofa and spreads it over his knees. Then she steals carefully from the room.

In the hall and on the stairway it is still as quiet as night. The gas flames are still burning as they had the evening before, as if she had just come this way.

But outside in the courtyard she plunges at this early hour into the even, colorless brightness of the early morning, in which the illuminated windows make their wondrously ghostly mark on the flagstones strewn with wilting, crushed chestnut blossoms.

A doctor coming from the inner courtyard of the hospital is walking through the trees. Seeing a woman walking toward the main exit, he stops and watches her attentively.

Somewhere a door is opened. Two nurses sweep past in quiet but quite amiable conversation. They too turn their heads and stare.

Elly does not notice. She stands in front of the porter's office under the great archway and rings the bell until at last the fat porter, quite without his usual dignified bearing and muttering sleepily, comes out in his shirtsleeves and, with a yawn, opens the gate for her.

She has completely forgotten that, when she left, she wanted to wait until the sun was all the way up, the gate unlocked, and the everyday routine under way in the courtyards. And now she is not thinking that she might be putting herself in a compromising position. —

In this moment she does not see people as dangerous spies and nosy gossips, but simply as brothers and sisters—she feels such a heartfelt union with them, so far removed from all petty doings—caught up together with them in the same life—and in the same death.

Thus does she step out innocently upon the deserted street as it dreams in the morning's gray dawn, hurrying her way homeward with rapid, buoyant steps, which echo almost happily from the stone wall that runs along the row of sleeping houses. Her mood is bright, young, and healthy and filled totally with an inexplicable joy.

And glowing red in the early morning mist the sun rises behind her, large and silent, wrapping the hastening figure all round in a solemn light.

ON THEIR WAY

— — — The higher they went, the shorter the long days of the Maytime sun seemed to become. Up by dark and gloomy Schwarzensee the cone shapes of mighty mountains were already blocking out the sun, while down in the deep valleys everything was still bathed in shining light. Down below the fruit trees were in bloom, and the lilacs were opening, and people as far north as St. Wolfgang were getting the first, small, sourish cherries from the South Tyrol. But up here, instead, there were still yellow catkins shaking on the willows on the far shore of the lake, new birch leaves were giving off their sharp and tangy odor from half-opened buds that, from a distance, resembled brownish autumn leaves, and on the mountain slopes the broad shimmering snowfields came down so far—as far as if the area bordered on a world of glaciers.

Later, the high summer would tend to diminish this grandiose aspect of the alpine landscape, yet even it would not destroy the infinite silence that prevailed with almost sublime grandeur. Here only birds and crickets seemed to have been given voices, mixed only with the isolated—lost—gentle clanging from the bells of the few pasture cows, their tones blending, beautiful and dreamlike, into the natural idyll as though they were part of it. — —

From the shore of the Schwarzensee a slender young dairy hand gazed, his mouth agape with wonder, toward the gentleman and lady who were approaching the dairy cottage.

They were not proper mountain climbers—tourists chancing an outing and perhaps still not knowing whether they might prefer to take a ride in a light donkey cart or risk improvising a walking tour up that way. This was evident from the gentleman's clothes, of which he had taken off the raincoat; in addition, the young lady in her broad-brimmed straw hat was wearing a skirt that appeared to be of a cut and length that would make it unsuitable for hiking for hours across mountain scree.

They stopped in the low batten door of the dairy and, speaking High German, arranged lodging for the night with the astonished dairy proprietress, Mali. Tomorrow at midday they wanted to move on, across the Mosau and down the Unterach as far as the Attersee and—and, well yes, the rest could hardly be of interest to Mali.

She had had to work the whole day and was about to go to bed. So without any particular show of enthusiasm she directed the strangers to the narrow wooden nook next to the hearth room and separated from it only by a wooden partition that reached just above eye level. Mali's huge bedstead was there, piled high with a straw mattress and, smelling strongly of cheese, a coarse woolen blanket that served as a pillow.

A line was strung diagonally across the room, on which several colorful aprons and calico skirts were hanging. In the corner, above a chest, hung a Bible quotation embroidered in gold beads and beside it a small shelf holding some painted dishes. All this was gathered under a cracked roof that provided the only shelter to cover the hearth room, the sleeping quarters, and the adjoining hayloft. And up into every joint and cranny of this roof the smoke that rose up every day from the fire permeated everything with its pungent creosote smell.

The gentleman and the lady looked around, put down their two pieces of luggage, and asked only for water for washing. Mali responded by bringing out a wooden bucket that was actually meant for the morning milking, which is why she asked that it be returned. Shaking her head she watched the two then as they actually walked out with the bucket to fill it with cold, ice-cold lake water and only then withdraw to their wooden sleeping quarters.

By that time Mali had already stretched out on the long, hard wooden bench beside the cold hearth; but as the evening cool came on she was beset by the coughing that she had not been able to get rid of from the winter, and, shivering, she pondered whether she should not rather climb up to the hayloft with the old hand and the boy. At first she may well have bid the strangers welcome with stolid indifference, just as she was accustomed to endure everything as the pasture does the storm, rain, and sunshine. But now she was confronting the unexpected and uncomfortable aspects of the situation; curious thoughts swirled about in her head, and tagging along behind them the secret concern about whether the unbidden guests would repay her for her lost bed rest with a small gratuity.

Then — — it must have been deep in the night—the wooden door to the sleeping quarters creaked, and the gentleman came in, feeling his way in the dark, his hand out in front of him.

Yes, well, was there something they needed, then? Mali thought to herself and immediately asked out loud whether there was still something he wanted.

No, they did not need anything at all, the gentleman calmed her, he was just going into the hayloft to sleep a bit longer.

She sat up in amazement. "To sleep?" she said, a bit offended, but she would have thought that her lovely bed would surely have sufficed for two people.

He laughed quietly. He had a youthful, nice-sounding voice. "You've given it a try, then?" he said, teasing her good-naturedly, said goodnight, and then climbed past her into the hay.

Mali did not answer. She stared ahead into the darkness, an alert listening look on her face.

Had she given it a try, then! She had had that bedstead since her parents died, and that seemed such a long time ago to her that just thinking back that far made her lose track. And then she had indeed had her young man she had liked, and a child from him—. That was a long time ago, too. The young man was long gone, somewhere out in the world, and the child had died young.

Now she herself was in her late thirties and had lost her teeth early and her thick hair as well. — —

Mali sat up on the hard bench; she was cold and she had to cough. She could not sleep this way.

And what strange people those were. In the evening they had gone and fetched cold water, in order to drive out the last bit of warmth; and in the night, well, then they slept apart from each other—.

The night air grew colder, and outside the wind came up, while the pale gray sky shone through the opening by the fireplace. Lonely and cold is how the nights really were now all the time—even in the summer.

But it had not always been that way. No, not always — — —

And Mali's thoughts wandered—roused for a short moment from her everyday sleep, like fluttering moths when a weak shimmer glides past them that reminds them of sun — —.

— — Once a tourist had come over the mountains. Not at all far from here it was, a few hours to the other side of the Schafberg, at the first dairy she worked at. A stormy autumn evening, near the end of September. The young man had gone up to sleep in the hayloft, but maybe it was the storm wind that came howling through, or perhaps the restlessness of the frightened cows in the stall had not let him rest, for deep in the night Mali heard him climb down and strike a match in the middle of the hearth room.

Her big bedstead with the flowers painted on it was there, not closed off in any wood stall. As in most of the dairy farms the bed was set up in the back, high above the oven hearth, right under the roof. When Mali looked down and saw his cigar glimmering in the dark, like a glowing cat's eye that was looking at her, she got up out of bed and began to dress, and asked him whether he needed anything.

It had grown so awfully cold in the hayloft, he said, he would rather walk around outside a bit and, as soon as the moon made things brighter, move on.

Then she offered him her bed.

Perhaps he had understood her to mean she was leaving it to him alone— but in any case he took off his hiking boots and, wearing only his knee breeches and loden jacket, climbed up to Mali, lay down on the bed and covered himself with the woolen blanket.

Probably only then did it occur to him that she herself was standing there at the foot of the bed, half undressed and at a loss, for now he invited her to get in and find room. "It's big enough for two!" He noted that with such a tired and thankful voice and with a satisfied yawn.

She climbed hesitantly over him and, in order not to disturb him, pressed close to the rear wall of the dairy cottage, whose cracks were chinked with dry moss. And while he proceeded to fall asleep almost immediately—soundly, so soundly, as if no avalanche could ever wake him again—Mali lay quietly, hearing the gusts of wind shaking the roof and listening to the deep, regular breathing next to her until it made her eyes fall shut.

— But before the gray of dawn, half dreaming and half waking, she felt herself bedded in his arms, felt his strength and warmth around her like an intoxicating power, and half dreaming, half waking, she succumbed to his strength. — —

Only when the late September sun came up did the tourist get up and on his way. Not for long, he assured her, for he had no intention of doing a regular long mountain hike but was just roaming about in the mountains to take a break from his stupid studies, and so he wanted to return that evening to stay overnight—this evening—and then again one more time—and one more time—.

Feelings of concern or foreboding did not trouble Mali when he shied away from saying good-bye to her because she was standing there before him like a person in a daze; and when she heard from far off his "God bless you!" as it echoed off the mountain walls she did not know that it was his last call to her. The whole day she went about her work so dazed and distracted, as if her poor brain were set up only to repeat constantly the same words: "This evening— and then again one more time—and one more time"—almost the only words spoken between them. And all the while she cleaned the dairy cottage of its dried-up spider webs and shook out the straw mattress and hung the skirts and woolen blanket out in the sun and scoured the floor, as if she were readying a bridal chamber.

Yet just as the sun was sinking behind the lake she sat down by the doorway and waited, imagining she could see him quite clearly before her just as he had been lying there in bed in the early morning, a dark green signet ring on his one hand and, visible and shimmering from his fine, soft flannel shirt—just above the monogram embroidered in it—his slightly exposed chest—so white, so white, like a boy's. He was sleeping in his jacket and with knee-length socks still on, his head, with his small dark mustache, thrown back, strands of straw from the tattered mattress in his rumpled hair, he seemed to Mali a young king, wearing the clothes of her people, a king in disguise.

The evening passed and night fell, but he did not come. Then she was sitting on the edge of her bed, her hands folded and her eyes glassy from intense watching and listening—and she waited— and waited.

Deep in the night a footstep crunched on the scree of the mountain slope down toward the lakeshore—at least it sounded to Mali like a step—and it came closer and closer —— and then went on by.

★ ★ ★

In the thick early morning fog that was brewing and steaming over the Schwar-zensee the two strangers from the evening before were standing on the shore. Though they had just finished their primitive washing up for the morning, their clothes looked rather the worse for wear for their session with the improvised night's lodgings—and in fact their young faces looked just as bad. Convers-ing tersely, they stared into the water that shimmered here and there through the fog cover like heavy, gray satin, and their features bore expressions of the greatest imaginable hopelessness.

"You're thinking what I'm thinking!" the young man remarked in embar-rassment after another pause.

She gave a meaningful nod, the way someone nods when sealing an entire fate. "You can't think of anything else—once the great and ultimate decision has been made," she answered.

He turned away from the mysteriously glowing water with a slight shudder, as if it had been hypnotizing him. "And yet—how little it would take and we could be so happy! Isn't that so, my dear Lisa?" he said, his tone melancholy, and he walked beside her up the slope toward the dairy house, "— a paltry bit of money! Life is beautiful after all! Our love would make it paradise."

"Don't start equivocating!" she admonished him with grim resolve, "what can that lead to, then? Do you want to live like some good little cobbler or tailor? No, let us remain great and true to ourselves—if you are not to be allowed to strive, free from common cares, to create works that might one day be immortal, and if I am not to be allowed to be the muse at your side—"

She did not finish. They were already near the dairy house, and through the wide-open doorway there wafted such a pungent smoke that they simply had to fall silent.

The wooden bench on which Mali had spent the night had been moved out toward the door; the gray-haired hand was sitting on it, bent low over the butter churn, making butter in intense silence, rhythmically ramming the heavy piston up and down. Yet even as he worked he turned his gaunt, alert face with its sharp nose and intelligent, light brown eyes with undisguised interest toward the two strangers as they came in. But the smoke from the oven hearth, where a random mix of moist brushwood was burning, so enveloped them that there was almost nothing of them to see. Right behind them came the boy, who crouched down by the hearth in front of the restlessly flickering flame that illuminated him brightly from behind, sucked on his pipe filled with crushed willow leaves, and looked on in pleased wonderment as the gentleman and the lady were on the verge of sneezing, coughing, and choking themselves to death.

"Why in the world don't they build in a chimney here?" the gentleman asked, his eyes tearing, "don't you spend enough time up in such a dairy house to make it worthwhile?"

Mali nodded; she was standing in the middle of the room, her skirts gathered up, the steaming wooden bucket full of frothing morning milk in her hands.

Of course they had been up there long enough: she herself for ten summers now and Aloys, the old hand, longer still, she said, simply using her hand to fish some small creature out of the milk to pour the strangers a morning drink.

But a chimney still would not be worth the trouble, she added, for the whole dairy house with its three occupants really existed only on account of the five cows, and the income from the cows was far from worth that much.

"Dear God!" remarked the lady, her voice choking, "— just listen, Martin, it's scarcely believable. We even become upset if our homes have something go wrong with the plumbing or the gas meter. To think people can live like this—and endure it."

Aloys had let go of the butter churn handle and was saying something very emphatically to the gentleman, his lively brown eyes sparkling.

The lady gave her companion a questioning look, unable to understand a single word of the dialect that flowed so easily from the old man's mouth.

"He thinks," the gentleman explained to her with a smile, "that really only in the cities are things made properly and nicely so as to fulfill their true purpose, while here all they have are miserable fragments that can't be made into something whole because there's a lack of everything. He seems to imagine our cultural world to be something of fairy-tale beauty."

The lady sighed and looked at the old hand almost with pity. Did he know the cities, then? she asked.

Yes, he knew them. Aloys rose, moved the butter churn back into the corner, and told with special pleasure of how, as a boy, he had gone away with a dealer in woodcuts: they made it to Linz and Graz, and he himself did beautiful carving. But then the man died, and he himself had come down with an eye disease. Since then he had been no more than a common farm- and dairy hand. With that, muttering in resignation to himself, he took up his ax and pick and made for the wooded slope above the pasture to fell trees.

In the meantime the gentleman had turned to the boy; he offered him one of his cigars to smoke instead of his willow-leaf pipe and persuaded him to carry his heavy rucksack as far as Unterach.

The lad turned the cigar longingly in his fingers, but he had no great desire to make the hike to Unterach. His whole life he had never been outside the circle of the dairy farm, except for his schooldays in nearby Radau.

Mali pointed out as well that he would have to be back before it became dark, since these days they were expecting a visit from the farmer.

"He'll be back long before then, and I know the way he has to take," the gentleman assured, "on the way back he need only look for the red markings that I'll show him. Now the whole stretch is most splendidly set up for walking," he added and pulled out the large, checkered plaid travel blanket that he wanted to lie on with Lisa outside as the morning sun broke through.

Mali shook her head and watched them leave. She took the giant copper kettle that hung from a bar over the quietly burning fire—and from the never-scoured metal belly, from which the greasy soot from time to time would peel off in black flakes—filled it with fresh water, and then, moving tranquilly, she sat down on the threshold. Mali actually had a proper day's work ahead of her, but she was neither especially diligent nor especially tidy, and she had no fear that the work to be done would not still be there when she turned to it.

Today was almost a holiday anyway, or at least an eventful day; Aloys had been incessantly sharing with her his speculations about the two city folk and his high regard for the world whence they came. She herself hardly knew that world and recalled no lasting impressions from her occasional outings there except for one hour that she had spent years ago in Salzburg on a carousel. That had been on a Sunday afternoon, and many little shopgirls and working girls were riding on it with her—one of them was riding a horse with an actual saddle, another was sitting on a raised royal throne, and she herself had climbed into a golden gondola. It struck her as an almost solemn occasion and not at all like merely pleasing entertainment; she also clearly noticed that most of the other girls were wearing expressions of almost reverent seriousness, not as if they were having a good time, but as if they were in a state of dazed rapture in the face of something grand.

And it was something grand, too: for the golden gondola glided with Mali into mysterious dreamworlds, even though she obviously was still sitting under the same canopy. You got on here to possess for a quarter of an hour everything that you had desired, to attain all that remained unattainable, to forget everything that weighed heavily upon you. The sounds of the music came like the good fairy in the stories and urged you to wish for the most beautiful things that you could think of, and you made the greatest effort to do so and had the secret feeling of being greatly exalted and omnipotent—.

Mali knew perfectly well that a carousel is only a carousel, a thing made out of wood and iron, of paint and gilded paper, but there had to be some kind of mystery about it that made sitting on it like being in church with the picture of the miraculous Madonna, only more beautiful.

The lady, she lived in a city and surely had little to do and surely rode on the carousel often—.

From the forest slope came the muffled echoes of blow upon blow. Aloys, who was working there, was also letting the presence of the foreign visitors disrupt his everyday thoughts. For they were rare and valued emissaries from that alluring distant world in which he had whiled too briefly and been disappointed, but that for years now had begun to become dreamlike for him again. After having told them all he had this morning and then, with heartfelt joy, having heard the gentleman repeat it all to the lady, he felt a deep happiness. It brought him closer to them— they had to feel that. Even though he was hired on up here as a common hand, he was still one of them.

When he walked farther down toward the clearing where the boy was working, ready to wait for him there with ropes so they could tie the winter foliage into bundles and take it to the stalls, Aloys saw the two city folk right in front of him. They were stretched out side by side on the travel blanket in the forest moss, and they nodded to him; the gentleman got right back into another conversation with him, and the lady sat up and watched attentively as he raked the wilted leaves together and put them in a pile.

Aloys was glad at heart: he told them about his youth with the wood-carvers of Radau, about how he had been the most talented of them all, and about the enthusiasm with which he had told them about his first visits to the cities. As a kind of bearer of culture and a prophet he had sat among them and inspired them to their best efforts in wood carving so that they could at least make their meager contribution to the world of beauty down there, in which they could otherwise take no part.

"But just how can you people up here believe that all in the cities that glitters is gold!" the lady remarked in amazement, after she had had everything that Aloys was saying explained to her.

But her companion gave her a nudge and threw in a few French words meant to keep her from muddling Aloys's cherished beliefs. And so he went on talking, getting deeper into the subject, and his fine, thoughtful face with the deep, expressive lines around the mouth shone with happiness while he worked with his rake, and large drops of sweat stood out on his forehead. Reluctantly he finally left his work when all the boy had to do was to tie the piles of leaves in bundles and carry them down.

The two young people in the forest moss fell silent for some time. The sun was shining down its warmth on the spring all around them, yellow butterflies were fluttering about the blue gentian shining in the high pasture grass, and over the Schwarzensee the snow-capped peaks stood golden in the morning light.

"They don't know what a beautiful life they have up here!" Lisa exclaimed, delighted.

Martin said more quietly: "Perhaps we too don't know what a good life we have down there. Aloys would consider it a grand mission just to hold even the most unassuming job there. But perhaps, too, now our feelings for all that is beautiful are just so extremely enhanced—"

"— Because we are taking leave of it all," she went on quickly and fell from her sitting position back down on the blanket as if she had been mown down.

They were silent again. They were both a bit pale from their almost sleepless night, lying there they looked like a pair of convalescents.

Martin avoided looking Lisa in the eye; when he did, it seemed too hard for him then to keep his proud composure. In that way too they knew that they were both thinking of death, of the death that was to put a voluntary end to their lives—as they had resolved—.

From time to time the boy walked past them, silently in his bare feet, a heavy mass of foliage on his back, bent deep under his load, his mouth half open in his simple face. And in the fresh breeze dry brown winter leaves were constantly blowing and flying out of the bundles of foliage, fluttering about him and sinking slowly, one by one, into the grass at his feet. It looked as though the spirit of death itself were striding on through the budding green trees—.

Martin noted this comparison, but when he looked into the boy's simple-minded face he was afraid of making mention of it.

Then it suddenly seemed to him as if Lisa were secretly holding back tears next to him. She had her head turned to one side, and there was a strange twitch around the corners of her mouth like a suppressed spasm. Deeply frightened, he sat up—.

But it was only a yawn that she was trying to stifle.

★ ★ ★

Toward eleven in the morning, the hand, the maid, and the boy gathered at the hearth around an earthen pot giving off a steam redolent of fat. The black iron pan—similar in size to the enormous water kettle—Mali had used to braise the dumplings and then left it to the city folk, for they intended to bake an omelet. Eggs were in short supply in Mali's kitchen, and the ones she had might have been lying around for some time, but they had to consider themselves lucky to find any at all. While Lisa struggled mightily to keep the sizzling pan balanced over the fire, her companion, in the absence of other dishes, plundered the cupboard in the sleeping quarters, taking from it two gold-trimmed banquet plates, the one with "May God keep you" inscribed in the middle, the other with "Live happily."

Right near the dairy house door, where a rough-hewn wooden table had been driven into the ground beneath some tall hanging birches, the two sat down to eat—with considerable hunger that was totally out of proportion to the modest omelet. They exchanged meaningful glances, as if each were trying to communicate to the other the question: "Do you know what this meal means? Do you know it is our last midday meal on earth?"

Lisa looked down at her plate with a pained smile and, reading its inscription, whispered: "May God keep you—that would have been too much!"

Martin wanted to respond in kind, but when he chanced to read the inscription, its emphatically bright golden letters sparkling so spitefully in the sun: "Live happily!" he fell silent, at a loss for words, and contented himself with returning her pained smile.

Seen from outside, the interior of the dairy cottage looked like a black hole, and the mechanically chanted liturgy that had to precede the meal at the hearth sounded almost somber, as if coming from the dark sanctum of a temple. And after the last word of prayer had died away, each of the three people, sitting there so close together on the wooden bench, dipping their tin spoons into the common dish, did so with such deliberate solemnity, as if they were only now beginning the actual ceremony, holy and calling for reverent devotion.

Only Mali's gaze would wander now and then over toward the tasty omelet outside the door and to the spoiled little couple dining out there, eating off the glittering gold dishes as if it were a holy day—bathed in cheery sunlight, blown around by the pollen from the blossoms—a picture of carefree happiness delicately drawn against the luminous white of the mountain snow and the deep blue sky.

The boy saw none of that, but just kept his gaze fixed on the dinner pot until it was his turn to reach in again, and old Aloys maintained with every careful mouthful the silence and grave composure of a man aware of the entire tragic burden of a life that must be lived in unspeakable toil for the sake of those few morsels of bread that it affords.

Hardly had the two city folk finished their meal than they wanted to leave right away. Glumly, the boy packed up his bag and the rucksack, and Mali stood there struggling to figure out in her head how much she had coming to her. Aloys stood up without a word; he took from the worm-eaten chest in the corner two goblets, one of blue milk glass and another with roses painted on it, and stole away with them to a small hidden spring on the mountain slope, known since olden times on account of the healing powers of its water as the "miracle spring." Carefully, carrying the two filled glasses before him, he returned, his eyes fixed on the precious liquid so as not to lose a drop of it, and proffered it in silence to the two strangers of whom he had become so fond. A good many tourists came by up here without leaving behind the slightest trace in Aloys's thoughts, for they too passed by the old hand without awakening his heart or his tongue. But these two had brought to life in him again a feeling of belonging to that world down below, from which they had come up here. He looked upon them as though they resembled at least those three angels that came to Abraham and "did as if they were eating."[1] And when each of the two slipped him a gulden as they shook his hand in farewell, then he respectfully took his shabby straw hat from his head. "God bless you! God bless you!"

But what he was thanking them for was worth more than money, although money did mean a lot to him as, trembling with joy, he knotted the two guldens into his only burlap cloth.

As they climbed slowly up toward the Mosau and the little dairy cottage soon disappeared from view behind the trees, Lisa remarked quietly: "How symbolic that was with the water—as if he knew—like a symbolic toast to death."

Martin said, changing the subject: "These simple people are happy with their illusions." Then, turning to the boy, he asked: "Do you like being up here in the mountains?"

"Nah!" he answered grumpily. He was annoyed about having to go along, and the idea that today he was stepping farther out into the world than he had ever been his whole life until now did not interest him in the least.

"Why don't you like being up here, then?"

"Nah. Because you can fall!"

Martin and Lisa laughed at him. Here there were no steep rock cliffs that a person would have to be afraid about falling off. Almost scornfully they gazed

---

[1] Aloys is referring here to Genesis 18:8, the episode in which Abraham "entertains" the visiting angels by providing them with butter, milk, and "dressed calf." In fact, in the German Lutheran Bible, as in the King James Version, the three angels do eat; there is no indication that they merely pretend to indulge in mortal activity. The author—or, more likely, Aloys—has remembered the biblical episode wrongly, an error perhaps intended to underline Aloys's tendency to overvalorize the visitors from the city.

along the mountain face: one like that they would not actually look for, if they—but of course they had decided on water, on a boat trip in the twilight that would not attract attention — —.

The boy let them laugh. He glanced fleetingly and with a cautious curiosity at the crosses that had been set up with pictures of horrible accidents. Except for the pictures in church these were almost the only ones he knew. All the gruesome stories he had ever heard were linked to such gloomy memorials.

Faster and faster they were descending now from the scree-covered mountain pastures of the Mosau.

From time to time Martin drew the boy's attention to the red-marked stones that they passed so that he would not miss the way back; then the narrow path wound steeply through the high rugged cliff walls of the Unterach, between which, far, far below, the mountain waters thundered past over a loud waterfall, raging and frothing and sending up a refreshing coolness to those struggling their way down.

They had all three fallen quite silent. Martin and Lisa looked at each other again—and then upward, back up the narrow mountain crest—. To stand up there, right at the top—and—a leap—. Their fantasy was laboring mightily, with pleasant shudders, for in reality they were no longer standing up there, right at the top—.

— And already they were leaving the half twilight of the mountain pass—when suddenly, with an unexpectedly sharp turn of the path, there opened to them, bathed in sunlight and in blessed splendor, like a painting of northern Italy, the blue shimmering Attersee beneath the May snow of its wreath of mountains.

The young dairy hand did not share their delight at this view; he stood there glum and sullen, his whole soul filled with the wish of not having to put one foot in front of the other with the straps of the rucksack cutting painfully into his weary shoulders.

Down on the lakeshore, dusty and hot, lay a small village in the oppressive midday sun. They went down, passing the orchards and the blossom-bedecked little houses, and when the tavern on the lake came into view Martin stopped the boy, took the rucksack from him, and slung it over his own shoulders.

"Such kind treatment would have been more in order at the midpoint of the journey," remarked Lisa.

Martin looked somewhat embarrassed. "The pack is devilishly heavy," he sighed, "but I don't want to enter the tavern alongside this heavily laden, nar-row-chested little fellow—"

Lisa smiled, but this time it was not a fateful smile, and she linked her tired arm in his. "It's good that Aloys isn't along!" she said, "he might experience his first doubts about the perfectness of people from the world below!"

The little dairy hand, who never tended to ponder the motives of human action, by now felt his goodwill toward the two city folk noticeably increased. And then when they even led him into the nice, cool tavern room and asked what he would most like to eat and drink, he felt extraordinarily pleased with the situation. Naturally, he most wanted to eat meat, for he had it only twice a year, at Easter and at Christmas.

"A sausage!" he decided.

And to drink?

"A beer!"

Both are placed before him on the colorfully checked tablecloth, and both are consumed by him with incredible speed. But then right away the waitress is there to take his order again, as if he were a gentleman.

"Another sausage!"

And to drink?

"A beer!"

And he becomes redder and redder as he eats, and hotter and hotter, and feels more and more happy. He likes it immensely down here in the wonderful hall, where it smells so good of beer and tobacco, quite different from the pungent smoke and sour cheese smell up at the dairy. Between the stag antlers there hang colorful pictures of the kaisers, and below them another picture in which a completely black lady with immense white teeth sits surrounded by cigar boxes and smoking a cigar.

When the smiling waitress approaches the boy for the third time he cannot, to his own shocked dismay, decide for yet another sausage and regretfully lim-its himself to another stein of beer. And of course he would like a cigar, too, he adds quickly, his gaze fixed on the wall at the lady with the white teeth. —

Far from his table, by the windows that look out on the lake, Martin and Lisa had ordered coffee with cognac. They were very quiet. Weariness lamed their limbs after two days of such unaccustomed activity.

Lisa stifled a yawn and remarked profoundly: "Up there it was romantic. A coffee table like this is not romantic at all."

Martin looked at her inquisitively. "I mean," she explained, "we shouldn't have had to come back down—we could just as well have done it up there, with a plunge — — anyway: that with the water was just our obsession—why does it have to be water?"

Martin had all this while been secretly fixed on the flat, almost keelless little boats that lay chained to the shore under their window. Such a boat they would rent toward evening—. "It's already too late now for this new idea," he answered quite wearily, "— right now at least I wouldn't be able to climb high enough. But your wishes are always very dear to me. — — We would just have to—postpone it—for another mountain outing."

She nodded uncertainly.

And now they described it all to each other right down to the last detail, completely forgetting their weariness. Their eyes became lively, their cheeks red again—.

Martin opened the window. "Here comes a steamer!" he exclaimed, "I think it's one that could take us home, but then we'd have to hurry!"

The shrill sound of the hissing steam and the clattering chains being cast over the dock filled the room.

They leaped to their feet, the waitress reached for their luggage—she had had no idea that the lady and gentleman wanted to leave with the ship. And what about the boy, then—?

Quickly they pay for him. Martin reminds him once more to set out right away so that darkness does not overtake him on the way back. In his haste—but also out of a wonderfully mellow feeling of good fortune—he gives the boy much too much money. And then away quickly and on deck. They make it just in time. With a shrill whistle the pretty steamer casts off from shore—

The boy looked one moment out the window at the steamer and the next at the money in his hand and then put his hand to head; he was a bit dizzy from the excess of pleasures and quite maudlin with joy. So that is how the world was that they did not get to see up at the dairy, that is how people were down below, full to the brim with euphoria and jubilation—and so now he is supposed to leave right away! Leave here, where people enjoy themselves so much, and where the people are so good and have it so good!

He does not like walking. He does walk, of course he walks, but with legs that do not belong to him at all. God knows whose legs they are.

First he saunters along easily, then comes the climbing. It is unbelievable how steep the walls are on the way up. And coming down it went so quickly—

it went remarkably fast—it was hard to keep up with one's own feet. But now neither his knees nor his feet want to go.

The cold in the Unterach makes him shiver. Where the path winds its way upward like a ribbon between the scraggly bushes, the boy sits down. From here he can still see the Attersee shimmering. Now, suddenly, he has eyes for it, now he sees it—blue, so shimmering blue and dazzling—an unbroken trembling and flickering of gold light that makes him dizzy until everything begins to sway and flutter in a circle. And there— there—in the middle of the lake a small dot—that is the steamboat. It sails on into the world of the wonderful community, likely to where it is most wonderful—.

From the mountain gorge comes a long—long resonating shout, announcing that one spiritual struggle has ended — —.

He goes down the mountain—unbelievably fast he goes down, as if wings were carrying his stumbling feet past yawning depths into which the waters of the Unterach go raging—. And the shout leaps along with him, from wall to wall as if it were racing with the boy, and it falls silent in the crashing and thundering with which the sliding rock scree plunges into the waters that surge up frothing and churning. — —

★ ★ ★

— — The higher one climbs, the shorter the long day of the Maytime sun becomes. Up on Schwarzensee night has already fallen in the early evening hours. Mali stands in her sleeping quarters, happy this time to be going to rest undisturbed. She is not going to wait any longer now for the boy. He did not come back at night. And if something has happened to him, God forbid—then there is no help for him, either.

But as she is lying in her big, painted bedstead, with her back stretched ramrod straight on the straw mattress, she feels her growing ill will toward those who lured the boy away.

Yes, that stems from the fact that they have been given the gift of speech for tempting and beguiling. Did she not experience the same thing herself? Was she not too—once, for a night—as if in a strange wonderland and letting herself be convinced that she was still there, even though she was really alone again even when she first awoke—?

And people got down off the carousel again, too. That was even after only half an hour. The carousel, too, merely tempted and deceived.

And at last Mali falls asleep with angry and mistrustful feelings toward the people in the city.

Only Aloys is still standing at the edge of the lake and listening into the night. Not that he would have been restless about the boy's not returning. He knows the boy is safe and cared for; he cannot fault him for staying down there if he does not come back. Nor would he envy him for it.

He has a premonition that he will not hear the well-known tread of the heavy mountain boots. Nevertheless he still stands and listens. Yet his thoughts are far away. His soul expands and takes its evening devotions under the star-studded sky in the silent night of the mountains. —

A REUNION

The hotel on the Stephansplatz in Vienna was—as always—booked solid and, on this particular midday, the site of lively activity. Though the season was well on toward late autumn, the flow of tourists headed for Russia or Italy, for Switzerland or the provinces of the German Empire, was still far from over. The two comfortably intimate dining rooms on the hotel's ground floor, with their old-fashioned arched windows facing out onto narrow Singerstraße, were packed full this noontime, and the headwaiter—tall and impeccable, his newly appointed apprentice, his piccolo, in tow—was wending his way solicitously among the dining and discreetly chatting guests.

At the wide glass door leading in from the hotel's foyer and stairway stood a slim woman in a dark traveling dress. Hesitating visibly, she cast a restlessly searching gaze about the crowded restaurant before finally deciding to open the door and walk in.

As she walked slowly past the occupied tables, she bowed her head a bit and kept on walking, purely out of embarrassment, even though the headwaiter had hurried her way, with an affable expression, to show her to an empty table. She went on right into the second dining room to the last single table in one of the raised window niches before she finally sat down and, in a quiet voice, ordered some red wine and one of the meat entrées from the menu.

Yet when her order came she seemed to have completely lost all thought of wanting to eat anything. She rested her right hand wearily on the table while with her left she fumbled, as if out of habit, with the small leather purse that hung over her shoulder and down almost to her slender hip. For clearly, her gaze had found its target. Eyes half lowered, she stared at one of the large round tables near the open double doorway back into the first dining room, where a company of five gentlemen was gathered together, caught up in animated conversation. The familiar assiduousness with which the staff served these gentlemen left no doubt that they were long-revered regular guests, taking their midday meal at their permanently reserved table.

At one point the hostess—a very young woman, and pretty as a picture—stopped by the table and stood talking in French to the man nearest her, a gentleman in his early forties with a clean-shaven, intelligent face and a gold-rimmed pince-nez. At once, the conversation at the table became louder and more jovial. Someone pulled up a chair for her, and for a few minutes she took a seat and tasted some of the fine wines that they urged upon her.

At that point the man with the pince-nez perched on his blunt Slavic nose looked up and noticed, sitting back at the last single table in the window niche, the lady in the dark traveling dress.

Just as soon as he caught a glimpse of her, he could not but notice these ineffably expressive gray eyes fixed on him, as if hypnotized, so detached from the people all around, so blind to the rest of the world. He stopped short in mid-word. A remarkable expression of incredulous amazement crossed his face. He stared wide-eyed, astonished, questioning—and then all at once he rose quickly to his feet. "A lady—I think I recognize a woman I know—please, pardon me," he said, excusing himself from the young hostess with a bow.

She turned in her chair, a move more involuntary than graceful, and watched him walk away. A profound silence suddenly prevailed at the round table as the men gazed more or less conspicuously after the tall, gaunt figure of their departing friend.

"The lady's a Russian—I'd wager!" murmured one of them, "that's obvious from her whole bearing, isn't it? Who knows what kind of old connections Saitsev's renewing over there. He seems to like living in Austria, in Italy, but still 'on revient toujours,' and so on."

The lady in the window niche blushed deeply as Saitsev hurried toward her with outstretched hand and easy manner, as though the people all around were merely part of a stage setting he had ordered up.

"Marfa Matveyevna! To think that such coincidences are still possible! and isn't life more pleasant for them! Imagine us—the two of us, suddenly, after such a long time, encountering each other in some hotel!" he exclaimed in Russian.

She let him take her hands in his as he reached out to her with eager warmth. Her excited blush lent a warm, girlish beauty to her pale, delicate features, which, while no longer quite so youthful, were still beguiling.

"It's no coincidence," she said, interrupting Saitsev in reserved tones, "I knew you were here, I found out from Ssasonov, he told me where you were staying—and the porter just now directed me in here—he said you'd be dining now."

"Well, if it's not a coincidence, then thank you, Marfa, thank you!" he chimed in, and held onto her hand a moment before sitting down across from her. "Really, if you'd written me ahead of time I would have met you at the station, looked after you. — How long have you been here?"

"Since this morning. And I'm leaving right away. I stopped to visit a colleague—we studied together, and now she's working here as a doctor. — — I'm hurrying back to eastern Russia."

"So, a doctor!" he repeated slowly, giving her a look of warm interest, "sure enough, a doctor! Now I remember. So you really did become a doctor—and on top of that out there in the steppes, where there's such a dearth of doctors, culture, comfort—yes, my God, such a lack of just about everything! So, that's how it is—and for years now, too!"

Her whole face lit up. She nodded, all seriousness. "And I'm not the only woman now who's gone out there!" she said quietly, "it's the women, you know, that's just it. Oh, how right you were back then with your lectures! I think that of all the beautiful, wonderful things that you said—and women were often there to hear it, when you were traveling from city to city—of all that, this was the most beautiful thing! That call to us women to take part in guiding and educating the people, in taking up the cause of culture among them. The way you called out to us: 'That too is the women's cause!' — — And yes, it is the women's cause."

She had overcome her initial confusion and was speaking with animated enthusiasm, her eyes sparkling.

Saitsev leaned back a bit, draping one arm over the back of his chair. He was listening attentively and looked thoughtful and deeply involved, as if he were struggling intensely to recapture the thoughts of those days. "Yes, of course!" he agreed, "I can well imagine. The young doctors hardly ever go out there at all—the men, that is. They get stuck in the few cities, no matter how much more difficult it's becoming to succeed there with all the competition. Of course! After all, to make a go of it in Russia in the most inhospitable, most remote territories out there in the steppes means denying yourself the most important things in life. Out there you've got to be doctor, priest, teacher, mother—in short, everything at once, but nothing for oneself. —Oh, I know it!"

"Yes, you do know that!" she interrupted him with a smile full of admiration, "if you were a doctor, you wouldn't have just sought out the more comfortable cities. Oh, how hard it must have been for you then, to leave your Russian homeland! Where your words were so inspiring! And where you yourself were so full of idealistic faith that things could become better for us in every way. And some things are better now — — I have much to tell you, later. Now you would be able to help in a completely different way and accomplish things along with us others."

Saitsev shifted a bit impatiently in his chair as she became so caught up in her theme. He remarked, somewhat hastily: "I would have had to go live abroad sooner or later anyway for my daughter's sake. She was the reason that I stayed rather long back then in the south of Switzerland and in Italy. Did you hear about that?—Since then I've always liked the south. I travel to Italy almost every year."

"But your daughter's doing well now, isn't she?" Marfa asked, distracted.

"Yes, thank you. She's completely recovered now, albeit in delicate health. She was married in Rome—I suppose you knew? My wife lived to see that. — — For a few years, before she died so unexpectedly, I had to move quite often, live in different places; in the end, we were living in Wiesbaden. — — That's how one becomes a cosmopolitan," he said, breaking off.

There was a pause. Saitsev's gaze, which, while he was talking, had rested upon Marfa's slim, pale face like a gentle caress, glided involuntarily now down over her figure and took it in, in every detail, with one long, all-consuming expression.

Feeling his gaze she blushed anew. Smiling, Saitsev said: "Do you want to know something wonderful, Marfa? You just said that you've been a doctor out in eastern Russia for years now. Fine. But sitting here now, that's not at all what you look like. No, not at all. Timid is how you look. As if you'd taken flight to this little corner, like a little girl who has absolutely no idea of how to get pushy and assert herself. Yes, that's just exactly how you look."

She nodded, hesitating. "Well, this place does intimidate me. The diverse, cheerful, vital turmoil of life here! And this city life, everything so foreign! Everything in such haste and so frenetic! You've got to know your way around. But I am so alien here. Afraid to cross the street or buy things in the shops. — — Back home, I'm not afraid of anything! I fear no one, I fear nothing! I know how to relate to the people there, and they have faith in my strength. — —How right you were to lure me out there. And you yourself—"

He interrupted her: "Marfa, what do you say we leave here . . . Isn't it unbearable to keep sitting here like this? I have my winter apartment right here in the hotel—I find that's where I'm most comfortable when I'm in town. Shall we go up to my place?"

"Yes, of course—if you're finished eating—I didn't just interrupt your dinner, did I?" Marfa said, signaling the headwaiter.

"We were all finished already and just chatting. As you see, there's just one straggler left at the table over there, but now you—" here Saitsev leaned over to look at the almost untouched dishes still sitting in front of Marfa while she was paying her bill, "—I think you mustn't remain so alone at mealtime, otherwise you'll always stay so thin and pale."

From the waiter, Saitsev took the short, dark winter coat she had taken off when she entered and laid it over her shoulders. Then they walked slowly past the row of tables to the glass door at the exit. Marfa walked along, her head no longer bowed, her eyes looking ahead, open and radiant, yet taking in as little of her surroundings as they had when she came in—they gazed into a kind of happy world that had quietly opened up for her. Saitsev guided her up a few steps to his suite. It was all by itself in the corner of a broad corridor overlooking the old Graben that leads into the square. She could hardly believe that these three comfortable rooms, so luxuriously furnished to his own special taste, were part of a hotel. She thought they were the coziest rooms she had ever seen. She was still standing in the center of the wide old Persian carpet—a memento of back home—that took up the whole middle of the living room, looking around in silence, when Saitsev, the sound of his steps muffled by the carpet, stepped up to her, put his arm around her shoulders, and, shifting from formal to familiar address, asked straight out: "And by the way, tell me, you, while you're out there caring for people so fanatically and wearing yourself out—who takes care of you? Why have you become so pale and gaunt? Why?"

She gave a start. "I—I have been taking care of myself," she stammered, her composure gone, "—in fact, I'm on my way home from a spa."

He leaned forward and took her wrist. "A spa? So you're suffering from an illness? You're suffering—?"

"Oh, no. Of course not. Just a little overworked."

"Exhausted!" he said, only half out loud, as if talking to himself, and gave a quick stamp of his foot. "Nonsense, that's what that is! You don't belong there at all! Why did you become a doctor? No, if there was one thing you had the aptitude for, then—it was more for writing poetry or something like that. You were one of those people who write their life like poetry, the way they think it's supposed to be, according to their lyrical opinion. — — I think in the end it was that lyrical side of you that took over and drove you out into the world to make people happy."

She looked at him uncomprehending and deeply astonished. Like an astounded child, that is just how she looked in that moment, with her thin face and trusting eyes. "Oh, no—you did that yourself!" she said slowly, addressing him still with the formal "you." —"You alone. From the very first idea right to the final decision."

He muttered something she did not understand. Then he began to pace back and forth.

Marfa kept completely still, and when he turned to her again she had sat down on the edge of an armchair.

"Am I really to bear the blame for that?" he asked, his voice subdued, as he came to a stop right in front of her.

"The blame?!" She smiled at him. "You deserve the credit for that—the credit for everything I ever did. Clearly, all by myself I would probably have been too weak to keep at it. Don't you know that? When you went abroad then, and I found it so hard, so terribly hard to remain behind. Only you, only your power to convince and inspire gave me the strength to do that—for the sake of our cause."

Saitsev held her gaze. "—Really 'for the sake of the cause'? For no other reason?" he asked.

She stared at him in silence.

Then he went on slowly, without averting his gaze from her: "I, at least, I was not speaking so purely for the sake of the cause. I was speaking for very personal reasons, Marfa. I was speaking for the sake of my wife and my ailing daughter—yes, precisely for the sake of this daughter, who lived with us, so suffering, so watchful, so jealous, in that way only such ailing people can manage to be. For the sake of those two—you and I could not remain together—that was why I could not let you go abroad with me. You know that as well as I do."

Marfa had gone pale. She made an uncertain, searching gesture with her right hand and stood up involuntarily. Her gaze darted about the room without fixing on anything specific. She almost made the impression of wanting to flee. But Saitsev, still standing right in front of her, merely opened his arms to her in silence. And without making a sound, she let it happen, let him take her in his arms and draw her to him.

He tilted her head back and kissed her on the lips. "How you're trembling," he murmured tenderly, and then, very softly: "I would like to ask you something, if I may? Tell me: is that why you came here? Is it?—Did you come here to get me back?"

It cut right through her. Dismayed, almost frightened, she looked up at him. "What—oh no, my God, how can you know that?" she said, now shifting to familiar address as well. "Yes! That's why I came, to bring you back."

He held her still closer. "Dearest! My darling, my dove! Didn't I tell you you're not a doctor—no, God forbid, a poet is what you are. The way you nurture and preserve an old love! Putting your trust in such remote happiness! Such a firm faith only a poet could have, hoping that we two might ultimately reunite after all."

"Happiness! Love! Reunion!" Marfa repeated, brushing her brow like someone awakening, as if having to struggle to grasp such ideas. "How do you mean that? No, oh no, I could not think of something like that. —I came only to bring you back to us— meaning simply: back to Russia."

Brusquely he let go of her. "To Russia?! Me? Fine, but how so?"

She reached tentatively for his hand. "Back there, Vitali. Where else, then? I told you already, back there you could achieve a thousand times more. And I— now I know so much more about it all, I've laid the groundwork—I'm caught up in the middle of it. And all the time I was doing it with you in mind. — — That's something that I never dared to imagine: that you could keep on longing for me—but I was sure: secretly you had to have a yearning for Russia and your work there."

She spoke urgently, persuasively. On her cheeks there were pale red blotches of excitement. Yet the longer she faced his gaze, the more uncertain her tone became, and she let her voice fall with the last words.

He reached out and softly stroked her hair—his gesture protective, comforting. "You are a foolish child!" He remarked, "in the world you're talking about I no longer fit in at all. I haven't just been sitting here these—what, ten years waiting for you to come get me, Marfa! I've lived those years, developing all the while a whole different way of life. I no longer think and feel as I did then."

Marfa stood stock-still. Slowly she let go of the hand she had reached out for so imploringly and let her own hands fall quietly to her sides. "But then—yes, then—we haven't found each other again at all!" she said, her voice toneless.

"We haven't? But indeed we have!" he countered quickly and emphatically, and leaning over her, he added with a smile: "Am I not really still that same young man with the lean, bearded face of an apostle and hair down to his shoulders? Still facing life so ineffably free of needs, yet at the same time so arrogantly full of demands? Now I want much less from life. But I do want you. I love you, Marfa. And so you will stay here, with me, as my wife."

"But of course I can't!" she exclaimed, beside herself, "I just can't. They are waiting for me there, they need me, sacred commitments bind me to them— bonds that you helped forge—" she broke off and suddenly clung to him aglow with hope; "—oh, do come along! That is the only way it can be—do follow me."

He looked down at her in silence. "—I—follow you?" he asked, lightly emphasizing each word.

She went deep red. "Not me! The cause!" she said, faltering.

"I once set you upon this cause—I guided you into this area, that's true," he went on, calmly, "but there you would be my guide and master, with me then your apprentice, your neophyte; you would be guiding me toward that cause."

Marfa shook her head vigorously. "No! Oh, no! I would do all that you wish of me!" she cried out passionately, "a thousand times each day I would bless you— and love you not less, but a thousand times more—"

"Yet I would cease to love you!" said Saitsev coldly, and took a step back.

Marfa pressed her hands to her eyes. She wanted to hide her tears, make them stop, but a choking pain welled up in her, and she began to weep.

Saitsev stood at her side for a few seconds, his head bowed. His eyes were slightly reddened, and from the veins at his temples it was clear that he was intensely agitated.

He paced the room a few times and then went to the wide window and stood looking out. The autumn gray of the late afternoon light rested on the genteel street scene outside, while inside evening darkness had already begun. Slowly the resounding boom of the Stephansdom chimes tolled five. The uneasy silence was interrupted when the room waiter knocked discreetly at the door to announce that Saitsev had a visitor.

Marfa awakened as if from a dark oppressive dream. "Yes, it's surely best if I go now," she thought. But Saitsev was just instructing the room waiter to admit no visitors. Then he ordered tea and dinner for two for eight o'clock, requesting that it be brought to the adjoining room and then announced only after it had been served.

When the waiter had gone, Saitsev turned to Marfa, who had been sitting there silently, listening in amazement. "That's fine with you, isn't it? wouldn't you also rather eat earlier? or would you prefer to have tea served before?

She shook her head. His words were so innocuous. Had something not happened between them just then, showing that they were estranged from each other in their innermost selves? And he did not deny it, either, he just seemed to ignore it.

Meanwhile Saitsev had brought some beautiful leather-bound albums full of large photographs and spread them out in front of her. "Wouldn't you like to see a bit of all the places I've been since then? Some of the many works of art I went on to see?" he asked, trying to cheer her up. "What fools we are for getting into an argument, when all along we have so much to share with each other."

And while he was taking care to push the pictures into the best possible light and Marfa leaned over them, absentmindedly, to have a look, he went on: "I really do have a whole world to show you, a world you don't know yet and thus can't really appreciate. To introduce you to a whole new world! How wonderful it will be to set it up around you until you are at home in it, to guide you from one pleasure to the next, from one insight to the next."

Marfa thought to herself: "Until I come to despise myself in this life of luxury! So that's the kind of world he would fit right into, without doing a thing."

Yet as she was thinking that, she followed mechanically along with what he was saying and showing her, noting the lively energy of his gestures as he spoke, and involuntarily she let it embrace her with the magic of old. His voice was speaking other words—but did they not have the same tone as before?

When Marfa kept her hand on one of the photographs for a few moments, trying to hold it steady, Saitsev reached for her hand and studied it intently. Marfa tried to pull away, she felt hot and flustered. "There's nothing to see there!" she said, halting and evasive.

"Nothing? Why there's everything to see there! Everything that you could ever possibly tell me about yourself. In this hand, which by nature was so small and delicate—and which one can now see has learned to come to grips everywhere and shirk no labor. That was very brave of this poor little hand! But now this hand should become small and delicate again, don't you think? It's supposed to be a pretty hand, isn't it?"

Marfa wanted to cry out: "No! No, it's not supposed to be a pretty little hand!

For always and forever may they remain strangers to each other, your hand so well-groomed, mine now grown so coarse."

But she remained silent, her heart beating in agony against her chest, her eyes shimmering with tears. His hand, which she wanted to push away, exuded a warm current of feeling, coursing into her limbs, draining them of strength, as if binding her to him — —

Then Saitsev took her in his arms and drew her to him. "Even I'd not have thought it possible—I didn't think I could do it!" he murmured, "that I could still love you—it makes me proud! Who of all my friends would have thought I could do it! It's as though no time at all had gone by since then—isn't it, really?"

She tried to stand erect under the weight of his arms, overcome by a strange anxiety and uncertainty. What he was so proud of—that was really nothing to be proud of—it was something all too human, is what it was—something that once they had both triumphed over with the help of grand ideals.

"—Strangers, oh, what strangers we are!" she thought over and over, yet ever darker, ever more nebulously the thought glided through her consciousness, as though it were whispering to her from out of the distant depths—far away from herself.

Saitsev had released her, his features were tense and excited. She stared into his face. "—Who knows—how often he's done this—" she tried to think, but then she stopped thinking, everything receding into mist-shrouded depths.

Saitsev moved to the door that led out into the hallway and locked it without a sound. — —

⋆ ⋆ ⋆

The previous day had been neither clear nor cloudy, neither warm nor cold, its weather so indifferent and indeterminate that it could have been any season.

Today was markedly late autumn. The dense night fog had lifted only to leave the streets slippery and wet, a moist west wind blowing through them, and a dense mass of cloud hanging low over the city.

Saitsev walked down Singerstraße, his hands in his overcoat pockets, turning to walk slowly back a few times. He had promised Marfa to wait that morning for her to visit him instead of going to look for her where she was staying with her doctor friend, a woman whom he did not know. But it was almost eleven o'clock, and she had not yet appeared. An intense restlessness had driven him out of the house ahead of time; he wanted to go meet her.

She could have taken ill. Her resistance low, she was in a weakened state as it was. He had to take care of her, above all. Yes, take care of her, make her flourish—.

His gaze lit upon a lovely girl who was just crossing the street diagonally, carefully lifting her skirt as she did so to reveal a pair of charming little ankle boots. He had to smile about the almost childish impatience of his desire to deck Marfa out like this until she too was a lovely girl—bring her out of her dour shell.

But Marfa was not coming.

No, he did not want to wait any longer in this dreary autumn chill. It depressed him, made him feel uneasy. And again he set out down quiet Singerstraße, walking, without a stop, until he had covered the short stretch to the multistory apartment building where she had said she was staying. A little white terrier trotted along beside him for a time, as if taking Saitsev for his master. Then a fine rain came drizzling down.

At the gateway of the building he was assailed by a deafening noise. In the courtyard there was a metal worker's shop, where long iron rails were being unloaded with a resounding clatter. Saitsev went up one set of stairs and then found the name on the door he was looking for.

A servant answered his ring. Asking about Marfa, Saitsev learned that she had left an hour ago. Where she had gone the servant did not know. He assumed she had gone to Russia. He said she had left a letter that the porter at the corner had taken to the hotel on Stephansplatz right after her departure.

So the letter was there, then. Yes, it probably was there, but Saitsev was in no hurry to read it.

The door closed, and Saitsev started down a few steps, then stopped.

Well, yes, why read it? These last confused lines had surely not been enough for Marfa to offer any clear explanation. She had taken flight. From that, he knew enough.

It suddenly occurred to him: "How stupid, how ridiculous the whole thing was, really. Her existence, her whole existence she had guided just according to my suggestion, because I wanted it that way—because we could not have each other. And now the only thing that stands in my way is my own suggestion."

Saitsev leaned over the banister. The noise came welling up from below, with a hollow piercing clatter, and it did him a world of good to listen to this brutal noise. His hand clenched involuntarily into a fist. Everything in him that was brutal strength suffered helplessly.

Leaning on the railing, he stood for a long time listening, without actually being aware of it, taking pleasure in the hard, shrill hammer blows as they made the iron vibrate and bend— trembling and glowing as it yielded obediently to the strokes—he listened as if the blows were speaking for him.

He himself had fallen silent.

PARADISE

She opened her fine, light gray wings and flew—.

Actually, she would rather have had completely white wings, snow white, but then they would have been visible to everyone, even when she went walking with them quite harmlessly—and even just thinking about how people would be amazed and find fault and gape she felt her movements become so heavy and self-conscious that she could make only slow progress through the air.

These unassuming little wings were really much better, so wonderful the way they nestled gently in the folds of her dress. Nobody had ever noticed that she had them. And, after all, the main thing remained, of course, that she could actually fly.

——Below her, gardens—ever, ever blossoming gardens, extensive springtime gardens, with anemones and violets growing in their lawns and the white and blue of new lilacs shimmering in their dense bushes. Countless songbirds were building their nests there, and their carefree jubilation and bold behavior made it clear how seldom they were disturbed at their work. But everything that blossomed and sang beneath the rustling long branches of the treetops sent its aroma and sound up to her as she hovered above in flight, no longer knowing whether everything was blossoming, smelling, and singing with such an intoxicating glow around her, or whether sound and light and color were not all flowing together into one pulsating hovering that dissolved into pure sunshine and bore her up higher and higher—.

From up above she also saw that here and there the gardens were fenced in and had closed gates. That is why no people were wandering about in them. For most people could enter anywhere only by going through gates or doors, and they had no idea at all how springtime looks from up above. They took their pleasure only step by step, from object to object, in the twittering of the little birds, in the aroma of the colorful flowers, and in the rays of the bright, hot sun. Otherwise amid such a springtime they would probably sink to their knees in helpless ecstasy— since they could not fly.

Hildegard lowered her wings and alighted slowly, reluctantly on the path, which was covered with windblown blossom leaves. At one of the garden gates stood a strange man, gazing and lost in thought and holding the silver grip of his cane up to his chin; he opened the gate and walked in, clearing his throat expectantly and looking about searchingly. He was a stranger only in the garden—for Hildegard herself already knew him. Only a short time ago her mother had introduced him to her—he was a friend of her late father, passing through on a trip—and intimated to her that she had to be courteous to him.

He looked quite likeable, too, with his pale, somewhat lined face; she had nothing at all against him, except that it bored her to make well-mannered conversation instead of flying.

For quite a while she walked along properly beside him and chatted in the manner in which, as she had learned from her mother, young girls are supposed to do; but then—actually out of pure incomprehensible distraction—she went fluttering just a little bit up into the air.

Just a little, but still in such a way that she ended up sitting on an elderberry bush. There she suddenly realized the inappropriateness of her move, and she went quite rigid with fright.

In the meantime the gentleman down on the path was, of course, much more frightened than she, he was simply petrified. His hand trembled as he lifted it to adjust his spectacles— clearly he was still hoping his eyes had deceived him, but still he did not dare to look too closely at the elderberry bush, for there was no way he could deny it: Hildegard had gone fluttering up there right before his very eyes.

Deeply embarrassed, she fluttered down again and went on walking along beside him, dejected, her face red. Both behaved, as if by agreement, as though nothing had happened; they ignored the incomprehensible thing that had just happened and from then on tried to go on talking harmlessly from where their conversation had stopped before.

Then Hildegard had an attack of high spirits and laughed out loud, so that her wings began to twitch. And the nice old gentleman completely lost his composure. She could see the sweat break out on his brow. His eyes grew large and ghostly.

"Please—" he said hoarsely and went pale, "please, what was that ——"

That was a critical moment, but it woke Hildegard up. She awoke still laughing inside, her fine head tossed back a bit on the pillow, and stretched her arm out straight with a languid, happy gesture.

Yet as soon as she opened her eyes and saw above her the unattractively painted ceiling of a cheap rented house instead of the broad glowing waves of the sun, which she had secretly been hoping for, the happiness and laughter of her features died.

Hastily she sat up, shook her tousled blond hair from her forehead, and listened to hear whether her mother was coming to wake her. Her legs drawn up, her hands folded around one knee, she sat in bed feeling bitterly cold, helpless, unable to fight it off.

Oh, the old gentleman! How often she still dreamed of him. Now one way, now another. Always in her dream he was old—but in reality he was not so old at all, only for her—oh, she saw him that way. Something about the very first impression had made him old in her eyes forever.

So in her dreams she was still playing tricks, then, in spite of everything. When she was awake she could no longer do that. But of course in her dreams she could still fly. And when she was awake she crawled along on the ground.

Hildegard turned her still-sleepy eyes toward the open window, an expression of deep reluctance and sadness on her face, looking to see whether some small ray of light might cheer her. All she saw outside was a foggy, gray, wet March morning. Early March, through and through. The day obviously could not quite make up its mind whether it should signal spring today or winter. Now and then it acted like autumn.

Close to the one-story house rose the immensely high, black, tarred fire wall of a proper tenement, indicating that the neighborhood was the outgrowth of a large city where the tiny yards suddenly turn into open field, where houses in the rear with all their intimacies seemed to beg for adjoining, enclosing neighbor walls, and where you have the impression you are getting a behind-the-curtains view of the stage setting of a city.

Slender little linden trees ran in a straight line past the house and intersected with a lane of equally sparse young birch trees that bore the grand name "Kaiserstraße." A suburb of the future was marked out here in the midst of flat fields with big signposts and small young trees.

The pastor of the suburb was walking past the one-story house with a robust old lady and tipped his hat in greeting when he caught sight of Hildegard's mother in the living-room window. The old lady held her lorgnette up to her eyes on its long stem and looked her way. "Of course, Frau Malten has her daughter visiting her—and during the last weeks they were away together—isn't it immensely strange?" she asked. "Only just now the young girl married the wealthy Alfred Neugebauer with his estates in the Tyrol. Right after that her mother travels away—but right away to meet her daughter—you must know what is going on."

The pastor shrugged his shoulders. "I haven't been informed. Frau Malten is not a member of my congregation. She's a Catholic. And besides that, as an Alsatian, she's half French. Of course, the daughter, following her late father, is Protestant, but I didn't preside at the wedding," he remarked in a tone as if otherwise such oddities naturally would not have occurred.

"That poor mother, I say! She's toiling away so diligently, giving her French lessons at the institutes, and now—but you really don't know—?"

"I believe no one knows exactly, there are rumors of—"

"Of: divorce!" the old lady cut him off quickly, as if she feared that he could get the interesting word out before she did.

"Divorce on the honeymoon! And people do say—"

"They say she's supposed to have simply run off on him—"

They lowered their voices and exchanged knowing nods. And now all at once they both seemed astonishingly well informed. —

Hildegard's mother had quickly stepped away from the window after the pastor's greeting. A delicate red came to her pretty face with its expressive dark eyes. She certainly had no idea what two people passing by chance might be whispering to each other, but one thing she did know: the conversations here in the suburbs, where the same people were always encountering one another, outdid the smallest small town when it came to gossip— and in any case it outdid in that respect the midsize Alsatian city that she had lived in until she became a widow. For the last few days she had been living here like a person without a skin.

When Hildegard, quietly and with her face lowered, carried in the tea maker and set it on the table, her mother's brown eyes turned to her with a gentle expression. And in this moment they resembled each other as do an older and a younger sister—as different as their features and figures otherwise were with respect to form and color. For blond Hilde was in appearance quite markedly like her father. But in both it was quite clear to see how the subdued quietness of their behavior was being imposed upon their natural temperaments.

Hildegard kissed her mother on the hand and on the lips and silently took her place at the table. Both would have all too gladly liked to speak about what was weighing upon their hearts, and for both it was the same thing. And since they both suppressed this urge, they simply swallowed down their words along with their tea, finding no topic of conversation.

Then her mother suddenly remarked: "In these next days—today, or tomorrow at the latest, Dietrich will be coming to see us."

Hildegard was so startled she dropped her spoon on her saucer with a clatter. "Dietrich? Oh, mother, that's just terrible. Why, then?"

"Don't talk such foolishness. What's supposed to be so terrible about that, then? You used to like this cousin a lot. And really you can't just crawl into a mouse hole. — — — And— I needed someone to help put the matter in order. — — At my request he was just down to see — — — Alfred Neugebauer in the Tyrol."

Her mother spoke these last words as if she had something in her throat. She herself found it embarrassing and quickly fell silent again.

Hildegard had long let go of her teacup. Her fingers trembling, she clutched at a dark leather briefcase lying beside her that her mother took to her lessons in the city. "Oh, Mama!" she said quietly, "then Dietrich too knows— everything. He's sure to talk about it. He'll likely even have to. Oh, Mama, why—oh, why did you encourage me too—back then? I certainly never wanted to leave you."

"That's nonsense, Hilde. All young girls get married. But not every one finds such a noble, excellent man, whom your father, when he was alive, couldn't praise highly enough. You know it yourself. You were devoted to him. You loved him. Not a soul could have guessed that you would be able to be so monstrous, so blind to your duty—"

Hildegard gave her an imploring look. "Don't scold! Don't scold!" she said very quietly, "what do you mean 'love'—? I love you a thousand times more — — it must have been something else entirely."

Frau Malten's features took on a look of forced, somewhat reserved coolness. "Nothing else. The other is sin, Hilde. I married right out of the convent, hardly knew your dear father. But you couldn't honor and respect any other—"

She rose from her chair, slightly agitated, and, in front of the mirror between the two windows, she put on her cloche hat and reached for her briefcase.

Hildegard followed her every move with a gaze that hungered and thirsted for tenderness. At last she could endure it no longer and embraced her mother. "Are you angry with me—?"

Frau Malten shook her head gently. The long kiss as she took her child in her arms was much more heartfelt than could have been expected from her words. Then she sighed and, more quickly than necessary, turned to the door in order to hide the fact that she had tears in her eyes. "If only the traffic in the city streets weren't so bad," she remarked.

With that she was gone, and Hildegard, her face pressed against the windowpane of the front window, saw her coming along the garden fence—quiet, composed, going about her tedious daily duties, her features again somewhat cool and reserved. But in Hildegard there still bloomed the joy at the rare tenderness that her mother had shown her, and she could almost have burst out in song. Then it occurred to her that there was not the least reason at all to do that. Her mother too had much weighing on her heart.

Outside a strong wind was blowing; it blew away the fog, and across the street she could see shirts and trousers fluttering on a long wash line. The garden in front of the house had its four or five arbors to show for itself along with just as many wooden enclosures, and they alone gave it its name, for there was not much more about it that was gardenlike other than these arbors, in which each of the tenant families could cook its own coffee or rave about the moon.

Hildegard thought with horror about what it would probably be like in the summer, when they would be sitting, arbor by arbor, with their fellow tenants! If only summer would not come! Or if only they were still in the Alsace, like when her father was still alive.

In the side rooms and kitchen she could hear the maid at work, and now, up in the mansard rooms where the poor people lived, a loud racket was beginning. Directly above the parlor, where Hildegard was standing at the window, a child was crying. It was that tormenting, incessant, moaning crying that her mother found so taxing. She could no longer bear to hear it. Hildegard had already wanted to go to the young mother upstairs—the woman had given birth a month before—but she did not know what she should say or do about such a crying child.

She walked over to the tea table, slowly cleared away the dishes, arranged everything in the kitchen that she would need for cooking, sent the maid shopping for lunch, and then, wearied by the small domestic cares that did not involve her soul, she took out a large decorative embroidery in a frame and sat down with it by the window in the living room.

Hildegard immersed herself in the delicate, fantastic pattern of leaves and lines that she usually thought out herself and for which she was often well paid—immersed herself in her work as people do in an interesting book that lets their fantasy take a pleasant stroll. She would very much have liked to have been much more expert in sewing, able to embroider the silk with all the strange things that forms and colors said to her. She thought that embroidery was the most lovely and beautiful activity for the daytime, like flying was for the night, and she darkly sensed a relationship between the two. But unfortunately she was able to take her pleasure in both only with interruptions.

After a while she let the lilac-colored silk, on which she had stitched leafless birch branches with hanging catkins and tiny stiff buds, sink wearily in her lap, leaning her head back on the chair and her eyes taking on again the anxious, uncertain expression with which she had awakened that morning.

She saw once again in her mind's eye the gentleman from her dreams standing at the gate by the garden, and she looked with unease and regret into the recent past. Yes, with regret as well, for she felt that she had behaved like a criminal toward him, like a criminal against what the law now simply demanded of a woman. And this feeling was the worst thing—

To whom could she talk about that, then—simply about the way she felt in her heart? Who would protect her from all those dreadful things: from the curiosity of the people and from her own tormenting doubts? Basically she was afraid of her mother, too.

Hildegard closed her eyes. From the Neugebauer estate she had stolen away secretly, although he surely would not have held her back forcibly. No, not forcibly, he was so good. That is why at the start she had trusted him so — — Then, when she arose quietly, even before dawn, to go on foot to the small railway station nearby, through which a morning train would have to be passing, she saw from the garden the light on in his room on the ground floor.

He was not sleeping. He was sitting in his long wrinkled robe on his corner sofa, bowing his head with its thick gray hair, his hands loosely folded. She was not able to see his face. But she knew how bitter and weary he looked. She knew it, and it cut her heart; and while she was running away from him, hurrying in secret, what a burning wish she had that she could also run away from this last sight forever—forever. Yes, and she arrived like a criminal at the home of her disappointed, frightened mother—

From behind Hildegard's closed eyes came tears, first one, then another, that moistened her cheek, without her raising her hand to wipe them away.

Then there was a sharp knock on the window at which she was sitting. "Good morning, little cousin!" said a voice from outside.

Hildegard jumped in surprise. Down in the arbor-filled garden stood a man in an English tweed suit, his light spring overcoat half open, a small, dark, felt hat on his head and a pince-nez on his nose. He nodded to her. Confused, she went to the hallway door to open it for him. It was Cousin Dietrich, whom her mother was expecting.

"Mama's gone out!" she said as a first awkward greeting, but she offered him her hands, both of which he had seized and was now shaking. He exuded a strong scent of tobacco, which, as she was not used to it, struck her as strange and bitter.

"Gone out? Well, that's no problem, little one. She'll come home sometime, won't she? Can't I make myself a little comfortable here with you in the meantime? Look, that wet overcoat, let's hang it up. So. And now don't let me disturb you," he remarked, following her into the living room, "I just saw such silken magnificence lying there in your lap. Aha!"

He bent appreciatively over her embroidery. "Isn't that quite frightfully tedious work?"

A stone fell from her heart when she heard him talk that way so pleasantly about harmless things, as if nothing unusual had happened. She looked at him gratefully. "It's a great joy, such embroidery. I think up the patterns myself," she said.

"Hmm. But still, it's horribly time consuming and taxing. Wouldn't it be much nicer to think up something useful?"

"But it is useful—it brings in money. But I'd do it anyway. I love it," she added, her voice warm, as if she had said about a person: I love him.

"That's not exactly the usefulness I meant. I meant there's something so superfluous about the thing itself—at best it's good for the superfluous leisure of the rich people who buy it," he responded, but, as he was speaking, he was looking at Hildegard with a great deal of serious interest. "I'll sit down with you, Hilde. Haven't seen you for two whole years."

"Yes." Sitting on the edge of a chair she gazed down awkwardly at her own slender hands; "you were traveling a lot? Where were you last year, then?"

"In England. There were all kinds of things I wanted to see there; among other things schools for boys, a few of which have instituted a whole new system. Half out in the country. They alternate between theoretical and practical work. Farming part of the time—not just the same old gymnastics and sport—in a word, something quite special. The important thing now is to get permission from the Culture Ministry here to try an experiment like that in our own country."

"You want to do that?" Hildegard looked at him with lively interest—"I had no idea that you wanted to teach. You always seemed to find it so boring when Father talked about it."

"Indeed I did, in the usual, subservient way—just as your father had to toil his way tediously all the way to the level of titular professor. —But what I'm talking about would be something quite different: a life in accord with my most deep-seated convictions. And that is the only life worth living, Hildegard," he said with spontaneous warmth.

"That must be nice! — — But doesn't that sort of thing cost an awful lot of money?"

"Some money—only a little of course—I can invest myself, and along with the money all my strength. But the rest I also believe I have already secured. The more money, the better, of course. For my cherished idea is that this school should also be open to poor boys."

The rapid, assured way he spoke and stated his views had a liberating, refreshing effect on Hildegard; before, she had always found him a little too casual and brusque. But now he drew her into a part of the world, a part of life, that made her momentarily forget herself. She would have liked to have said to him: "Tell me more, much more!"

Dietrich had stood up and, with a glance to get Hildegard's permission, took out a lighter to light his cigar. As he did so he cast an attentive appraising eye upon the long, low living room, turned to Hildegard, and remarked: "I'll stay here a little while. I mean, out here with you two, as long as I have all kinds of things to discuss with your mother and you. Later I'll find a place in the city. Here in this suburb there are surely more than enough vacant rooms."

Hildegard looked confused and went deep red. She had not thought any more at all about the immediate purpose of his visit. Now that forced itself upon her. And he, who had been chatting so nicely and harmlessly, now went right ahead talking about it.

"Well? Isn't it fine with you if I stay a while?" He leaned down to her with searching eyes and, when she did not answer right away, he took her gently by the wrist. His hand did not quite go with his manly, somewhat lean figure; it showed the first signs of corpulence and had hard, curved fingernails that made her think of well-trimmed animal claws. Hildegard's fine fingers twitched; suddenly distracted, she looked down at his fingers. If only he would leave! What good was it that he was able to chat so nicely. She would much rather be sitting all alone, hidden in a small, dark mouse hole.

Dietrich stayed leaning over her for a few more seconds; he was no longer waiting for an answer but instead studying her face very carefully. His hand grew hot around her slender wrist. "I think it was time I came," he said.

* * *

Hildegard's mother was visiting Dietrich in the room that he had rented for a month right near them. While her nephew was going about the room and taking the last things from his suitcase, Frau Malten was studying some letters and papers lying before her on the table.

Then page by page she put them all back and bowed her head. "So, it is taken care of!" she said quietly; "and that it happened in this way—with this agreement—you must admit, is proof of how high-minded he is, how unusually good—"

Rummaging about in his things, Dietrich, somewhat irritated, muttered: "Becoming fond of Hilde is really, in the end, not a major feat. Aside from that, there's really no special goodness about it. He really had to agree in the end anyway. — —"

Frau Malten shook her head. "Another man would take revenge. After all, she had vowed before God and the community—"

"That alone just doesn't do it!" he cried out a bit too animatedly and forgot about his unpacking. "And the fact that Hilde, in spite of all the conventional nonsense that you people bring girls up to believe, was able to act so instinctively, so naturally—I'm sorry if it bothers you, but I like it. It just shows up the folly of her perverse upbringing."

"I brought her up in a way that I can answer for," Frau Malten replied, quiet and serious, "— we women all suffer more or less, believe me. Whether or not it's preceded by a brief passion doesn't make it any better. In the end, duty decides and brings peace."

"Brrr! Well, yes. I do know this view, yes," Dietrich remarked, and held back what he was about to say. He thought of Hildegard's father, the frail scholar, struggling with his worries and cares, who had surely also been "noble and good" but had probably never sensed to his dying day how much temperament and youthful ardor had to wither away in the charming woman at his side, until: "duty brought her peace."

Frau Malten might have been thinking the same thing, only in an entirely

different way. Her face, now calm, showed that trace of forced, somewhat reserved coolness around the corners of her mouth that had cowed Hilde. She
stood up wearily and said: "You think so freely and inconsiderately about all
matters of piety and morals. But you are still young, too. At my age, when life
is behind you, a person really has an uneasy, burning feeling that she can pass
on or bequeath to her own child only one precious thing, and that is the sum of
what we have learned from our most difficult, most personal experiences. But
children see that as strictness and withheld freedom."

Dietrich stood in front of her and, with his sharp, kind eyes, looked sincerely
into her face. "I don't think we should go on arguing this case any longer,"
he answered, "I'll help you put it in order—and then— yes, then there is, of
course, one thing I'd like to know: whether in spite of these reproaches you
like me enough, and — — in short, whether you think I am a decent fellow,
through and through, whom you can trust to have an influence on Hilde."

She gave him her hand. "Make her happy again for me!" she said quietly
and went out. She went with slow and reluctant steps. Perhaps it really was her
fault that everything went the way it did. She had not known any better.

She thought it was so fortunate that, when the time came, she was able to
keep Hilde from all the dangers of youth, from sin and passion. Were not the
two just basically one and the same? When, in the course of her own exemplary
marriage, her own hot blood, her fantasy, would storm and rage, then they
were only holding out to her mysterious joys behind which really only sin was
lying in wait. What if she had been able to follow those impulses when she was
single—?! And Hilde? she was the same—

That is what she felt, but she could not talk to Hilde about it. When she
looked into her child's eyes, she found it difficult to say the word "sin." For in
these eyes there was something that reminded her of her own youth so long,
long ago. It awakened darkly something in her own past life—some kind of
dream, long-forgotten and banished—a dream in which the full flaming power
of youth and passion had risen up so triumphantly, like a picture of naked
innocence bearing witness to heaven. —

Dietrich stood thinking a few moments, whistling to himself by the table,
on which a disorderly array of things were lying about. Mechanically he picked
up one thing, then another, only to put it back down again distractedly. He
picked up a paperweight that he did not even think he had taken along—a
funny thing made of imitation bronze: three little pigs in a row, one smaller

than the next, and all three with their hindquarters removed and replaced with penholder, pencil, and eraser, all made from the same imitation bronze.

Dietrich turned it over in his hands. About a year ago, at Christmas or New Year's, a merry widow had sent it to him so that he might think, when far away, of pleasant times that he had spent intimately, albeit unfortunately briefly, with her. —

Such items occasionally popped up among his practical, sensible traveling things and then would disappear again. In general, his experiences with women did much the same. Occasionally they happened, as if by roguish chance, to get in among his serious plans, thoughts, and studies, and because of their lesser value he barely paid any attention to when and how he would likewise happen to lose them.

Dietrich gave the three pigs a vigorous little push so that they tumbled over; he had been seized by a sudden impatience. Outside it was quietly becoming twilight: now Hilde would have to lay aside her eternal embroidery and go walking with him as she had done yesterday.

In the very next minute he was already on his way, and after a few strides he was standing at her living-room window, ready to knock, as he had done a few days ago.

But he did not get that far: Hilde had seen him coming and hurried, already dressed to go, to meet him at the door. As he shook her hand in his somewhat too forceful manner, her face, this day, gave him a happy, expectant smile.

"You certainly are an obedient little girl!" he remarked, pleased by her prompt arrival. "You see, I like that. Will you always be so nicely obedient when I ask you to be?"

"Yes," she said softly, "if you always do it as nicely as you did yesterday. I had to ponder that for a long time. Nothing but new and interesting things you told me about—or rather the way you judge and view everything, that's new and interesting for me. —Let's head for the woods," she added, "that's where the sun keeps shining the longest."

Her mother stood at the window and, lost in thought, watched them go. But they did not notice that. Even as they were walking down the street between the sparse little avenue of trees, they were already deep in conversation, as if yesterday afternoon's exchange were seamlessly joined to today's.

"After a long dry spell, when the May rains come, then the foliage grows— palpably, visibly—in mere hours, and it gains in luster and sap," Dietrich expounded, as he cast a protective eye on the delicate figure beside him, "—you strike me that way, too. A pure pleasure, with a few refreshing drops of water, to wash from you all the dry and dusty things bound up with your upbringing. Why shouldn't you, with your receptive mind, not learn to look at life as it really is in all its hundredfold connections?"

She looked up at him gratefully and eagerly. "You—help me do that!" she said in a childlike tone, "when I hear you talk like that, then I too would like to do and become something quite capable. Not just sit there by myself as I've done until now—"

"—With your eternal embroidery," he completed her sentence mockingly.

"Oh, no, you, I won't let you scold me about my embroidery, it has enough pretty and interesting things to tell me, too—but as a man you're not likely to understand anything about that"— Hildegard stopped and looked over toward the other side.

"What is it, then?" he asked impatiently, "you're not going any farther?"

"No, it's just—let's go the other way," she pleaded, "we can get around to the woods that way, too, and—here we'll encounter acquaintances."

"But at most it will be just people passing by, what harm is that, then?" he remarked, made alert by the anxious tone of her voice, "do you mean they aren't supposed to see us going walking together here?"

"Oh, that's not a problem—that part of it. But—I wouldn't like it if they were to greet me or perhaps—perhaps even talk to me."

"Hilde! are you afraid of people, or what? or what is it? Are you this way when you go walking alone?"

"Alone?" her eyes suddenly widened as if the notion frightened her, "—if I can avoid it now I never go down that street by myself, where there's nothing but familiar people or at least nothing but people who aren't complete strangers living in house after house. I always take the back way and disappear into the woods. They don't go there. And I like most of all—most of all, not even to leave our parlor."

Dietrich was silent for a moment. Then he took her gently by the hand and said emphatically: "Come, let's continue. Right down that street there. Right past those people there. To morbid fear we must not yield. You must overcome that quickly."

Hildegard gave him a frightened look. She half turned with her body, as though she wanted to get away, and then her eyes wandered along the windows of the facades of the closest houses, which only in a few streets of the suburbs stood as close to each other as they did here. But instead of running away, which had been her first impulse, she almost mechanically obeyed the gentle pressure of the hand that held hers fast and right away gave her the direction and let go only then. She obeyed against her will because she was ashamed not to; and just now when, out of an open window on the second story, a young girl waved and called out to her a few words that they did not understand but that were accompanied by dramatic hand clapping, Hildegard greeted her back as a fleeting redness crossed her face.

They encountered only a few workers, and only at the very end of the street did an old lady approach Hilde slowly and inquire at length about how her dear mother was.

Dietrich remained a step back and watched Hildegard as she answered in a small voice.

"For your dear mother it is surely a great joy to have you back with her so soon—she surely must have missed you—are you staying—for long, then?" the old lady went on to ask, with a gaze that signaled motherliness and that was meant to express, between and behind her words, her sympathetic understanding.

"I—I don't know yet," Hildegard answered helplessly and went pale. Her heart was pounding as if to burst when she said good-bye and returned to Dietrich.

Although she was keeping her eyes lowered, she felt that his gaze was fixed on her face, and that made her suffer intensely, for she felt as though it were a silent appraisal of her strength. And so she tried forcibly to pull herself together, but could not do so with this gaze upon her. She kept struggling for a moment and then, at the edge of the spruce forest they were approaching, she suddenly burst into tears.

He drew his brows together. "Well, so!" he said calmly. "But it doesn't matter; even tomorrow it will be better. For tomorrow we'll avoid the people just as little as we did today, and I'll send you along these feared paths on your own—until you're no longer afraid of them."

"No!" she begged, beside herself, "—never again—I can't do it. Why did you—that's cruel of you. For you know why—oh, of course you know everything."

"Yes, Hilde. And right from the first moment I arrived here I also knew that there would be more important things for me to do here than what I was to discuss with your mother about your matter. Namely, to talk all this foolish shyness and embarrassment out of your heart. Just how can you let your life be made bitter by these stupid people? You aren't cowardly, are you, Hilde? Don't you know what can be the most important thing of all? To hold one's head up when people revile us."

She was walking very slowly at the edge of the woods, which the sun was bathing in its last rays. It was very quiet around her. Only a woodpecker was still hammering diligently away with a steady rhythm high up on a spruce branch.

"I'm not cowardly!" Hildegard said haltingly and shook her head, "hold my head up—I could do that too. If the people were disparaging me unjustly. People would not depress me—if only I myself didn't—"

"You're being childish!" Dietrich stood still and took her measure with a wide, smiling gaze. "You're condemning yourself— because by chance you've been talked into thinking: you are supposed to do this and do that; no, Hilde, don't be frightened so fast. I won't mention anything as long as you don't want to talk about it yourself. Only I wanted to take this opportunity to tell you that what you think you have to condemn yourself for is the same thing that has very, very much raised my opinion of you and my respect for you."

Hilde stared at him. He spoke the last words emphatically and earnestly. His eyes did not lie. He had never lied at all, as long as she had known him.

"No one judges as you do," she said hesitantly, "that can't at all be—no, no one, really—"

"No one?" He came closer to her and went on, lowering his voice: "Really, no one? But I think someone does, someone else: you yourself, Hilde. You yourself judged that way with your immediate feeling, when you took your irrefutable initiative—in the deciding moment of your action. Everything else came after that—your reason, which is still not an independent reason but instead is letting itself be guided along by traditional chatter. Oh, how much greater you women are in your first feeling than in your second judgment, which has been twisted around for you to the proper way of thinking. Afterward you're all pitiably stuck—no longer equal to your task—you see, I even have to spring to your aid to put you back on the right track again! But that doesn't matter because you really were bold and magnificent, girl—your nature and your sacred imperatives made you that way, raising you high above hundreds, yes hundreds of others who in your place would now be sitting in comfort and their 'duty'—and wealth."

Hildegard had half parted her lips. He could see clearly how everything in her was listening to him, astonished at first, but also thirsting and longing—

and the longer he kept on talking to her, the wider and more credulously her eyes rested upon him.

The tears on her cheeks had long since dried in the mild spring air. She was still pale—but now pale with inward feelings that no longer had anything in common with fear and humbleness. When Dietrich fell silent she took a deep breath. She bowed her head in its simple, dark, broad-brimmed straw hat and seemed to be thinking. So serious, almost solemnly serious she looked as she did so that he dared not interrupt her thoughts.

The woodpecker up on the spruce branch went on hammering diligently with his long, hard beak, while from some distance away came another bird's muffled answer. The departing sun immersed the clearing around the woods in soft, gold-red tones, and although scarcely a bud on any of the bushes dared a tentative opening and the sandy ground was covered with fallen leaves from the winter and spruce needles, everything was aglow in deep warm tones of color as if offering a smile to greet the coming spring. The narrow stretch of moss along the edge of the woods was simply ashimmer with emerald green, and the same greenish tinge decked the bark of the old tree trunks and the brushwood along the path.

Hildegard walked on slowly; she gazed, without speaking, far out into the luminous landscape.

But Dietrich, although she was not talking to him, understood that she had come close to him in this hour—that it was as though she were inwardly leaning on him—thankfully, trustingly. The expression on her face was one of almost blissful peacefulness.

Suddenly she said: "Spring is still hardly here, is it? But we can feel it. — — You know, springtime and I, we are mysteriously related, we share a secret. — — And without spring—the early spring down there in the south Tyrol—I wouldn't be here."

"You wouldn't be here? You mean you'd be down there on the Neugebauer estate? I don't believe you."

Hildegard turned around to face him as he walked along behind her on the edge of the mossy path between the woods and the tilled winter crop. "You just have the wrong idea about me—for all I know," she said gently, "but I do know: it was the spring. Nothing else. Of course, it is hard to explain. Spring had come. It greeted us when we arrived. It was blossoming around our room. It was on ground level with wide, wide French doors, which led right outside— out into the garden. Such a beautiful thing I had never seen before—at least not when I was awake. I moved about in it all as if intoxicated, I almost ached with joy. Twilight was just beginning when we arrived—as it is now. Then it grew darker; in the starlight we could sense the spring more than feel it—except the nightingales proclaimed its presence the whole night through, and the sweet aroma—oh, the aroma—"

She broke off. Then she went on, very softly: "Then something so miraculous happened to me. I don't know how to say it. It was like believing in paradise. Yes, that was it. A belief in my paradise. Something like when someone lets you look into the depths of your soul, so that you simply know: it's waiting for you. It's not there yet, but it's waiting for you. And while you're experiencing that while the spring all around you is telling you that—as sweet and clear and longing and blissful as never before—you are suddenly supposed to cast yourself in that very same moment out of paradise. And follow someone who wants to take it away from you! Who wants to make you believe that every other garden does the same thing!—See, then you're seized with such a senseless fear—such an anxiety that you'll lose it, that you'll desecrate it — — as if all depended on you, on you alone, whether spring might ever return again at all—even whether the sun is still the sun."

Hildegard's words became increasingly disjointed and passionate, but the tremulous tone of her voice lent them a strange eloquence; in her excitement she had impulsively stopped walking, and the power of what was moving her soul for a moment broke through her gentle reserve—her eyes glowed and flashed in deep fire and all her movements took on almost a devout rapture, even enchantment, as if she were growing—

Dietrich leaned against a tree in front of her, virtually enveloping her in his steadfast, delighted gaze. His eyes too flashed, as she spoke, with a special fire while he consumed this image of her standing there in the sunset among the dark spruce and tearing the veil from the secrets of her soul. He hardly heard what she was saying; yet the way she was saying it—with a temperament that, like a magic spell, transformed her gentle girlishness into a rare and passionate beauty—that captivated him and made him, too, feel enchanted.

"The rogue! the rogue! Unable to conquer this woman! Unable to bring about this transformation!" he felt his heart cry out in scorn and excitement and suddenly felt his self-esteem flattered to the point of ecstasy by the fact that he could influence Hildegard with his words and wisdom.

Something within him rejoiced mightily. On the one point that he was a superior power for her, he had already triumphed over her: she was following him. That is what the girls he knew did, most of them. But what kind of girls they were! He avoided the girls of his own class—he even avoided the women of his class because he believed they were the embodiment of boring discrimination and conventionality. "But you—Hilde! My sweet!" he thought, deeply stirred.

Hildegard seemed to have forgotten him. She was looking out into the landscape again, and with wide, open eyes, in whose gaze, now lost to the world, the passion of her words was still resonating, she seemed to be dreaming of something that had no connection at all to him and to the real surroundings of the moment.

It made Dietrich impatient and restless. He felt this fairy-tale moment here in the sunset must not end without giving him something. His whole being was drawn to Hildegard—impetuous, yearning. He said in a subdued voice: "You have cast a spell on me, Hilde; will you make it right again?"

With that Hildegard looked up, awakening, returning to the present, and without her having listened closely to his words, her face lit up with a smile of joy and pure ecstasy. She blushed and, at the same time, reached out her hands to him. "Oh, you!" she said, taking a deep breath, "what great fortune and wonder for me that you came! I don't know myself what you have done to me. You have made me free. You have shaken from me something terrible whose weight I bore, bent double, day after day. Perhaps that will come again— but surely never as heavy as it was. And if it does—then you will help me again, won't you?" she added, childlike.

He held fast to her hands and sought with his own gaze to fathom and hold fast to hers. "— Did you hear what I said, Hilde? — — Will you help me?"

She looked at him in honest amazement. "I—help you? Oh, how should I do that—you are so much smarter and stronger and braver than I. I will always obey you when you advise me to do something. That is good, it makes me feel so well protected."

"Always obey?" he asked, his voice restrained.

Hildegard nodded.

"— And do everything that I say, whatever it might be?"

"Whatever it might be!" she exclaimed cheerfully and looking happy; "— if it's what you want, then surely. For I am so grateful to you!"

★ ★ ★

The three of them were sitting at midday around the already half-cleared table enjoying the first genuine day of spring. So hot was the March sun flooding in through the opened window that it could have occurred to them to dine outside in one of the garden arbors instead of inside.

Hildegard had in fact made this suggestion, but it had been rejected, simply on account of those passing by who would be sure to peer over the fence and smile at their premature idyll.

"That would certainly be possible!" Hildegard admitted, "then we would just have to laugh along with them, Mummy."

The forenoon heat of the kitchen, or perhaps also the sun's warmth, had colored her cheeks red; she looked radiant, and her mother's spirits were lifted in secret joy at how the five or six days of contact with Dietrich had seemed to waken in Hildegard all her former youthful high spirits. Dietrich himself was very taciturn. He smoked in silence and watched as Hilde poured the coffee into the little mocha cups. In the smile with which she handed him his cup, in her whole bearing, now so cheerful, and in the expression on her face there was something that put him off— something that did not have to do with him. While she remained the same toward him, he felt the urge to be closer to her than before, and having to feel his way toward her so uncertainly was putting him in a turmoil of excitement.

As they were sitting together in near silence, they heard from upstairs a pitiful child's whimper. As quiet as it was, it still made Frau Malten wince. The fear that the crying would become louder was enough to torment every nerve in her weary head.

"I was just about to lie down in the next room for a little rest; this afternoon I must go back to the institute in the city," she remarked sadly.

Dietrich pushed his cup away and listened for a while. "Haven't you ever inquired what's wrong with the child, then?" he asked, "it sounds terribly weak and ailing."

Hildegard answered his question with a shake of her head. "Those people have been living here only a short while," she responded, "and they're said to be very poor—we hardly ever see the woman—the man doesn't come home until very late—only a small, pale lad often plays out back on the sandpile in the yard."

"Why don't you go up to them and see whether something can be done; as a fellow tenant you could have long since helped them with some advice," Dietrich said.

Frau Malten stood up to go lie down a while. "Perhaps that would be good," she said hesitantly, "before, I always kept Hilde from going. It's easy to become too close with fellow tenants. Who can know what they're like and how they'll act?"

Dietrich made a sort of derisive face and shrugged his shoulders. "Hilde really isn't a porcelain figurine that could be damaged by every little contact," he remarked, "for heaven's sake don't let her become too soft and sensitive. Life is there for us to relate to."

Hildegard gave him a look of agreement from across the table. She felt that everything he said flowed out of such a clear, solid outlook on life, which he spoke up for with a forceful will and that really helped to make things better. And if all he did was merely show her the way into the midst of life and bring her a short way forward—then, full of faith and trust, she would find her way through to her paradise.

She stood up and went into the other room to see that her mother was comfortable on the old divan. Then she came back into the living room and stood at the window. Her supportive gaze at the table had filled Dietrich with secret satisfaction: a warm joy suddenly rose up in him. Basically Hilde already did belong to him inwardly. Everything else would come about of its own accord. And anyway: she was at that age when girls fall in love, and if it was not a success the first time—perhaps merely because the man in question, as a friend of her father, struck her from the start as too avuncular—well, then, all the more certain it would be the second time—this time.

Or perhaps it already was a success.

The good dinner wine, which Dietrich had brought himself, and the aroma of the coffee after dinner seemed to cheer him so pleasantly that he was no longer assailed by the fatal feeling of Hildegard's detached unapproachability.

Through the blue veil of smoke that enveloped him he looked over at her in an almost detached way until she slowly turned around. With her back to the window and lightly resting her hands behind her on the sill, Hildegard exchanged only the occasional word with him—in a low voice, so that it would not disturb her mother.

At last they fell completely silent. Only Dietrich's eyes, always fixed on the same spot, spoke—blinking a little from the glaring sun, which was shining so brightly on him—but still full of ill-disguised excitement, from which it was easy to see, in the silently dreamy comfort of this lethargic midday pause, how it conjured up image upon image before his soul—.

And while the midday weariness left even him feeling slightly paralyzed, he

was seized at the same time by the longing—hot and irresistible—to lift his
arms, leap up, and draw Hildegard to him—. Just once, like this, to close his
hands around her white, delicate neck—but firmly—firmly — — until at last
his mouth and her lips — — .

To marry! How long could it still go on, anyway! So directly after these
divorce formalities— He almost could have stamped his foot with impatience.

Hildegard was not looking. Still leaning her back against the window, she
gazed out before her, her face serene. In reality she, too, was occupied with the
most peaceful thoughts; she was just combining a gentle nuance of pale rose
with light gray and looking for a dark background for it, still without knowing
to which forms of nature this fantasy for a new embroidery should fix itself.
The workings of the lines usually came to her separately from the colors; and
usually only from them did she develop the realistic plan.

Then she looked up and unexpectedly encountered Dietrich's gaze, blinking
and fixed upon her. At first her features took on a look of dull incomprehen-
sion, as though this gaze could not be meant for her but rather for some other
object entirely unknown to her. Dietrich's head was resting almost on the back
of the chair because he had slid down imperceptibly in his seat; his left hand
was in his trouser pocket, where it held tight to his lighter and was sharply
outlined in the checked fabric—he had just been about to relight his long-
extinguished cigar. The vision of Hildegard seemed to have made him forget
about it; unnoticed, the cold ash fell on his coat and shirtfront.

Hildegard gazed long into his eyes—. He smiled. She had gone pale.

Neither of them spoke a word.

★ ★ ★

Then Hildegard went slowly to the large basket standing in the corner, where
she kept her silk thread. She pulled it close, sat down near the window, and
began to spread out the fine, colorful strands on her lap, bowing her head deep
over her work.

A few minutes passed.

At last Dietrich, his voice forced, remarked: "Does it disturb you, perhaps,
that I'm still here? If that were so, I really would leave at once."

Hildegard, her voice friendly, responded: "Oh, no! What are you thinking?
Please stay just as long as you like."

He touched his brow nervously. The friendly tone sounded icy. Something
like: "Just stay, I'm done with you anyway." To gain some calm he said to

himself: "She's just shy." But unfortunately at this moment nothing at all about Hildegard could be called shy. On the contrary, she seemed to him so absolutely sure of her bearing. Her tone so high pitched and cold. Like hard glass that resounds shrilly to the touch.

A sudden anger welled up in him, he could no longer bear watching her at these doings with her stupid silk thread—and on top of that in such triumphant contentment, as though she knew of no greater pleasure. Yes, there she sat, full of contentment and the innocent pleasure of feminine cruelty. He would not tolerate it.

Dietrich stood up and walked over to Hildegard at the window. She did not move. Then he reached his hand into the delicate, colorful silk to pull it away from under her hands. But she held it fast.

"Stop this stuff now," Dietrich said impatiently, while he found it strangely appealing to feel how the rustling silk pushed back and forth between his fingers and hers as they touched.

"But why, then?" asked Hildegard, and against her will she had to laugh at him.

Dietrich saw the roguish look playing about around her lips, and excitingly it crossed his mind: "Don't you laugh! Watch out! Be nice to me! I won't bear it any longer: I'll make you sorry."

Out loud he answered: "Because I would most like to throw out the window everything that you waste your thoughts on so blindly."

Hildegard shook her head. "You'd probably never be done with that," she said casually, "for it's so nice to dream while I'm embroidering. And that just happens to be my favorite thing to do."

Dietrich let go of the silk and remarked coldly: "Ah, yes. There's a tendency to hysteria with you women."

"A tendency to what?!" Hildegard looked at him, baffled.

"To hysterical behavior. Obviously you're one of them. That's where all your talk about dreams comes from, and all the premonitions and feelings—that all passes only when you women have been introduced to a regulated and useful feminine life."

Hildegard was too taken aback to answer right away. But the rogue was gone from her eyes. Astonished and incredulous is how they looked, and now they turned in reproachful earnest to Dietrich, who appeared to be looking indifferently out the window. "Shame on you!" she said softly, "—you shouldn't have allowed yourself to say such a thing—especially not you. You— whom only a few days ago at the edge of the woods I trusted so completely—in whom I confided—"

"But that's just why!" he persisted, "you gave me a kind of right to be your guide—That's why it's up to me to alert you to your aberrations. — — You sit there and lose yourself in dreams of impossible things, and by doing that you lose your eye for things as they really are."

"— But when those things are ugly!" Hildegard was almost ready to say, but she kept silent, and her animated features were a picture of agitation, contradiction, and vigorous defense.

But at least no more indifference! Dietrich thought, approvingly. Nothing left but girlish moodiness! and he would soon put an end to that. His influence on Hilde he would never misuse! He would much rather make her into a sensible, happy woman.

"You yourself were talking about our walk in the woods, but have you forgotten how it went?" he asked insistently, "how, right before, you exhibited all manner of shyness, all manner of trumped-up anxieties toward people? And that I should force you to shake them off—at the start, you didn't want that either— later it was all right with you because that had made your life difficult. Now you think that all kinds of other notions you should be allowed to keep because they might make your life more beautiful—but they are just as deceptive and unwarranted."

He leaned down to her slightly and offered her his hand. "And now, be good—shake hands; obey me."

Hildegard's cheeks flushed a hot red. She shook her head. She didn't offer her hand.

"You're not giving me your hand?!—Are you serious, Hilde— ?"

Hildegard looked as if she were about to jump up. Then her mother came out of the next room. She was already wearing her little coat and hat, ready to leave for town, and was looking for her parasol. "It's so wonderful outside, you two should accompany me a ways—to the next station," she said as she walked in.

Hildegard almost ran to her. "Dietrich will want to do that in any case—he was about to leave already anyway," she said somewhat hastily, "so the two of you can walk together, can't you? I would rather stay, for I would like so much— so much—to work with my new silk patterns."

"As you like, my dear." Her mother kissed her, and hesitantly Dietrich took his hat. He made a grim face, and his brows drew so close together that they formed a sharp line at the bridge of his nose.

But Hildegard looked past him. She found the parasol, brought it to her mother, and gave her several bright and affectionate nods as the two left.

Dietrich had had to go.

Taking a deep breath, Hildegard stood for a moment in the middle of the room. Yes, that was good. But she would have liked it better still if he had had to leave alone. She missed her mother.

On the chair by the window and on the floor beside, the silk strands lay scattered about. Hildegard's gaze took in the scene. Her eyes and her cheeks were burning. He really was wrong—of a person's most intimate life he understood as little as he did of the colorful silk there— A person had to have the right to compose her own life in as delicate colors as she wanted. —

Hildegard walked slowly into the next room and, distracted, straightened the pillows her mother had used on the sofa. Then she stretched out where her mother had lain. If only she were still here by her. She gazed blankly up at the ceiling. She tried to force herself to think about unimportant things.

Up on the ceiling a kind of sky had been painted. Four chubby-legged cupids against a clouded blue background. One in each corner, they were holding between them a star-covered ribbon, and out of a strange cornucopia in the middle—into which unfortunately iron hooks had been driven to hang the light—fantastic flowers were falling onto the ribbon from every corner of the heavens. It was supposed to portray something like a paradise— Hildegard looked at it full of defiance and anger and scorn.

Then upstairs—right above her—a door creaked. Heavy steps crossed the hall upstairs. Otherwise there was no noise. No noise from the children. So strangely quiet it was up there today— Then clumsy little feet came crashing down the stairs. That was the boy who usually played in the yard.

Hildegard remembered that she had wanted to go up there. Why not now? At least it would make her think of something else. And at least she would find out how to put an end to the frequent disturbances for her mother. Resolved, she stood up, walked to the hallway, listened once more, and went up the narrow wooden steps to the mansard rooms.

By the low landing there were two small doors without nameplates. Hildegard knocked at the one that was above her living room. An indifferent voice called out something. Hildegard opened the door and stood hesitating on the threshold.

The sparse room with its shabby walls was dim despite the bright morning outside; the brown linen curtains on the windows were drawn shut. Not far from the window sat a young woman with disheveled hair, her hands clasped over her emaciated breast. At the rear wall stood an iron bedstead with a straw mattress on it, and beside it a cradle—an elegant but faded wicker baby carriage with broken wheels, which looked as if it had been donated.

The woman did not move, and she did not look up.

Hildegard closed the door behind her, took a few steps forward, and said hesitantly: "Good morning. I wanted to ask how your baby is doing. Yesterday it was crying so."

The young woman nodded. "That's right. Johann was crying a lot," she acknowledged phlegmatically.

"Can't something be done about it?"

"No. Nothing can be done."

"Little Johann is ill, then?"

"Ah, well now! He's not ill."

Hildegard stood hopelessly and pondered what she could say next. This would be of no help to her mother and her sensitive headaches. "Is the little fellow sleeping there now? May I look at him?" she asked quietly.

"Oh, yes. But he's not sleeping," the woman remarked in a strange tone.

Hildegard approached the wicker carriage. The red, already well-worn cradle curtains with red and gold tassels were pulled way back. Anyone approaching the cradle could see the child's head at first glance.

It was lying there blue and bloated. Its jaw hung slack, the eyes, wide open, were looking almost threateningly at Hildegard in their glassy dullness.

"Oh, God—the baby—little Johann!" she cried out in horror, "just look, he's dead!"

The woman shook her head. "No. He's still dying," she said.

Hildegard looked at her in horror. She was sitting there in such apathy and saying such things.

"But perhaps we can still help, surely!" she said, quite beside herself, "we can—I'll call a doctor at once—"

"No doctor can help him now. Just leave it. It's not an illness."

"But what, for God's sake, what is he dying of—?" Hildegard went right up to the woman, tears filled her eyes. She so bitterly regretted not having come up earlier.

Then the woman looked up for the first time. With hard, weary eyes she answered curtly: "What's he dying of? Of the fact that his father has no bread and I have no milk."

Hildegard was silent. Her face, both cheeks, slowly went a deep red. Not a soul in the house—no, not a single person had known how things were with the poor people. And such poverty existed a hundredfold. She knew it, but how little it had forced itself until now upon her fantasy, her sympathy, her desire to help.

Now she felt that her being here was merely an obtrusiveness for which she would have liked to have asked forgiveness. For now she, a stranger, arriving unbidden, could do nothing—

Then clumsy little footsteps came tramping up the stairs. Someone shoved and scratched at the door that she had almost shut, and then a little boy of about three years old pushed his way into the room; his patched smock was covered with sand, and he came trudging over to his mother, lifting up his face so that she might wipe it with her apron and blow his nose.

Hildegard stood by silently and watched the bowlegged little fellow with his resolute movements. Her heart was full to the brim. She would most liked to have picked him up and hugged and kissed him. But she did not dare to do that. She just ran her hand hesitantly through his blond hair.

"If it doesn't trouble you—if you would let me—I would so like to take the little fellow with me downstairs. I would be grateful if you would let me play with him. —But perhaps you wouldn't like that?" she said, stammering.

The woman gave her a rather surprised look. She clearly could not grasp why Hildegard was talking so many useless words about such a simple thing. She shrugged her shoulders. "If you want to—it's all the same to me," the woman answered with her deeply indifferent voice, and then she wiped the boy's snub nose one more time—"go downstairs with the lady, Rupert."

Hildegard took him by the hand, while he looked up at her, mouth open and interested. "I thank you. He'll have such a good time that he'll like to come again. And I—may I come back again?" Hildegard asked and held out her hand to the woman.

The woman gave her hand a quick touch, and now she stood up. "If you like!" she remarked, still as surprised as before.

But as she said that, something was working in her face. She stared over at the cradle, then she walked ahead of Hildegard and opened the door to the stairway for her.

In the moment that Hildegard stepped out, their gazes met. They hung upon each other for an instant, and it was as if they gave each other a silent hug.

Hildegard's wide, dark eyes said so eloquently: "I did not know! Forgive me! I shall never forget you. Neither you—nor the misery of life."

And the other woman's red, tired eyes, numb with sorrow, answered in silent response: "Thank you."

Very slowly Hildegard went down the wooden stairs, step by step, holding the boy's hand. When they were standing downstairs in the entryway by her rooms, she felt the warm little hand in hers give a pull—instinctively he wanted to take the usual way out into the yard, where the nice sandpile was. With a serious gaze of critically comparing inspection he looked through the open door into her sunlit parlor. But when Hildegard disappeared for a moment into her clean kitchen and then came back with a small pot of leftover bouillon and a piece of white bread, then he followed her, as fast as he could, into the living room. He could tell from the little pot that it had to be something good tasting; he flared his little nostrils.

Hildegard chatted with him, seated him at the dinner table, and took great pleasure in feeding him. She pondered in her mind how she would have him down here more often and how she would be best able to help the poor woman.

She felt herself to be so immeasurably and unjustly rich and happy compared to her. —And like a child who knows about as little about real life as the small boy there. —His mother knew what misery was. And what happiness was, too — — — a happiness perhaps that Hildegard could barely sense: to bring life into the world. —

When the little fellow had eaten his fill, Hildegard took an old box of glass buttons and shook it out in front of him. She showed him how to lay out figures and shapes with them. From time to time she listened to see whether it was still quiet upstairs—

Then she heard a step. But it was from downstairs. Someone was opening the hallway door.

Dietrich came in. When she jumped up, startled, he stayed in the doorway. He saw how quickly the joy faded from her eyes, how her movements expressed fear. He felt a quiet shame well up in him. Hildegard could be so captivating when she showed her feelings without reserve. Back there at the edge of the woods he had found it so totally enchanting.

His presence lamed this full upswing of her soul. "You have a brand-new visitor!" he remarked rather awkwardly.

She nodded. "From upstairs. I'll tell you about it later. —"

"I can imagine!" he said, without looking at her, and he sat down by the child at the edge of the chair. —"Do you love such little urchins as I do—?"

She stood across from him and did not answer. He glanced up briefly. How pale she was! But that passed. He would surely love her so much—as much as he would never before have believed possible. And with an imploring gesture he reached out his hand to her across the table.

Hildegard sensed darkly that she would now at once have to spread two light gray wings and let them lift her up—high, high, as in her dream. But she also sensed darkly how it is in feverish dreams: as though something in her were helplessly, powerlessly beating its wings—and suddenly she didn't know whether she was flying—or falling—.

Then Dietrich drew the playing child to him. He looked at Hildegard, almost a bit timidly—and at the same time gently kissed the child on his blond hair.

And Hildegard slowly laid her hand in his.

Reaching out over a paradise.

INCOGNITO

She stood in almost reverential silence before the high mountains that looked down upon the twilight dark alpine village; she barely noticed how cold she was in her thin summer wrap.

Her small suitcase was still lying on the back seat of the carriage; to a pretty, plump woman who was just hurrying up, the coachman, without stirring from his driver's seat, was expounding at length upon how they had him alone to thank for this guest; for down in Innsbruck the young lady had said only: "somewhere in the mountains!" and with that he had directed her here to the Schöneberg hotel in the Stubai Valley.

The hostess merely gave him a nod and pointed to the beer parlor; then she took charge of the few bags the lady had brought and began to extol her rooms to her. The best of them were still empty—so late in September hardly anyone came up here, and so she was to choose as she liked; and as for the beds, there were none better to be found in all the world.

"And what is this here? is it part of the hotel as well?" the woman interrupted these outpourings and pointed with outstretched arm to a very small house that was situated right near where they were standing, apart from the main building and half hidden among the trees right by the slope.

What that was? Well, that was the summer cottage. Of course it was part of the hotel, and in the summer it was always booked; now it cost only a few guldens a day—did she perhaps want to stay there?

The young lady was already walking toward it, looking at it with delight. Yes, of course she wanted to stay in it! Like a lovely plaything with its cladding of carved wood, it peeked out of a thicket of wild, red alpine creeper—so cozy and apart, as if it could not possibly have anything to do with a usual hotel business.

Right away, then, Resi, a rather young waitress in Tyrolean garb, was sent out to the summerhouse with pitchers of water and fresh bed linen. Resi threw open the shutters and began to put the two tiny rooms in livable order. Then she brought the lady the guest book and asked her, just for this first evening, to take her evening meal on the public veranda until everything here was in order.

The young lady opened the guest book and entered her name and residence: Anjuta Ssapogina from St. Petersburg—and, very quickly and rather casually, made ready for dinner. As she was looking in her suitcase for her etui, comb, and brush, a few books fell out, tattered paperbound books, which she pushed impatiently aside.

"If just for a short while I wouldn't have to hear anything about that—anything about books and profession," she thought and suppressed a sigh as she ran the comb through her splendid gold-blond hair, its natural curls fastened at the back. Now she had had enough of that for a time. Actually, it was not a vacation at all, having to travel around and always be thinking about where she might find like-minded people and collaborators—. Well, here in these magnificent mountains there was no such thing—no one would talk to her about those matters here. And then she would at last really and truly be able to get some rest—from all the hustle and bustle and work of the winter months that scarcely gave her time to breathe.

Slowly she walked across the dark meadows to the veranda that Resi had mentioned, a small covered structure of wood across from the hotel building. Resi was just standing up on a chair to light the lamps that hung over the tables; now she was adding kerosene from a metal can, pouring it into the holder of an already burning lamp.

"You! Resi! If you do that again, I'll wring your neck. You're just plain hopeless!" a blond young man called to her from the already brightly lit corner of the veranda, where he was sitting alone with a bottle of Tyrolean wine.

Resi laughed, climbed quickly down off the chair, and turned her child's face to Anjuta Ssapogina with a roguish wink as if to say: "he's not being serious!" Then she began to explain the dinner arrangements to her by pointing out that what was on the nicely decorated menu was not available at all, while on the other hand there were diverse other things that she could recommend warmly. Anjuta liked listening to her, for her friendly manner was like that of a lively child, yet she could not communicate with Resi, whose rapidly spoken dialect mostly eluded her.

Then behind the table in the corner the blond young man stood up and offered to help; he advised her to try a piece of the cold roast chamois and introduced himself to Anjuta as Erwin von Stein from Graz.

Resi hurried off to fetch her roast chamois and left the Schöneberg hotel to the sole two late-autumn guests for themselves, sitting there at adjoining tables and exchanging the first conventional conversational pleasantries. Anjuta looked Herr von Stein over carefully and found that he was still quite young, trim and slim of build, with solid shoulders that tended to broadness and that in his brow and eyes he was possessed of a surprisingly handsome, open expression. When he asked whether she had come up from Innsbruck, she told him that she had wanted to travel on from there to Vienna, but in the meantime the mountains had lured her away.

"So you like it in the mountains?" he asked, visibly pleased.

"Oh, the mountains!" she said in her soft voice, and the indeterminate color of her eyes seemed to grow darker, "I used to love the plains, that's where I'm from. And it is beautiful there, too, where it is boundless, or at least appears to be so. But when people come to the plains, they immediately become human themselves, serving people, and they're no longer untouched and unapproachable. It occurs to me now that that's why the mountains have the effect they do. As if one were seeing nature itself as it rises above all that's human and looks down upon it. No matter how many small settlements might grow among them they still retain something so primeval." She broke off and looked at him, shaking her head. "Only in Russian can I say exactly what I mean, of German I have only a superficial grasp," she remarked quite candidly.

He looked at her with an interest that surprised even himself. Something strange and feminine about her he found appealing. "I can understand very well what you mean," he answered, and when Resi, who had brought their dinner, had gone away again, he added, "but I would like even more to hear you say it in your mother tongue; there is so much music in that language. I can't understand it, but at the technical institute I knew a fellow student who was a Russian and who often spoke Russian. He was a strange person in any case—always ready to accomplish something extraordinary while others dither about, always brooding about ideal goals."

Anjuta nodded. "Circumstances make many of us that way. They create martyrs and fanatics. Men do not live for themselves—they live for a higher cause— if they are at all able to be enthusiastic about something," she said, but then fell reluctantly silent, as she thought to herself: "a person really is after all like a machine that's set in motion for some specific purpose! Now I myself have to start talking about these matters again."

"What masculine men such an attitude must produce. And such men—what feminine women must inspire them," he remarked, looking at her with a gaze of respect.

"No, indeed not!" Anjuta thought to herself, "ecstasy alone does not produce masculinity; such men forget how to act, they often just explode," but she said nothing.

"Later we lost touch with each other," said Erwin von Stein, taking up the conversation again, "I went to the architectural academy; he transferred to the university. He was more scientifically inclined, although I wasn't at all. I chose architecture in order to keep my studies based on art—even though it is supposed to be a professional field."

"What would you prefer to do?" she asked.

"I would prefer to serve art free from any bourgeois profession, and in fact to serve the least lucrative of all the arts, lyric poetry," he responded with a smile that nevertheless struck not at all as self-deprecating but rather as serious and innocent, "and your countryman said that was purely a matter for women. But I cannot find that many women can or should write poetry. Instead, they should make the man into a poet."

Anjuta smiled too, she looked at him, amazed and attentive. "So you believe that's what women are suited to do," she interjected, drawing him out so that she could observe him undisturbed.

"Yes, but of course only those who have remained women," he remarked. "Not the so-called emancipated women, those students and female fighters for all possible rights. About them we'd rather not talk at all, would we?"

"Oh, no, for God's sake, no!" she put in hastily, looking almost startled, which made him laugh. All he saw was that she wanted to avoid that topic of conversation.

"I'm really happy that we agree on that," he said, full of conviviality, "for I must tell you that on this point I am downright unjust. I don't oppose such women on principle—on the basis of some theory. I have no theories at all. Such matters I have barely pondered—let the philosophers among us do that, shall we?—But it just goes against my subjective taste—just as some people have idiosyncrasies about cats or spiders. Better the most indolent, most unhelpful woman than one of those involved in intellectual or professional pursuits."

When Anjuta once again had nothing to reply to that, he could not keep from thinking: "Perhaps she is less intelligent than she looks. In any case she's one of the quiet ones. She engenders good feelings just by being near."

In the meantime she had pushed away her plate and stood up. "Now I want to go over to my little castle," she said, "where it is really as charming as can be. Oh, had I only found my way to the mountains earlier—my oldest brother would have come along. He would always have found rest and recovery here."

He had stood up and was accompanying her to the edge of the veranda. "Was he unwell?" he asked sympathetically, and gazed into her face, now grown so serious and pale.

"He was ill for some time before he died," she answered quietly, and gave him her hand, "good night! I'll find my own way across the dark meadows."

"Good night!" he called after her, "the meadows are wet with dew, and the grass is high! I can see that the dew is soaking you and the hem of your dress is dragging in it."

She stopped in the meadow and lifted the hem of her dress. And then she hurried for the small, bright-shining opening of the door, in which Resi had been so considerate as to place a light. Inside in the little parlor a lamp was burning on the table, and in its light Anjuta saw the carved paneling of the walls with all the antlers and stuffed birds that decorated them all around. The adjoining bedroom was little more than an alcove. But through its single wide window the snow-covered mountains shimmered in magnificently.

Anjuta unpacked her small suitcase, threw most of its contents into the drawers of a low bureau beside the bed, and undressed. As she did so she noticed that the hem of her dress had been dragging that way across the meadow because it was hanging down torn. At home old Natasha, who used to be a servant for her parents, took care of the sewing for her.

A small photograph of her late brother she had placed on the bureau. Now she reached once more for its black leather frame and looked at it thoughtfully by the light of the candle.

Ah, if only he were still alive, how much nicer it would be for her in the world, she thought a little sadly. Since childhood she had loved him so much. And, after her parents died, when she went to live with him, how well they always got along together. His life was completely filled then with his political-literary weekly—and he, he completely filled his little sister's life. Then, of course, she could help him only with minor things, with proofing the galleys and mailing out the issues. But had she not ultimately given up her own plans, joyfully and readily; had she not turned from the studies she had already begun in the natural sciences just to work for him and with him? How ambitiously she let him explain everything to her as she pursued her studies and wrote the driest reports and articles for his paper. Yes, that had been a beautiful time.

Anjuta had put the photograph back in its place again, climbed into bed, and put out the light. But she could not fall asleep. If she could just for once stop her thoughts from constantly turning around this weekly paper. Of course, that had become more and more impossible since her brother's death, as she was now acting as coeditor, along with her brother's friend and collaborator Sergei Wiranoff. Since then the weekly had taken on more than one female coworker and was in collaborative contact with the women's movement abroad.

During her current trip, Anjuta was becoming acquainted with many such women; she had visited their organizations and made speeches to their members, speaking on matters that usually went beyond what the German emancipation movement was allowing itself to do. Yet doing so she found that even the smallest emancipation of the German women was evident in their outward behavior. Would young Erwin von Stein likely have otherwise spoken of them with such disapproval? He likely had no idea at all how superficially he was judging. But he was probably also one of those who are afraid that the woman of today is becoming too much to cope with —— .

From time to time Anjuta sat up in bed and listened. How strange it was here at night! In the wainscoting there was a constant creaking and scurrying, likely from weasels or rats that were living between the wood paneling and the outer brick wall. Outside the wind was singing a quiet song in the trees, the creeper vines were whispering to each other, and a narrow, calm stream that flowed past the little house was chiming in with its muffled murmur.

It would be quite easy to be afraid of sleeping here alone in the dark, especially for one of those delicate princesses that Herr von Stein preferred because they were better recipients of his poems—and ideas[1]—Anjuta went on thinking and laughed into her blanket. But still she was not happy. She listened to the wind, and her tired, overworked mind yearned for sleep, for a child's sound sleep, and most preferably with a dream as well; then she would dream of how she had so liked to perch on the arm of her brother's chair at his desk and how he had forgotten about continuing his writing as he stroked her hair—.

---

[1]The original achieves a subtly critical jibe at Herr von Stein with its use of the verb *an-dichten*, which evokes the act of writing poetry for or about somebody, but is more often used to describe the act of "ascribing," "attributing," or "imputing" qualities to someone in a possibly misleading or illusory way. Accordingly, Anjuta here is differentiating herself from those "princesses" to whom Herr von Stein likes to write his poetry and to whom he is also inclined to ascribe specific, traditional feminine qualities and attitudes.

* * *

The next afternoon Anjuta was coming back from a wonderful long walk when, a half-hour from Schöneberg, she encountered Herr von Stein. Even from a distance she had recognized him from his clothing, which she found quite becoming: at any rate this olive-colored loden vest suited his boyish build, with its matching belt drawing it tight around his hips and its opening at the neck exposing only a strip of his fine, white shirt collar.

"I'm glad that I've run into you," he said and tipped his hat. "You've already ventured out so far all by yourself. Do you like it in the mountains as much as you did yesterday?"

"More and more by the hour," she answered, "I've been wandering around for hours. I wanted to find some alpine roses."

"The time for alpine roses is over by the time midsummer has passed; up here pretty well everything has withered by now," he remarked, "but if you want some autumn decorations for your room, then allow me to bring you some; it's shrubbery and prickly when you try to pick it."

"Good, bring me some," she said in friendly fashion, "besides, I've been looking more at what's around me and above me than at what's at my feet. Right down into the valley the mountains are so white, so white! The snow is getting close, isn't it?"

"Now at this time of year, yes. Now at any moment it can overtake us even here with its big flakes, as soon as a few clouds darken our sun. —Actually, you're dressed much too lightly for our mountains," he added, with a glance at her suit.

Anjuta gave a carefree shrug of her shoulders. "I'm not staying long at all. The friends I'm traveling with can arrive any day now in Munich or Vienna and send a message for me to Innsbruck, and then I'll join them. I left the bulk of my luggage in Innsbruck, including a plaid bag with my warm things," said Anjuta, and sat down on a grass-covered piece of rock where she had the most beautiful view. "I'd like to take a bit of a rest here and gaze my fill."

The young man pointed out the individual villages and mountain ranges that stretched out before her, and doing so he also began to tell her about the country that she had come to like so quickly. He described the beauty of the mountains and valleys, which stretched for miles around, in seasons when there are no tourists and they lie in lonely magnificence. At such times he had often roamed about in the Tyrol, Carinthia, and the Salzkammergut. The farms where he stayed overnight and the mountain life of their inhabitants he described to her as well, and so too the splendor of the silent mountain lakes that no steamers crossed but that one had to row across in a small boat if one wanted to continue on. He told of the strange magic of the landscape when, at the start of spring, the fruit trees begin to blossom or when late in the year the last leaves fall.

Anjuta listened without interrupting him even once; she found that he was especially good at telling, with a warmth in his voice that approached things quietly and seemed to draw more from them than mere words to sketch their basic contours.

When he fell silent she raised her head and said: "I don't know whether it's your voice or what you're saying, but I can well imagine that things shape themselves into poems for you. And also that it must make you very happy to write poems."

"Is this the first time that's occurred to you? Haven't you always felt that whenever you came to grasp and understand a poem?" he asked in amazement and seemed to hold back a further idea that was just on the tip of his tongue.

Anjuta shook her head. "I've had little to do with literature. I know less about art and literature than you likely think," she admitted with the frankness that people have when they know they have had a thorough but one-sided education; then she added quickly: "But that's of no interest at all. I'd rather hear you tell me more in this nice fashion—much more."

He sat down not far from her and said, his voice low and his steel-blue eyes fixed upon her, imploring: "As you wish. But I've been talking the whole time, and you've said nothing at all. There is something so quiet about you that I would much rather be silent in order not to lose inadvertently a single sound that you make. Say something to me, tell me about something, whatever it may be. Yesterday evening you started to, a little."

"Oh, what a shame, why do you bring our conversation back to that!" she remarked with regret, "do you want here, in this area, to hear about Russian men and the situation in Russia—? I'm not a German, and I find it hard to discuss abstract things in your language. That's why I strike you as quiet. Because I could tell comfortably only of the most simple and commonplace things."

"Well, do that. I would really like to know what you would find to be the most simple and commonplace things," he said with a smile, "what occurs to you right now? Make a story out of it for me."

Anjuta gazed out upon the landscape as it took on a crimson hue in the rays of the setting sun and cast its bright reflection on the two of them. She was in a light and happy mood, and she had to smile.

"What occurs to me just now? I'm thinking of a strange little playhouse that I lived in when I was a child. My 'summer cottage' here in Schöneberg makes me think of it. It was in the garden, not far from our estate house—my parents were landowners and had, besides me, four sons, the youngest three of whom have long since settled in the interior of Russia. When my brothers grew bigger and the house was always full of all manner of half-grown boys, my father had this little cabin built for me and my playtime activities. Then I could watch the noisy doings of our boys only from afar, and now I often wish I could always watch all activities only in that way. — — The little house was located behind a stand of nothing but birch trees, and it was painted white itself, with crudely painted flowers around the window frames — — but I don't know how to describe that to you so that you could have a vivid impression of my little house and my childhood happiness," Anjuta added, and she looked almost shyly at her companion. She did not know herself how she came to tell about this.

The gaze that met hers was so serious and reverential that she became still more confused and stood up to go.

He had looked at her as she spoke and thought to himself how this small delicate figure, with her head full of blond curls, did not at all belong in this noisy world, but in a very quiet happiness, in a happiness like the one he tried to convey in his poems.

But he said nothing, and they made their way back exchanging only an occasional word. Anjuta gazed ahead so peacefully that one could have thought she had forgotten her companion beside her. But she was thinking of him and listening to him speak as he had spoken to her before. And she looked, as if he had revealed it all to her, beyond the rocky masses of the mountain cliffs and out into the infinite distance; she saw the broad valleys stretching out and the lonely lakes dreaming in the green ravines, all as untraversed, untouched as paradise. And in an inner vision she saw two people walking through the silent landscape, like the people of paradise, like the two first people—a man and a woman. So far from all the hustle and bustle, from all the trouble and strife, in blissful oneness with each other, alone and by themselves—a man and his woman — —.

The mountains, so high, soon captured the sun. In Schöneberg dusk was already falling. Anjuta offered her companion her hand and went into her summer cottage.

On the table in the little living room several letters were waiting for her. She heaved an impulsive sigh; newspapers and magazines she did not have sent on to her from Innsbruck, but she could not do that with letters.

She lit her lamp, closed both windows to lessen the evening cold in the room, and then slowly she read through her letters, one after the other. One was from Wiranoff, the good fellow, who was now looking after the editing in Petersburg all by himself and taking care of her work as well. What he wrote was sad, but that was not from the work but because he missed having her there, she was certain of that. There was no more loyal friend than Wiranoff, she knew that as well. A friend who had loved her for years and was waiting for the time that she might one day give in to him. In the weekly they did indeed have a common interest, a common child: they belonged together.

How he would surely freeze if he were sitting with her now, Anjuta thought, and wrapped herself more tightly in her one woolen blanket. Wiranoff had a penchant for keeping his overcoat on, even inside; often he might not have put on a suit jacket under it—he was more than careless. But that was easily forgotten and forgiven by a look at his inspired, honest ascetic's face with its lean, high cheekbones.

She had to answer him at once. The second letter required no hurry; it was from Ludin, the editor of a rather impoverished literary journal. He, too, was abroad this autumn to establish new connections and was to meet Anjuta on their way back. But clearly he was already eager even now to tell her all the news personally, for Ludin could not have his fill of chatting. In addition he was well suited to the purpose of his trip, he was something of a social talent.

Anjuta reached for the inkwell and paper, stood up again, and walked back and forth in the room. All her thoughts were already back on the old track again; Wiranoff's questions about the journal and reports occupied her, she saw before her the various familiar faces that surrounded her every day in the big, dusty editorial room and that crowded around her tea table in the living quarters in back. Yet for the first time she was amazed that among so many men she never felt quite right in her female sexuality. Quite a few of them had flattered her, others wooed her, and each had loved her in a good, serious, respectful way, with the better part of themselves. But still she felt she was among comrades and had always pondered a possibility of marriage only from that perspective.

Suddenly Anjuta stopped, as if startled by the sound of her own steps, as she walked back and forth with firm tread. She realized that she had been walking about with her arms crossed behind her and her brow furrowed, like a brooding field general.

She seized the lamp and stepped before the oval mirror that hung above the table. "I shall surely become old and wrinkled before my time," she suddenly thought, "work in such a profession makes a person ugly, and the constant sitting. If my small figure does not remain slender then I've lost it. — — But that is a small and modest sacrifice, a little bit of feminine beauty given in the service of a great cause," she went on thinking and felt a fine, painful sorrow.

And then she put the lamp down quietly and began to write. Yet she remained distracted, made a few false starts, and finally stopped.

If it stayed so cold, what in the world was she to put on tomorrow? She had brought along a white flannel blouse with Russian embroidery on the shoulders, and it was pretty. But the belt no longer looked very good; it had long since been worn bare. If she took a bit of time she could sew a new belt out of a piece of flannel.

Anjuta stood up and took out her sewing things. As she did so she remembered the torn hem of her dress. Should she tend to these things now instead of writing her letter? Did she want now, for the first time in her life, to make a conscious effort to dress up for someone?

No, she still did not want to do that. Not dress up. She gazed steadily at the light and felt a burning in her eyes, as if she wanted to weep.

Not dress up. But rather cover up something—hide something. And perhaps most of all that of which she had previously been most proud.

And Anjuta sat and froze and sewed until deep into the night.

★ ★ ★

Some traveling singers and zither players who had come from a festival in Mieders were resting the following afternoon in Schöneberg. When Resi brought dinner to the summerhouse she had all sorts of wonderful things to tell about them and tried to talk the Russian lady into taking a look. But Anjuta had no desire to do so; outside a strong wind was blowing, and the sky was growing ever darker; she had to move the table at which she was diligently writing her letters today right up close to the window to have enough daylight.

She still had not finished her writing when a large dark shadow fell upon her papers and she saw Erwin von Stein's loden vest by the window frame. He greeted her and, by way of explanation, raised the hand in which he was holding a large bunch of ferns, red berberis, dog roses, and mountain ash.

Anjuta stood up and opened the door for him. "That certainly is friendly of you!" she said and took the fresh autumn branches and fern leaves from him.

"And that's not the only reason I've come," he answered a bit awkwardly as he stepped inside, "I wanted to let you know as well that even this evening or perhaps early tomorrow morning I'll be going down to Innsbruck to bring back your bag with your warm things."

"But that's not at all necessary!" she exclaimed happily, "I could also have all that sent to me, if I must have it. Just think what a long, long way it is with the cart that drives up here."

He shook his head. "There's a much shorter way that you didn't know about when you came. Barely a quarter of an hour downhill from us is the little railway station at Patsch, and from there one can reach Innsbruck the quickest way by train. Who is supposed to send you what you've left in the railway depot? And — — I would so like to be allowed to do something that is useful or of service to you."

She did not answer right away as she was busy with the branches. As she did so he took a close look around in the small, wood-paneled parlor, as if he were looking for something. "How foolish a person can be," he remarked after a short pause, "I was here several times before you arrived and looked at the little summer cottage through the window and imagined how cozy it would be to live here. And just now I thought it would have to look just like this, just because you're living here. That's foolish, isn't it? And I've still completely forgotten as well that you arrived here with almost no luggage."

Involuntarily Anjuta too cast her gaze around the room with its many antlers, stuffed birds, and wall carvings, where nothing spoke of her presence except the table covered with papers and a pair of gloves that lay forgotten on a chair. There were a few things in her suitcase with which she could have made it a little bit more habitable, but she had felt no need at all to do so.

"Perhaps it's less the lack of luggage than the fact that I don't have any particular talent for decorating rooms," she said candidly.

"You don't believe that yourself!" he said, "where there's a woman living, then things bend and yield to suit her personality, as if they were given life, in order to resonate with the melody of her personality. I would surely be able to prove that to you, entirely without words, just by pointing out one thing, if I were allowed to visit you at home where you live. — — But I will prove it to you even now from a more minor thing."

Anjuta had taken a dusty vase of green glass with gold and red flowers on it from a corner of the other window bench and was filling it with water. "Well?" she asked curiously, and thought to herself with a heavy-hearted feeling: "it's good that he's not seeing me at home where I live!"

He had moved close to her and lifted a few of the scattered ferns and branches from the table. "That's all!" he said with a smile, "I want only to watch how you arrange and order these things and which ones you leave out and where in the room you put them. Some of them don't necessarily need water. — — But each in its own place, touched by your hand, will reveal something about you and your ways and workings."

Anjuta's entire face went red. She had never had much to do with arranging flowers and tried to bunch together the whole bundle and stick them in the water. "Why do you attribute precisely to me these qualities that might befit some other women," she said, embarrassed, "you certainly don't know—"

"Because for me you are the perfect example of a woman—of woman in her finest silence and simplicity," he cut her off, his voice low and passionate.

The branches were trembling in Anjuta's hand. She saw only unclearly the red berberis so bright among the green fern, her heart was beating so wildly it hurt, and a strange anxious feeling came over her, as if she were to perform not some simple manual task but as if she were standing there with her hands full of heavy, aromatic roses and did not know how to weave herself a wreath of them.

She did not know how beautiful this shy apprehensiveness made her in the eyes of the man standing beside her by the table and gazing at her uncertainly. She did not know that in this moment she looked as young and dear as she really still was, in spite of all the seriousness of her profession and life's work— a blushing young girl standing beside a young man.

The room was growing ever darker than before. A gust of wind whistled past the windows, and at the same time big white flakes of snow were falling just outside the window and dissolving, even as they fell, into sparkling drops of rain. From the hotel they could hear the zithers; now loud, now quiet, the wind carried the lost tones over to the two in their silent room.

Anjuta had let the branches fall back on the table and closed her eyes, as if to a light into which she did not dare to look. All she felt was how two gentle hands were very tenderly holding her face and lifting it up — — and then— then she did not want to know anything more or feel anything more than that he was kissing her—that he was kissing her awake.

★ ★ ★

Snow and storm were doing their best around the little house all through the evening and the entire night, and Resi was convinced that her Russian lady really had been afraid out there alone, for when she brought her second break-fast, the first one was still standing untouched beside the green vase with the berberis branches, and Anjuta herself was just getting up.

She looked pale, but that was not from the storm and the fright, she said to Resi, smiling, and gazed in jubilant delight out onto the delicately snow-covered landscape, which lay there outside her windows in the occasional ten-tative ray of sunshine. "My paradise!" she thought again, and never before in her life did she think she had ever seen things bathed in such infinite beauty as today—as though a whole new morning of life had begun for all things, as though they were in secret league with her own mood. Whatever she looked at seemed to become beautiful for her, and the merest occurrence nestled at her feet just as in paradise the plants and animals gathered around people and found peace in their company.

The golden darts of the sun broke through the last clouds and shone high above the most distant mountain peaks, and then their brightness turned pale again, and the first mist wove, quiet and silver-blue, around the distant moun-tains. Anjuta was still abiding, dreaming, at her window, for now quite, quite near was the hour when the train had to arrive at the small railway station in Patsch, and she would not have to be alone. Alone, she could neither do nor take up anything; alone, her whole being was an attentive and patient waiting. She felt as though she were no longer here in the far-off summer cottage, but instead returned to the little garden house on her parents' estate and still a child through whose door life was yet to make its entrance—the young, beginning, carefree life, with songs upon its lips and flowers in its hair.

And was that not really the way it was? What had she experienced since then that had touched her most intimate self? She thought with a smile of what for years she had considered to be her most serious struggle and a form of sacri-fice: the fact that she had given up her own chosen study of the natural sciences in order to help her brother. One course of study exchanged for another—that was really all it was! Was it not really quite immaterial which one she chose? Just how could she imagine that it mattered in the least?

No, it made no difference, and nothing came of it but more books again, and book people, and papers, and thoughts about papers — —.

The tension grew in Anjuta to the point of pain. The shadows of the trees in front of the house grew longer, the sun stood deep in one of the cuts between the mountains she faced. Why had he not come yet? He must have missed the train—but why did he do that? How could he do that to her?

It could be something else, too; perhaps acquaintances in Innsbruck were keeping him, or an unexpected errand. In any case he was coming soon—what sort of unusual thing could possibly happen to him between Innsbruck and Patsch?

Her restlessness was foolish, she talked herself out of it, but she was no longer able to control her inner unrest, which was only trying to find all kinds of explanations. In essence she was not worried that something had happened to him or about the distance from Innsbruck to here.

No, it was just that she could be torn from him, even if he were to come into her room this instant—she feared the unspoken distance between him and her, about which he knew nothing, of which he had no inkling.

Could she change that she simply was who she was? One of those women whom he avoided and found depressing? He loved her quite naively and un-aware—because she did not wear a pince-nez and have short hair, and so he did not have the least suspicion. Now she was dreaming a fairy tale—yes, that was it: a fairy tale, as if she were in paradise; but out of this paradise knowledge would soon and quickly have to drive the two of them.

An irrational anxiety came over her. The hours dragged by and did not bring him back. She stared out into the evening and felt as if she should fall to her knees and pray. Yes, as if she should pray for release and salvation from her guilt, for a miracle that would let her return to the days of her innocent child-hood and early girlhood. She raged with such anxious wishes against her pure, courageous, and able life—only because it had grown independent and hard-ened and would not fit into the blossoming garden of lyrics and love.

She had sunk down by her chair and pressed her face into her hands. Then she rose to her feet and was almost frightened by the way she was. She could have been in no more grave and anxious a mood than if she had been a guilty person facing a judge. With the first man whom she loved she felt ashamed of all about her that was not feminine, almost as deeply as a girl is ashamed of her lost purity. She would have liked to wrap a cloak around herself, a white-gold cloak that would cover her entirely and make her whole past invisible forever to the man of her love and her desire.

Anjuta wrapped a blanket around her shoulders and went outside. There, not far from her door, the narrow white gravel path wound its way down toward

Patsch, the path Erwin had taken down early that morning, accompanied part of the way by her. Tonight, with the last train, he surely had to come! He surely would not leave her alone in her anxiety and uncertainty.

She could take it no longer and ran more than she walked, down the steep path into the depths. A few times she stumbled, the bushes on either side clung teasingly to her dress to slow her down, and the twilight around her became darker. Then there were steps, uneven steps carved into the rock and the stony ground, and finally she saw the shimmering lights of the station.

Flushed and trembling from her exertion, she arrived at the bottom. She wanted to sit down in one of the dark arbors that stood by the little station house, just as a train from Innsbruck was coming in. But perhaps it was not even coming from Innsbruck, she no longer knew; she stood still and looked silently at the train doors as they sprang open.

And then her heart gave a mighty beat and seemed to stand still. In the lights of the station platform she recognized her leather bag. From the bag her gaze made its way upward, and she was just about to hurry forward, but then her foot held back. The man carrying her bag was all wrapped up in a large coat, but if it was Erwin, then he must have undergone a strange change.

It was not Erwin. She took a few steps in his direction and stared at him with wide eyes as if he were a ghost. "— Ludin!" she cried out.

"Ah, well, can it be? You're here, Anjuta? How so, then? There, you see, I'm bringing you your things, Herr von Stein had me do it," said the Russian.

"Herr von Stein—" she murmured absentmindedly.

"Yes. You see, I met him carrying your bag just when I was getting your address from the post office. Well, then, of course, we had a talk. I really like him, this Herr von Stein. Sociable fellow, isn't he? But do we go up on foot here now?"

"Wait a bit. Not right away. We can sit down in this arbor here, Ludin. I'm very tired," said Anjuta, struggling with the words as she walked slowly toward the arbor. "Why didn't he—why didn't Herr von Stein come along, then?"

"Why didn't he come along?" Ludin slid the heavy bag up onto the bench in the arbor, "yes, well, how should I know that? Eh? He didn't seem to be in any hurry. So I've brought you your things now."

"Did you talk to each other for some time?" she asked quietly, uncertainly.

"Yes, of course we did. We drank a bottle of wine together. From the outset he was so engaging, really almost cordial, this Herr von Stein. That's how people are in this country, I suppose? But he found me quite interesting, too, if I do say so myself. Just imagine what all I could tell him, can't you?"

"What, then—tell him?" asked Anjuta, still more quietly, and in the dark arbor she closed her eyes and clenched her fingernails into her own hands—"what all did you tell him, then, Ludin?"

"Well, about our weekly and about Wiranoff and about you—yes, especially about you in particular, that's what he mostly wanted to know about, of course. And you can just think how I praised you, Anjuta! Our first—our editor, I said, and she writes articles—. But are we to keep on sitting here, then? Couldn't we go now?"

Quiet and grave, she nodded to herself as if in a deep dream. "Now we can go," she repeated apathetically.

★ ★ ★

A small handcart with Anjuta's bags stood by the railway platform in Patsch, and Resi, who early that morning had wheeled it down herself, unloaded the few items from it and time and again gave Anjuta's hand a trusting farewell shake before resolving to hike back up to Schöneberg, where her employer was impatiently waiting for her. And just what should she say to the Russian gentleman, she asked, suppressing a laugh, when he wakes up and finds that the lady has disappeared overnight after he had arrived the evening before to see her—.

"He'll sleep for a long time yet, Resi, and then he'll just come along after me to Innsbruck," Anjuta answered and nodded to her again.

Yes, he was sure to follow her back right away, full of surprise and newborn loquacity—but at least just as long as he was not there right away. No, anything but that! Just that he should not be around right then!

The little station stood in the bright morning sunshine, a few chickens were pecking about in the short, scorched grass by the arbor. Anjuta went into the station house, ordered herself a glass of wine so that she could sit outside in the arbor, and then took a seat at the wooden table to wait, her arms at her sides, her hands folded in her lap. Her train would not be coming for some time, she had left so early just to get away from Ludin. And it surely would not make any difference anyway where she was—nothing made any difference until her fate was decided in Innsbruck.

Or was that not just one last delusion? Had the matter not already been decided? Yesterday evening, over the bottle of wine that the two of them had drunk together down in the hotel—.

She could not bear trying to imagine Erwin's feelings. When she did she felt as if she had been stripped and pilloried—. Put in a pillory of praise—and that was the worst kind.

And then as he listened a blush of shame must have risen to his cheeks—shame at letting her dupe him like that: for, after all, she had silently approved of his views—and perhaps laughed at him behind his back? After all, she had so willingly let him go on talking to himself about his fantasies and dreams—perhaps so that she would not make him feel her superiority?

Anjuta groaned quietly to herself—that was almost unbearable. And now it would also be unbearable to meet again—. Or was there not, perhaps, she thought in a sudden surge of hope, a bridge, an understanding, a harmony—? If she could know now how he really felt deep down—whether he was angry or sad.

An arriving train awakened her from her thoughts for a moment. But it was not her train, she was going in the opposite direction.

Then, as she was leaning back against the arbor wall, she saw on the narrow path that led up from Patsch, not five paces from her, a man leaning in the shadow of the trees.

He had probably just arrived. But she had the wondrous feeling that he must have been standing for a long time now, leaning against a tree—a long time now. There was no sense of urgency in his bearing, he stood uncertainly, idly, poking about in the grass with his stick. It was Erwin.

He had turned his face partly toward her, yet he was not expecting to find her here, and the vines of the arbor also sufficed to conceal her from his gaze. Silently she looked at him, her lips moving quietly.

No, he did not look angry. And not sad either. He looked out of sorts. Out of sorts like someone who is about to face an embarrassing, unpleasant task, something he must force himself to do, and is now standing and hesitating.

Now he was moving slowly away from the tree he had been leaning on, taking out his watch, and then sauntering a short stretch up the trail with reluctant steps until he disappeared behind an abrupt bend in the mountain path.

Anjuta did not move. She was still sitting quite quietly, her hands folded, the sun shining in on her, sparkling bright through the foliage, and the chickens scurrying about pecking in the grass beside the arbor.

The feverish restlessness had suddenly died out in her. Her mouth took on a fine, arrogant expression that made her look older, and she lined up all her thoughts like soldiers meant to defend her against the attack of some other sudden new weakness. She could be loved for her own sake and without being anxious about whether she possessed all the virtues of an acquiescent little girl. She was loved and catered to for her higher virtues!

She was ready to stand up and walk out to the platform where her train was drawing ever nearer, coming at last to take her away from here and back to an existence more worthy of her, to an existence of work and capability and strength—to her life back home.

Then a hot ray of sunshine fell directly upon her through a gap in the foliage thinned out by the coming autumn, and the ray glided with its trembling light over her countenance and over her shoulders and gave her a glowing—glowing kiss on the nape of her neck—.

Only a few passengers got off the train. A Tyrolean farmer with his boy, who was carrying a heavy green rucksack on his shoulders, walked past the arbor and into the station.

Anjuta did not notice. She had pulled the scarf from her neck and bowed her head low — — —.

A DEATH

Esther was climbing up the carpeted stairs just as the gas was being lit; on the first landing she opened the door to her apartment and stepped into the still unlit hallway. As she was taking off her coat, still wet from the rain, she listened at the adjoining children's room. Only then did she quietly open the door and step in.

There lay the little twins, sleeping peacefully, their cradles side by side; the little girl had one fist up to her mouth, the little boy had his brow furrowed into a look of great gravity. At the window sat their old nurse, whom Esther's foster parents had sent from the province, wearing her pretty cap and knitting in the twilight.

With a smile around her mouth and eyes that endured long past her brief look at the scene, Esther withdrew without a sound into a room next to the dining room that faced out in front onto one of the broadest, noisiest streets of the capital. The curtains were drawn shut, a pretty old brass lamp burned over a round corner table, and in the calm glow that it cast over the finely shaded, matte-finished, gray-brown wallpaper there stood out from the middle wall, white and bright and surprisingly beautiful, a marble relief in a simple wooden frame depicting two laborers, their upper bodies half bare, hard at work at the fire of the forge.

Esther sat down at the table by the lamp and began to sew. But after only a few minutes she stopped again; there was nothing pressingly necessary about what she was sewing, and she would have so liked to be doing something necessary.

She thought: it really had been good in earlier times when a household resembled a small kingdom that still had to produce and create everything by itself and where the wife and her maids would spin and weave and, working on a grand scale with all the servants, take care of everything that life required.

But nowadays and especially in such a big city! Here life was lived in regulated comfort, and every street corner could provide just what was needed.

All at once Esther stood up, taking a deep breath as she raised up both arms so that suddenly she seemed almost too tall for this small room and, in her powerful, easy bearing, full of such a noble plasticity of her lines, as though she were posing here as a young Juno for some invisible artist.

Since she was no longer carrying the twins and now almost no longer nursing them, she felt as if she had to do something useful—as if a long, precious holiday time were past, during which she had had to do nothing because the all-powerful, wonder-working force of life was doing with her what it wished.

The fine smile in her dark eyes deepened, as though she were gazing with a smile deep into herself. The twins would not be the end of it! She would eventually have her big, bright nursery—the prettiest of all the rooms in the house—full of darling children, of boys and girls — —.

Downstairs the house door slammed shut with a bang, and she heard the rapid, loud steps coming up to the first floor. Esther let her arms fall and went to meet her husband in the hallway where, even before he pulled the door shut behind him, he pressed his lips, his beard still moist from the autumn frost, to her hand and lips.

"You've come just at the right time," she remarked, cheerfully fending him off, "for a moment I didn't know what I was to do with myself."

"That's something that can hardly happen to me, unfortunately," he replied, "I come rushing home like mad from the new buildings, just happy if I don't have to stir again right away. In addition, I've brought you something exceptionally interesting," he added, stepping into the small room with the hanging lamp and pulling a pack of newspaper pages out of his coat.

"What is it?" she asked, reaching for the pack.

"Do you know that recently, in Paris at a private exhibition of young painters and etchers, there was a display of Eberhart's reproductions of your father's works and besides that his own etching *Lonely Journey*?"

Esther unfolded the pages, her face transformed, now serious, moved. "Yes, I know! and this is something about it?" she asked quickly, but then immediately laid the newspapers back down on the table. "Not now. I would rather read it later, when it's quiet—later, after we've eaten," she said, and put her hand under his arm, "you must be tired and hungry. And dinner is already on—just come."

"But I'd be happy to wait if you would really like to read it right away, Esther," he said sweetly and followed her into the dining room, "— it's interesting indeed—and it could give Eberhart, in his loneliness and delicate health down there on the Riviera, a proper boost of the spirits, I should think."

Not answering right away, she sat down across from him at the table; her eyes checked the dishes to make sure nothing was missing, and her hands served him with calm, friendly attentiveness. But her thoughts were still dwelling on the conversation they had begun, for after a pause she said: "Don't you think as well, Georg, that he'll no longer be able to doubt himself so much. He'll be able to admit to himself: my father is great as a sculptor—but I too can accomplish great things, if I really wish to, even though I only do etchings."

"Why do you say: even though I only do etchings?" her husband asked, astonished. "Do you think your foster father is more than his son simply because he's a sculptor?"

"No. But it did always seem for him to be the greatest thing to be able to do what his father could do," Esther responded, "and of course he was supposed to become a sculptor, and that's what he wanted to do. And what did he do later, when he had turned to etching? He did etchings of what Father created and helped in that way to make Father more famous. That's so natural, too. You don't know how that was from early on. When you were close to our country estate, when the big factories were being built out there, that was already the time when Eberhart became ill and moved away."

"But even still, before that too, I would often visit your foster father in his studio in the city," her husband remarked and poured himself a glass of red wine, "and certain conflicts and differences are plain for anyone to see. Eberhart, with all his doubts and artistic aberrations—as far as I can make him out—is, quite simply, a modern man. Your foster father, for all his truly considerable greatness as an artist, might not be one."

"Oh!" Esther said slowly and leaned back in her chair. "You can't judge a person like Father in that way. So infinitely kind and understanding he was to Eberhart, he was always the embodiment of love for him. And never did he hold him back or force him; and how early he even let him travel away as soon as Eberhart felt that restless need to leave, even though it was difficult then to make the sacrifices to enable him to do so. How long Eberhart was in Paris. But he himself admitted that he couldn't be creative there, that he was just standing around, 'leaning against a lamppost,' as he said. So he felt drawn back home, and at home he suffered because he had to admire so much what he himself was not able to accomplish."

The architect stood up and lit a cigar. "Poor, ailing fellow!" he said. "But a fellow who had it in him, I think. So many a man goes to ruin—but they aren't always the worst. All in all: it's a hellish struggle just to survive."

He kissed Esther's brow and went over into the small living room. She stood up, rang for the maid, and then followed him to the table under the hanging lamp where the newspapers were still spread out.

Esther unfolded them slowly, one after the other. When she had found the part she was looking for she sat back in the corner of her armchair and read, resting her brow on her hand.

And soon she stopped reading, but instead just kept on gazing—gazing at the short, black, fine-print columns of lines as if into a vast, twilit, distant landscape where she saw the figure of Eberhart wandering and waving to her.

"A narrow, dark, wooden frame holds an unusual sheet," read the reviewer's report on the exhibition, "— a small etching with a broad border. Right in the foreground a piece of land, just a strip, a simple home in a bright garden. And nestling up to this shore: the sea. Its waves have just broken, and as they now draw back they carry with them, as if in triumphant high spirits, a small craft, while the wind, bearing seaward, helps them; the wind fills the sail so that the boat goes shooting out as if borne on mighty wings. The man in the boat has turned his eye seaward as well. His will is like that of the storm: striving outward at full strength! On mighty wings. But he is resting his oars. Could it be that, where he hopes to find greatness, there is only the infinite? Perhaps! Perhaps in the next moment he will turn his head back toward his home. But it is already small and distant, and the storm wind's mightier hands are driving him on: there is no returning home. —This is: Lonely Journey. The etching can tell a story, and what it tells sounds like a fate. That is the result of the mood that the refined delicacy of the technique brings to expression in every nuance. We see the man's form only from the back, but what expression there is in the line of his back, what a leave-taking is expressed in this figure. The waves under the boat are less in motion than those at the shore, and farther out they are more and more thinned out and still, and finally, where they touch the horizon so far—far away, they are very finely drawn with a delicate, dry nib. And then— beyond that—the gouge ceases completely and gives way to a pale, shimmering infinity."

Esther raised her head and looked over to her husband, her eyes wide and distracted. He was sitting bent over his newspaper column on politics and, as he read attentively, from time to time puffing out his cigar smoke. Without really being aware, she watched him for several minutes. She noticed how the ash grew longer on his cigar without his taking it out of his mouth, and how finally a small gray curl of ashes sprinkled down onto his vest, its top button open. And as she took that all in she actually saw only Eberhart before her—saw him cast out in his lonely boat on the boundless sea—yes, lonely and cast out in the storm, while she herself she saw harbored and protected in her cozy haven.

She had been to the sea more than once with Ebert. The country house near a northern German city where her foster parents spent most of the year was not too far from the Baltic coast. And so it was with such feelings and moods, with such desires and bitterness, that Eberhart must have stood on the shore then, listening to the storm and the shrill cries of the seagulls and letting the shimmering mist in the distance act upon him. She had never thought of that. When she was with him by the sea she had not resisted letting herself be lulled by the rhythm of the waves, by their eternal rise and fall, which, like the breathing of the earth, lifted and lowered its mighty breast of waves. In her fantasy there was no small boat cast adrift, no raging storm carrying it away into the alluring distance, no confusing shimmer and glitter of the pulsing waves. Everything seemed to dissolve into the rhythmic song of the infinite totality—lullaby and hymn in one—.

When it was time to go to bed, Esther's husband stood up, yawned emphatically, and laid his cigar aside. He knew exactly what time it was without having to look at a clock. And he had a good right to be tired early, for he had to set out early in the morning again tomorrow, and each of his days glided past quickly and busily, with no other immediate goal but to make new efforts and climb higher up the tree, branch by branch.

Esther had gone out quietly to close the window in his room; since the restless twins had come along she slept alone with the children. When she returned after a while, her husband took her in his arms and said with a smile: "You're still like a part of them out there—of your foster parents and the whole house—a living part that feels each and every thing in its flesh and blood. You are a loyal soul, Esther. I think a little Jewish orphan like you—that becomes more an inborn part of the family than the members of the family themselves."

She put her arms around his neck and pressed her head with its heavy dark braids to his shoulder. "All you did was read and smoke," she said, embarrassed, "you really don't wish to talk a while?"

"I don't wish to disturb you!" he responded, keeping his voice low, and gave her a kiss.

★ ★ ★

In the middle of the night Esther awoke. Some dream, even though she could not recall it, had wakened her with its force. It was not entirely dark in the room, since for the children's sake a small, shielded night light was burning. But its pale shine seemed to fill the whole room with nothing but single, ghostlike shadows, with amazingly many shadows, as though it had merely divided the complete darkness into nothing but parts, like a thick, dark mass.

Esther turned over on her back and closed her eyes, but she could not get back to sleep. Her mind began to work; she thought of the etching, of her old foster parents, of the love that hung, tender and caring, upon their lone, ailing son. And he himself rose up so clearly in her thoughts; like a slender shadow he emerged from the dark corner beside her bed.

He was slender, in fact quite frail, with his fine limbs and his fine face. His father always said he looked like a pen and ink drawing. His bearing could often strike as a bit stiff if he was not slumped over from tiredness, and there was one position in which there was something of an old man about him. Now and then he would laugh about it himself.

He also used to avoid physical exertion as if he really were an old man, and Esther recalled how he did not like to walk long distances or carry packages. One day he met her just outside their parents' yard as she was about to hurry to the next village carrying gifts for the poor people. He called to her: "Stop right there! Please just stand there so heavily laden! You're pretty as a picture the way you're standing there—so tall and so strong and so good—and with such a cheerful face crowning your heavy treasure of gifts. —Are you really and truly so good? Are you a Saint Elisabeth or some such?"

She shook her head at his enthusiasm, which had made him ask her to stand still instead of helping her with the packages, and then she replied to him openheartedly: "I'll tell you a secret, Ebert. But don't laugh at me, do you hear? I've come to like the poor people only because your father is making them the object of his art. I came to like poor people of bronze and stone before I knew real poor people. Do you understand that? About his art I surely understand very little— or about art in general. But I do understand that the gaunt, often sorrowful faces attract him more than the most beautiful and that I am closest to him among those who hunger and suffer and toil."

As she said this they were walking side by side between the summer fields over which the larks were rejoicing. Eberhart's lean, nervous hand ran over the trembling leaves. After a short pause he said, in his pleasant, slightly mellifluous voice, which he rarely raised: "You are wrong about Father's art. It does not spring from any kindheartedness, nor does it mean to make pronouncements with its choice of poor people—it is much too high and pure and free of tendentiousness for that. In the working—and often even starving—folk Father simply finds gestures and physical lines whose beauty speaks to him more clearly than do the conventional or covered or withered physical forms of our class. That's a matter of taste. But if his works did have to preach something, then it would not be about some lack that arouses sympathy but about a capacity that the folk possess that awakens our curiosity."

"But all the gloom and misery?" Esther asked. "I have known it ever since I have been visiting them. And he too must look for those elements."

Eberhart responded, hesitantly: "Yes, in his works he does give them more beauty than they really have. He sees more than is present. That's how Father's eyes are. With such eyes it is possible to see what one wants to see, what one can use. I don't have such eyes, unfortunately. So I would be destroyed as an artist if I dealt with poor people."

For a while they walked on in silence. Then Esther asked innocently: "Would you prefer to seek models among us happy people?"

"Among us happy people?" he repeated, astonished, and stopped in amazement. "No! I would probably only keep on finding poor people. But there are other kinds of poor people, tortured by other torments, consumed by other fevers—poor people in whom is fermenting and gnawing all that our time wants to bring out in the modern human soul and does not yet know how. And of these poor people, too, it can be said that they are the true workers and still the eternally unpaid, who work on for those sated, satisfied, and possessing people who take their ease upon what they have acquired or inherited."

Esther recalled that conversation so clearly, clearly right down to the gentle tremor of his voice as he was saying the last words. But as attentively as she had listened, she still did not know what to respond. She could not imagine how all that he said could be hewn into stone. And so she was silent again.

Eberhart used his walking stick to lop off the head of a poppy that hung out over the path, and he remarked in an irritated tone that his voice so often took on: "You see: my art could never talk so clearly to you as my father's does. And even if in this single case you have misunderstood his art—no matter, it acts upon you nonetheless, and so you live with it and in it. In my art you would not live. —And anyway, it doesn't exist at all."

With that he let her go on alone from the edge of the village, for he could not bring himself to enter the cottages of the ill. So he leaned, waiting, against a tall aspen, struggling to gaze with his eyes slightly squinted up into the sky where a bird circled over him. But Esther moved on calmly, happy and a little impatient to hand out the rich gifts she was carrying in her arms.

But now, this evening, his art really was speaking to her, speaking to her out of another person's description of his picture. His art had suddenly acquired an eloquent voice to speak to her, and Esther felt as if she had to heed that voice, as if she had no time to sleep. Eberhart still had so much to say to her! If she could be with him now! She had not understood him then—not on this point and perhaps not on many others. Would his life have otherwise become a "Lonely Journey"? And still, they had grown up together, from Esther's eighth year on. And had she not hung upon him with all the strength of her soul? But she felt as if she had always been able to understand totally only her father. As high as he towered over her, they still shared a common language.

When Father was sitting by the sea, then he too was probably listening to the great rhythm of the great waves and not to the allure of the distance—so Esther still thought, and then she fell into an unrestful slumber.

At morning's very first light she was awakened by the baby chatter from the two cradles at the side of her bed, and in spite of her bad night's sleep she awoke fresh and strong, feeling, as always, the same sense of well-being about the babbling noises that, with the gray of dawn, would greet her ear as the very first sounds of the day. Her nocturnal unrest she had completely forgotten; all morning she was always so totally in demand that her thoughts would hardly even have found time to go beyond the warm circle of activities of womanly and maternal care. But today she finished everything more hastily than usual, as if in the course of her quiet, caring concerns something more important could easily be overlooked. After her husband had left and the twins had had their bath, she wanted to sit by them in the nursery with a piece of work—but then came the sharp tone of the electric doorbell in the hallway.

It was the telegraph messenger. He brought a telegram for her from her foster parents. He brought news that they themselves might likely have only just received.

Eberhart was dead.

He had died of a hemorrhage. Yesterday evening when she was sitting by the lamp reading about his etching in the newspaper and so longing to see him— he was already dead — —.

Mechanically, Esther went in to see her little ones; she took the little girl on her lap and stroked her absentmindedly. The boy cried impatiently; then she reached into his cradle and shook the brightly painted jumping jack at the child, who had been named for Ebert.

Ebert was dead. He had died in the moment in which he had suddenly begun to become so clear to her, just as if he had had to say something more to her. An immensely frightful feeling of loss and emptiness came over her; a strange, sharp anxiety lay upon her heart—not sorrow. She felt her heart beating wildly and thought, still as if half numb, that as a result she must not nurse the little ones toward midday as she usually did.

And then: she had to write home. Home where pain and despair prevailed, and boundless, inconsolable sorrow for their only son, beloved more than anything. She could imagine her mother in this pain—but not her father. She could not picture him submitting helplessly to this blow of fate.

Then she dropped the jumping jack and pressed her face into her little girl's thin blond hair and wept long and hard. She virtually burrowed into her sorrow for her old parents so that she would not have to look into the suffering of her own soul. And in her sorrow she wept, too, of course, for the brother. —Only the brother?—Had they not loved each other as well?

No, she had never really been able to believe that, she doubted to herself that it was so, she had denied it to herself and tried to forget it. And how could she believe it? As infinitely rarely as she had seen Eberhart strong and assured and happy in life, she had just as rarely seen any sign—that he loved her.

But now it came over her; now, when he was no longer alive, she was assailed by those rare moments full of life as if her fantasy were using them to ward off his death and were nurturing and enlivening him with all the most vital things that it knew, as if that would call him back to life.

For once he had gazed into her eyes, radiant and laughing, and kissed her hands and spoken to her of his wonderful future as an artist. She was sitting at the window and sewing. But, as he spoke, her sewing had slid to the floor, and quite enraptured she sat and listened to the flowing stream of life that suddenly just emanated from him, until, taking a deep breath, she said: "Oh, Ebert, how wonderful it must be to be able to create! And how much you surely have yet to create, and how great it will be!"

Then he bent over from the window railing he was leaning on, bending down to her, so that she saw his mouth right above her— this voluptuously formed, beardless, tender mouth she so loved.

"Do you know what that would involve as well, Esther?" he asked, much more softly, "do you know what I would have to have as well? I would have to be able to triumph over a person so completely that she would believe in me, full of enthusiasm, and look up to my works as though they were already created. You see, that would give me self-assurance! To have triumphed at least once, to feel once that I was lord and master! You don't know how small and weak it makes a person to have always to admire and revere!"

These last words he had said barely audibly. Esther did not move. His hands embraced hers more tightly, his gaze looked more deeply into hers. A gentle autumn rain beat against the window and darkened the room.

"Make me your lord and master—over you—and then in the future I shall be so, too!" murmured Eberhart. "Repeat after me: my lord and master."

"My lord and master!" said Esther, caught up in the moment.

"Dear, dear Esther. Dear—Esther! Now you have cast a spell, do you realize that, too? How could he not emerge strong and great and triumphant to whom you are willing to bow down and pledge yourself?" — — — His voice sounded full of happiness.

Then she thought he loved her. Then she reached out devotedly and long-ingly for this love. Why had it been only this single blissful hour? Why could he not hold onto her?

Eberhart spent the time after that in the city, in his father's studio; Father told how he was working so hard that he had no rest, no chance to come home. But then when he did come he looked just as weary as before.

Esther was waiting for him at the gate. And then they walked silently, hand in hand, deeper into the autumn garden, with the colored leaves falling on its gravel path, soft and gentle, as in a dream, without a single gust of wind.

And suddenly he burst out: "It's insane living like this! I would ten thousand times rather be dead. Better dead than a bungling amateur!"

"You're not an amateur!" she said sadly. "Someday you will realize your visions. Just think of what you said last time."

"What I said!" he repeated and laughed nervously. "That's right: I spoke words. Are words important?"

And at the old garden bench that stood beneath a rust-brown chestnut tree he sat down and drew Esther down to sit beside him. "All that was nonsense, Esther, all that was only longing. Helpless longing, do you understand? Oh, I am so tired! I can't go on living alongside Father, I'm not even good enough for that. Not even as an errand boy. Not as anything!"

She wanted to answer something, console him, but then she felt his head resting against her neck, and on her neck she felt his tears. Deeply moved, she kept silent. She had never seen Eberhart this way, he had never shown anyone his most private self in this manner. He wept quietly, his whole upper body trembling, and she did not stir; it was the first time that she had ever seen a man weep, and she was almost astonished that it should be just the same as when women wept. A boundless sympathy for him overcame her.

They sat for a long time holding each other like that, and he quietly poured out his sorrow, and she consoled him quietly, as well as she knew how. And she also felt as though he were becoming more calm and liked her talking to him. When it began to become damp and cool, she stroked his hair gently as though he were a big, dear child, and reminded him that they had to go. "It can be bad for you if you stay out any longer," she said, standing up from the bench, "and back at the house they are sure to be looking for us already."

Eberhart ran his hand over his brow and looked up in surprise with his still-reddened eyes, as if remembering the present again only now. And all at once she saw something of an irritated look in his gaze, something almost hostile. And at the same time he was actually staring at her, his eyes slowly taking in her figure and her face, rejecting, cold, and with such a strange look that Esther blushed deep red.

"What's wrong with you, then?" she asked, put off, "is something wrong?"

"Something wrong? No, what do you mean?" he answered, embarrassed and angry, "what do you mean wrong? Because I'm looking at you? You're wonderfully beautiful, Esther, for our artist's eyes—flawlessly beautiful. That's why I'm looking at you. Am I not allowed to? Well then, forgive me."

With that he left her standing there and went into the house.

What had she done? how had she lost him? or had she perhaps never possessed him? She could never understand this transformation; but even then she began to sense the truth darkly in her heart, when on the evening of the same day she had to go into the living room and saw Eberhart crouching on a low stool by his mother. The two were not talking to each other at all—the mother was a dear, simple woman, who had likely truly possessed only the earliest years of his childhood and who in this household retreated all too modestly behind the others. He had his head in her lap, and she had her withered hand on his head.

When he had heard Esther coming, he had jumped to his feet and gone to the window, straightening out his suit. He had blushed.

So he was horrified to let her find him this way. Did he hate her, then?— Or perhaps he hated himself, because he had let her see him weep earlier—her, for whom he so much wanted to be the strong, triumphant artist—the "lord and master"?

As often after that as she met his gaze, it was always the gaze of irritation or hostile rejection that she saw, and never again were they close in a warm and heartfelt way. Only after Eberhart had been sent south did his letters begin to seek out and call to the Esther of before, who had been his playmate and friend since they were little. Never did he remind her of those two strange days. But he did write to her as one writes to a very dear person whom one can send loose pages and words, diary entries, banal and profound things at random and all mixed together. There were even discussions of artistic technique, of which Esther understood nothing. Her fine ear detected in it all this lonely, longing tone, and she answered like a sister and felt herself more the keeper than the possessor of the pages she received. When she became engaged, this correspondence too became more fleeting, and then it died out.

So now Ebert had known no one to whom he could still speak. He was completely alone. And in the end he died. And now he needed no one.

But Esther felt as if she were to blame for his isolation. With a power it had never had, with domineering force, the memory of Eberhart—now that he was dead—forced itself into her life, into her most intimate life.

Esther stood up; gently she took up the little girl, who had fallen asleep in her arms, and bedded her down in her cradle. The old nurse came in and tended solicitously to the other baby; as she bent her head in its large white cap over the child, she looked up a few times with her intelligent, inquisitive eyes at the young woman. But Esther did not notice; she stood lost in thought at the wide window and stared out onto the bright, loud street where the people were rushing about in the noisy midday traffic and the vehicles were rattling past each other.

She did not notice any one particular thing, only the cold, businesslike haste of the whole picture that engulfed any individual thing and fit it into the general hubbub. Then she noticed a neglected brown poodle that was running about without its master among the carriages and horsecars and giving various passersby an inquisitive sniff. Its curly hair hung down over its eyes in unshorn disarray, so that it had to take the trouble to lift its head before it could recognize anything clearly. Some brushed him aside with a kick; a few times a coachman would strike at him with his whip, and a rear wheel would graze his back without actually catching him. Esther looked in distraction at the helpless, frightened efforts of the animal, which finally sat down, resigned, in the middle of the street and trustingly awaited its fate. Half absentmindedly she thought: "Any other breed of dog would put his nose to the ground and set out after his master, and the poodle, this most clever of all breeds of dog, has such poorly developed instincts that it does not resist being trampled by life passing by, sitting there and pondering deeply where his master and his goal may be." But the longer she watched, the more she felt as if from the misery of the poor dog something was calling out to her with human voice and force.

And in involuntary horror she reached for the window latch, as if it were up to her alone to bring help —— —.

★ ★ ★

In the meantime, a gray-haired man in a traveling coat and a black slouch hat had entered the house. He rang the bell at the apartment, but, instead of having himself announced to Esther, he went at once into the nursery and walked quietly up to the two cradles.

Esther already had her arms around his neck. "So wonderful that you've come, Father!" she whispered and looked at him with anxious, tender eyes and kissed him repeatedly, "are you on your way—there?"

He nodded and leaned for a few moments over the cradle in which the little boy lay, looking in silence at the small, sleep-reddened face between the blue curtains.

"I'll be traveling on even in the next few hours," he said then and straightened his somewhat heavy, midsize build, "I must go there—bring him back to his home, you know."

"Yes, bring him to Mother, don't consign him to foreign soil. But were you able to leave Mother alone now? How is she holding up?"

He ran his hand over his brow: "Mother was expecting it. — Just think, she actually expected it to happen. His letters may have had that tone, but how can someone read such a thing out of them and accept that it will happen? Do you understand that? You see, I believe she had already mourned and wept for him before he—before he was dead. And now she has set up all the pictures of him around her and sunk totally into her memories. —Esther, it's horrible to see that. To see how she has already grasped so completely that he—that he—no longer exists at all."

Esther led him away from the children and into her little living room where they could be undisturbed. There she sat down beside him and took his hand in the pair of hers. "Oh, that you are here!" she said again; "it is such a consolation to have you here. I find it a consolation. It was horrible to be so alone with that news."

He bowed his head slightly, brooding in silence to himself. He and Esther had loved each other very much and always understood each other. They found it a refuge to be able to sit together in silence in this hour.

Esther's gaze hung upon her father's face. It looked less pained than stunned, astonished. His eyes, bright, almost childlike in their alertness, looked out from under his bushy, gray-blond brows with a strange, surprised expression. Esther suddenly thought how one night she had dreamed that a person dear to her had met a horrible end and how in her dream her first feeling had been a lone, resolved denial of the dreadful fact. From this strained, intense act of will she had now suddenly awakened.

Such an expression, something of the denial of a fearful dream, was etched upon the face of Eberhart's father. Her heart tightened, and tears came to her eyes. Clearly, no matter how much he struggled against it inside, he could not awaken from this dream.

Then he raised his head, stroked her hand, and began at once: "Isn't it true that you corresponded with Eberhart a lot two years ago? He wrote only to you about—about how he was feeling. Isn't that so?"

"Yes," she replied, hesitating.

"I know. I know, those are the only words from Eberhart that reveal the truth about him. He was reticent toward me. And, when he was at home, perhaps toward you, too. But the separation from you opened him up. That separation was something very painful for him, but it opened him up."

Esther blushed deeply. —She did not answer.

"Give me his letters to read, Esther—now, here."

She rose from her chair, her heart beating. "You cannot be serious, Father! You know that Eberhart insisted that no one should ever see these letters. And then— then as well there was always a small rift between you two—you know that—and Eberhart was often excited when he wrote."

The old man made an expansive, weary gesture with his hand. "Ah, child, as far as that's concerned; what was between us had to be, what human being would pass judgment on that! — — But the other thing you said: that these letters were meant only for you—ah, I know, I know—." He, too, stood up, and as they faced each other eye to eye he added, his voice resolved and insistent: "Esther! That's just why—precisely why! Those letters hold fast a piece of Eberhart's soul. I must have them, read them— with or without your permission. What do I have from the pictures your mother is surrounding herself with? I yearn for this picture of him. Let me have it!"

Esther wept. There was something in his words that moved her deeply. Just as she herself was doing, he was stealing around this dead person astounded and afraid, wanting to look into his heart—and solve his riddle—and understand him.

The old man took her face in his hands and gently forced her to look at him. "It costs you a struggle," he said softly, "perhaps even a struggle with your conscience that will leave its mark. But fight it through and yield to it. Obey me, Esther."

When had she not obeyed him?

In silence she left the room, and when she returned after a few minutes she handed him, her eyes downcast, the bundle of letters tied up in a thin silk ribbon.

Almost heavy-handedly he reached out to take them and took them to the window niche where, far back among the curtains, there was an armchair. Esther could not bring herself to be there; she went out and saw to it that some refreshment would be ready before it was time for him to travel on.

Only after some time did she enter the room again. The old man was still sitting in his chair in the window niche reading the letters without noticing or acknowledging that Ether had come in. From time to time he let the page he was just reading sink, and looked ahead with visionary gaze at the empty gray-brown wall across from him as though something were happening there before his eyes that demanded his most profound attention and that he found highly compelling.

Esther had seen him like that a thousand times at work in his studio. Watching him, she almost forgot his actual reason for reading these letters. Totally gone from his features was the somewhat fixed, rather astonished expression. But there was no sorrow in it, either. Only an intense struggle of the spirit.

Esther sat down quietly by the tiled stove on the edge of a chair and, her eyes wide with amazement, looked over at the old man. She could not understand that Eberhart's letters had not had a different effect on him, more emotional and touching. But this old gray head with its strangely commanding expression so fascinated her that she was not able to tear her eyes away from him.

And as she sat that way, watching silently, there emanated from him in a miraculous way something of the consolation that she had instinctively expected to feel in his presence—just now, when he was not concerned with her at all. For she felt deep in her heart: he, the bereaved one, had in some way come to terms with death—he was moving this way as he read silently and gazed ahead with his eyes so childlike bright. Somehow he had awakened from the terrible dream in which he was to know that his son was dead. How he had done that, Esther did not know, of course. But she felt that strength and peace were emanating from him and that the frightened soul could take flight to him.

For a long time they sat in silence.

Then the old man laid the last letter with the others. His eyes were aglow with inner joy. "I did not know him as he really was; no, I did not know him!" he said, totally caught up in his impression, sunk deep into himself. "Oh, my dear child, what beauty lived in this soul!"

Esther stood up impulsively. Then he turned to her and went on excitedly: "What was struggling in him and tormenting him was full of infinite beauty, because it wanted to find expression and blossom into a strange new bloom of art. —He was sure to triumph."—

Esther went to him and embraced him. "Oh, Father!" she said softly, "if only you could talk about it to me! If only you could stay here!"

He seemed only now to remember that he soon had to travel on. He stood up, distracted. "—Stay here? Do you think so?—No, child, I cannot do that. I must go back home—you know, return home now to my work. I see him before me—I see him bright and grand before me—I never saw him this way before— I never saw any person this way. I never looked so deep into people's souls—or I saw only into very simple souls. He—he would surely have been able to do that with his own wounded, longing soul, so resonant and sensitive. I shall raise him up like a victor! And then you'll come, won't you? and see him? He shall come to resemble himself as he never did before."

Full of excited, glowing joy he spoke. It was utterly impossible to think of reminding him of the purpose of his journey, of his son's corpse.

Esther almost dreaded it. "Father! he is dead!" she wanted to call out. But she remained silent and held closer to him.

★ ★ ★

Days, weeks, months went by. Winter came early with snow and blizzards and the frost on the windowpanes. For Esther it was an imperceptible flowing on of life; she often felt as if, alongside it, she was leading another life all for herself alone that had nothing to do with the changes of the seasons and her daily relationships. Of Eberhart she seldom spoke. For when she mentioned him once to her husband, she felt that he was not thinking of the same thing, even though he used the same words to express his thoughts as she did. He had hardly known Eberhart, and in his way of talking about him there was often an unintentionally sweet friendliness toward Esther; in reality he was now concerned with his professional life, which was placing higher demands on his time and concentration. But she was always thinking of Eberhart: she lived still turned only to what had been, ever deeper into the past; her memory wandered like a reaper over fields that had long since been mown, carrying out a second harvest, gathering—and gathering—. Sometimes it happened that for a moment she moved or used a phrase the way Eberhart had done, and then she felt happy and excited, until she thought of what caused her to do it — — and then she felt a sudden loneliness draining everything of its color and burying it.

Esther lived for her husband and their children, but when she married she had already experienced her disappointment with Eberhart. Before her betrothal and for some time after it, of course, he had written her those letters that she had had to give her father to read.

On one of those days when Esther was disturbed and sad about a new letter from Eberhart, with its doubting complaints and the despair about his own talent, her father had spoken to her for the first time about her husband's proposal.

She was in his bedroom, busy rubbing salve on his right arm, which he used so much and which was somewhat prone to gout. "You were created to care and tend, to be a wife and mother," her father had said and stroked her hair, "and you must marry young, Esther. And that's not enough for your strong, blossoming strength: this house with us two old people and then Eberhart's tales of woe. Doesn't he carry on as if you were supposed to be helping him?"

She did not want to talk about the content of the letter, but because her heart was heavy with his worries and because she did, after all, believe in his future, the words passed her lips: "Father, he carries on as if he were in bondage."

"You often speak as if from the Old Testament, Esther. Don't let yourself be misled by your sympathy. I want to tell you one thing: now there are women who must support and guide their husbands, and there are men who like that. That is suicide for the woman."

She blushed, but at the same time she felt something cool in her nerves.

In her mind she beheld that scene when, on the garden bench, Eberhart had poured out his sorrows and wept — —. Her father had unknowingly said what had to make her feel deeply uncertain. It was as if, merely at his bidding, Eberhart had turned back into her brother.

In the meantime, her father had gone on talking, cheerful and openhearted. He told her about how joyful it would be here in the house if someday she were to come visiting with little foster grandchildren. He had a quite remarkable idea of exactly what kind of grandchildren he wanted, and he knew as well what the father must be like. He wanted boys, but there should also be a girl, and she should turn out just like Esther herself, he said tenderly. In the end he caught Esther up in his mood, and while they were chatting together there in the bedroom, he in his shirtsleeves, she still holding the jar of salve, the pair of them, like two children, painted in detail the picture of a whole, bright future, rich in children, the two of them full of trusting belief in the creation of their own fantasies.

Esther had felt like a bride, like a wife, and like a mother, even before her father spoke the name of him whom he had chosen for her — — —.

If she could hear him talk more often that way, then she would feel lighter at heart, Esther now frequently thought to herself. But she heard nothing from home. Her mother, who wrote only seldom and, in any case, awkwardly, only once informed her about something in greater detail: she told her about Eberhart's bust, which had just been finished and was being brought out to her to be set up at the country house.

On the evening that Esther received this news she came quietly into her husband's room as he sat at his desk looking through plans and calculations. "Well, so you're visiting me now, dearest?" he remarked in a friendly way, without disrupting his work.

Esther knelt down beside him at the desk and leaned her face on his arm. She said quietly: "Let me travel to see my parents for a few days. I long to go there."

Her husband at once laid down his pencil and looked at her long and thoughtfully. "You've received letters?" he asked.

"A short one from my mother. She isn't accustomed to writing, you know. So I do not hear much. Father no longer writes. Mother says he is working night and day. Since he returned he's been working without a break, as never before. He hardly goes out to see her any more. She's all alone — —."

Esther stopped. Then, as though she had, against her own will, let false motives for her request creep into her words, she added still more quietly: "In addition, he's completed a marble bust of Eberhart."

"And you'd like to see this bust?"

"Yes, Georg. I have thought of everything and also put things in order for the children. I want to be back on the third day."

He took her face in his hands and lifted it up to him. "Tell me one thing: would you insist on this trip even if I wished you wouldn't go?"

She became a little paler. But her eyes gazed upon him, steady and devoted. She had no thought of disrespecting his will. She had lived the entire time with inner worries that did not concern him, but hearing this question she felt put back in her assigned place; never had she felt so deeply and clearly as in this minute that her father had paired her not only with a certain man but also, in this one, with the only man she would follow and serve as his wife at any cost.

"Then I won't go!" she said.

He kissed the smooth black crown of her head. "I thank you, Esther. Of course you shall travel. Even tomorrow. I'll take care of it, you dear. What I wanted to know was something else that I did not wish to ask you straight out."

She closed her hands around his as they rested on his papers. "What is it, Georg?"

"I wanted to know whether, when you take this trip—whether you'll return to us again as the same person, from your parents —— and from this bust."

Her blood surged in a dark wave to her face, throat, and neck. The way he spoke of the children and himself together as "us" touched her in a strange way. Suddenly she knew that he, too, had been suffering this whole time and that he had noticed her distance from him and felt hurt by it.

Still kneeling, she pressed her brow against his hands. "I was on a journey, Georg—but I am back with you again at home," she said, full of regret. —

Toward noon of the next day Esther left. Before twilight she arrived and rode by carriage out to the country house and her foster mother, who did not know she was coming. As if deserted, the long, one-story house stood in a vast field of snow; in the garden the bushes seemed to be struggling to stretch out their bare branches to reach beyond the oppressive weight of the snow; in the tall linden trees at the entry a couple of ravens were cawing out their welcome, and from the yard came the happy whimpering of the old guard dog, pulling wildly at his chain, having likely sensed a friend's arrival.

The maid who greeted Esther at the door led her through some cold, empty rooms to the small boudoir where her mother was sitting in her armchair and knitting—quite sunk into herself and obviously heedless of the goings-on out by the entryway. All the more boundless was her joy at the sight of her foster daughter; so vigorous and strong was the old woman's expression of happiness at seeing her again that Esther had the impression her arrival had awakened a dead person, and she secretly regretted not having announced that she was coming.

The small room was still the same as ever, only the many pictures of Eberhart at various periods in his life had not been there before. On two of the photographs hung a withered wreath. The bust, however, was nowhere to be seen in this room, where Esther had been sure she would find it.

"Look at the pictures, child," said her foster mother after the first storm of greeting, "do you remember them all? Look, in this one he's still quite little, so little that you couldn't have known him yet. I think it's my favorite picture. Back then he still belonged only to me alone. Ebert used to like to sit on my lap—but I wasn't allowed to tell him stories—. Can you imagine that? He told me some. Maybe not actual stories, but still all kinds of strange things that he talked about."

"So this is Eberhart's room for you two," Esther murmured, and she wanted to ask her question about the bust.

"This is Eberhart's room for me only," the old lady interrupted her in a strange tone, "for Father, Eberhart's room is probably his studio."

"How do you mean that, Mother?"

"I mean simply that he's probably together with him there when he's working. In addition, he thought only of Eberhart as long as he was working on the bust. And since then he's kept on working and working that way—he's quite immersed in his plans and ideas, he says, and he feels as he did when he was young. — No, Father doesn't like to sit in here with all these pictures and wreaths. He's stopped going to the grave, too. The wooden cross is still there, imagine. And now really a marble stone could be placed at his grave."

Esther kissed her hands and tried to calm her. "He is thinking of him in his special way," she said softly, "but don't you have the bust in here with you?"

The old woman made a dismissive gesture with her hand as soon as Esther mentioned the bust. "Here? No, it's not here. It's in the front room where I don't go. I can't bear seeing the bust. The bust made him forget all his sorrow—if you only knew how happy he is now. The poor boy himself who's lying out there he's completely forgotten with his work on the bust. —— And it's not Eberhart at all, either, this bust, it's not at all my poor, pale boy. It's supposed to make him look after his death the way Father would like to have him so that he makes him happy. —— It doesn't make me happy, I can find no consolation in this stone. I bore him, I lost him, nothing will bring him back to me . . ."

With these last words she sank back into her chair again and looked so sorrowful and bitter that Esther's heart ached. That is what the great and lonely grief had done to this gentle woman, who had always retired so completely behind Father and his will. Yes, she was isolated after Eberhart's death, but not because Father was around less, but because with the death she had lost him, too, from her heart.

"Just go and look at it," the old woman said wearily, as Esther, moved to silence, wished she might be able to take her mother with her back to her home and to her children, "just go and then come back to me. It's in the third room. You'll have to have seen it by the time Father comes for dinner."

Esther went through the adjoining dining room, through a second living room, and finally came to the so-called stateroom of the house that usually no one entered. There, across from the window, on a black pedestal, stood Eberhart's life-sized bust.

Esther almost cried out when she saw it. The room was no longer light, but no more light was required for her to see Eberhart there completely lifelike before her. In Esther's breast something contracted, trembling, something of pain and jubilant joy, as though she were seeing him again, a person she thought was dead, as though she were encountering him again, resurrected, here in the cold silence of this room —— but as a person in whom all worldly cares had fallen silent and all timorous despair had grown still—as a person triumphant in salvation.

She stood still and barely breathed. From the shoulders of this Eberhart her father's hand had gently taken the everyday garment, that gloomy gray she had always seen him wearing; it had bestowed upon him that garment of spiritual grandeur that he so seldom wore for others to see but that he nevertheless did possess, hidden away deep in a precious shrine, as his secret cloak of royal purple. Yes, she felt it was he, the Eberhart of that fleeting hour when he had spoken to Esther of his commanding love and his golden future, when he had believed in himself as her lord and master and in happiness ———.

But with a barely noticeable half smile he was looking past her and slightly upward as if into a vast distant vista, and his brow was aglow with pure clarity, and his tender mouth seemed to tremble as if caught up in the ecstasy of someone beholding a revelation—.

And suddenly she understood: she had found him unmanly, not man enough and not sufficiently master of himself to master a woman and a woman's happiness—but this only because the full strength of his manliness was still caught up in a bloody and inexhaustible struggle for something higher and grander, indeed for something more divine.

She had not been able to understand that then—but what did that matter? He had stopped for a moment by her, and perhaps for a moment made her the victory sign and symbol of his own soul— yet she was not important. Quietly the regretful worry, the strange unrest about having failed him and consigned him to his loneliness, quietly the anxious sorrow of this entire past time vanished from her heart. And in peace she bid farewell to Eberhart: one more time her soul greeted him—and gave him up to the totality of the universe, in which he meant more than she.

She stepped back from him with a gesture of reverence—back into the circle of her own feminine being that embraced her close and dear and that she understood completely and that she belonged to completely.

In her thoughts she recalled Eberhart's etching, *Lonely Journey*, which she had found described in the newspaper shortly before news of his death arrived. And she thought of the wonderful, golden autumn day when Eberhart embarked to spend the winter in the south—on his "lonely journey." That was when she had seen him for the last time. For the last time they stood together at the seashore, and he looked out into the distance, uncertain and hopeful, and she listened to the monotone murmur of the waves, to this steady rhythm of the eternally bound rise and fall of the sea's waves, which seemed to her like a hymn and, at the same time, like a lullaby.

There, high above, a dark swaying stripe drew across the sea—a long line of migrating birds fleeing the autumn, heading for the sun. They both looked up at the bobbing, black dots in the sky.

"They're leaving the nest of home, as you are," Esther said sadly.

He was not listening. Pale and silent, he held his hand up to shield his eyes from the glaring light and looked far—far out to sea.

"Don't you think," he said hesitantly, "that a great yearning is like the birds' heading south—a sign that somewhere life is in bloom—?"

AT ONE, AGAIN, WITH NATURE

Almost all who encountered her turned their heads; yet no one could have said what was so striking about her. Even in the by no means extravagant Königsberg her English walking suit had to be considered the model of correct apparel for a lady of the finest circles who, on this cloudless September evening, was still out for a bit of a walk in the light of the setting sun. Her finely built, slender figure with its slim, sloping shoulders moved on with easy gait, and only seldom did she look up; yet, when she did, her wide-eyed, calm gaze never lost its expression of profoundest indifference to the bustle of the people and carriages around her. When she crossed the street without looking around, one could think every time that only felicitous chance kept her from being run over. In her right hand with its suede glove she was carrying a gray-brown bundle that was not easily identifiable, swinging it imperceptibly back and forth as she walked, like someone returning from a country outing on this summery autumn day and bringing back something lovely, her joyful thoughts still focused upon it even as she entered the city.

The evening breeze played in her soft brown hair, which she was wearing loose, so that under the small, man's straw hat she was wearing it fell just to shoulder length, where it was neatly trimmed all around without any natural wave or artificial curls. The individual lights already going on in the store windows and street lanterns threw restless yellow reflections on her face with its still-youthful features. At the wide open doorway of a large fruit and delicatessen store with its lights already on bright she stopped. She leaned over the baskets full of fruit that were set out to each side of the doorway, took an apple, a plum in her hand for a look, an expression of almost cheerful disdain playing about her mouth as she did so. One of the shop boys in his white apron came along and was about to ask what she wanted, but the proprietor of the store, a hearty, portly man who had been standing at the counter, noticed her out there, went up to her right away, pushing the zealous boy aside, and greeted her with great respect.

"I had already begun to fear that our dear Fräulein had traveled away again without coming around one last time," he said.

She straightened up, returned his greeting with a nod, and stepped into the doorway of the room redolent with the smell of fruit, fish, and spice. "Do show me your hazelnuts!" she said as she raised the thick bundle in her hand. The shopkeeper reached for it quickly. It was a bundle of hazel, its nuts, nestled in among their jagged leaves, of gigantic size and umbellate shape, like grapes on the vine.

"God, Oh, God!" cried the shopkeeper.

In the meantime the boy had brought a handful of hazelnuts from the barrel and offered them to the young woman. She rolled them around and let out a pleased laugh. "Such poor little things! Grown without any proper tending!" she said in a tone as if she were talking about neglected workers' children; then she went on: "Very well, Herr Gesellius, do we have a deal? More than the quantity we mentioned I cannot supply. I was quite sure of what I was doing, and even by spring I had finalized most of the deals. We've only an extra-rich harvest to thank for the fact that I can still close a deal with you."

"Certainly, certainly," the proprietor hastened to reply and looked at the imposing brown bundle almost in ecstasy—"my God, if only I'd known earlier! I could surely order many more. But, in addition, dear Fräulein, you will still be sending me the sample of apples we agreed upon, won't you?"

She nodded and turned to go. "Yes indeed," she confirmed, "and what I wanted to tell you as well: with this size and quality of the hazelnuts there's a new trend involved that will probably prevail this season even here in Königsberg. These nuts, once disdained, which people used at best to give their children to munch on, are now becoming a dessert fruit. They are finally taking their rightful place. People serve them as they grow on the bush, in such bizarre bundles. You shall see, it's becoming the fashion. In Copenhagen, where they've been trying to imitate me since I sent them the first samples, it's already as good as fashionable now—."

These last words she spoke from out on the street as the man accompanied her out the door, bowing all the while. With a much brighter, much less indifferent face she went on down the street to her nearby hotel. On the way she pulled out her watch and, after giving it a look, hurried her pace.

When she entered the hotel the porter approached her to announce that two ladies were waiting for her in her room; "the one for some time now," he added.

The bright expression vanished from her eyes; wearily she climbed the few stairs and entered her room with a look of such fixed indifference that it seemed to hit the two ladies there like a cool draft. Nevertheless the one of them, a pretty, young blond girl, jumped up in sprightly fashion and went to her with outstretched hand, visibly delighted and calling out in a cheerful tone: "Cousin Irene! how happy I am to see you again! I would have recognized you anywhere at once, despite the dreadfully long time it's been. — — —You know, I wouldn't let them turn me away because—"

Irene shook the hand offered her but right away let it glide limply out of her own and cut her off: "Thank you, Ella. I'm a bit late, it's my fault. — — You ladies likely don't know each other yet, do you?—Ella Werner, my cousin, who is to travel with me tomorrow to our uncle's estate— Frau Doctor Fuhrberger, but, if you please, a doctor on her own merit, not by way of a husband—one of the leaders of our German women's movement, who intends with her speeches to ignite ideas in the heads of the poor women here in Königsberg."

Frau Doctor Fuhrberger, a small but very ample woman, whose feminine corpulence contradicted in something of a humorous way the man's vest she was wearing with the still starched linen front and boyish necktie, shook her head reproachfully. "No—no, from you, Fräulein von Geyern, from you in particular such mockery is something of a sacrilege. That is: of all women in the world, you especially should be involved in our struggle in an active way. I feel it—yes, I would like to say: I sense it—and I know as well from a word that you recently let slip what you think of men and how sympathetically our views are linked."

Irene von Geyern had taken off her hat, sat down across from her two guests deep in a soft armchair, and slowly slipped her suede gloves from her hands. "The fact that I am against men does not by any stretch mean that I am for women," she remarked, shrugging her shoulders, but quietly, wearily, without the previous trace of irony in her voice, as if she were afraid of becoming involved in a tedious and boring debate.

Frau Doctor Fuhrberger looked at her, all the while smiling and sure of victory, full of desire and strength for even the longest dispute, and answered her challengingly: "Whoever thinks as you do, whoever asserts herself in a manly way and faces up to men, such a person has already felt as well the desire—no matter whether she admits it or not—to be allowed to share in all the rights that men have in order to be able to act as they do. Oh, just believe me: the most intimate heart even of women's unspoken yearnings we know full well."

"Really?" Irene asked, her voice weary and her large, calm eyes taking on a strange look of sadness that was far, far removed from ridicule, "yes, that may be so, yet you've deceived yourself in me with your hopes and challenges. I find no appeal in what men possess. Man's right is to take part in everything— and I don't care to be part of anything."

Her cousin Ella, who during the conversation with the new guest had been neglected with a touch of familial intimacy, was leaning back in her chair the whole while without joining the discussion and, lost in thought, was looking at Irene's hands as they lay limply folded in her lap. She still remembered so well from her childhood these wonderfully fine hands—Irene had the hands and feet of a princess—but back then they had been white, with delicate blue veins, while now they were brown from the sun and rather broad for all their delicacy, with fingernails that, while still nobly formed, were cut short and completely unpolished.

Irene's hand almost contradicted the rest of her appearance, being, as it were, the most robust and now least aristocratic thing about her looks. Her pale features no sun had been able to turn brown, and her light brown hair, combed back so simply and artlessly, left bare her unusually beautiful but marble-pale brow. This hair detracted a bit, with its rather light, faded-looking color, from the impression of Irene's beauty; Ella kept looking at her and felt a genuine impulse to imagine her being white-haired, her young face framed in snow white — —.

Who could know what old memories that might have involved; Irene, when they were both very little girls playing with dolls, had often looked like a little old woman, as is often the case with children wise beyond their years. This sadness in her gaze, which she had shown just now when she answered Frau Doctor Fuhrberger, she had then, too—but not in certain moments as was now the case, but constantly—that vast, quiet child's sadness, incomprehensible even to itself, that looms, like a giant wall, dark as night, behind many a small human soul and casts a shadow over its radiant life. —

Ella was so enjoying the advantages of undisturbed observation and immersing herself, as she looked on in silence, so deeply in her old passion for the little-girl Irene of her childhood days, that she gave a confused start when Frau Doctor Fuhrberger stood up and declared with uncalled-for vigor that she now must finally pedal away again, all the more so as she had come by on her bicycle only to take leave of Irene with yet another assertion of the love she had for her, against which all resistance would be useless.

Irene politely accompanied her guest out of the room and into the hall of the hotel, while Ella looked forward impatiently to the moment when she would finally see Irene alone and be able to greet and kiss her with a warmth other than she had shown in the company of the other woman. She was already imagining how Irene would soon have to come back with a deep sigh of relief— and she already felt her tongue itching irresistibly to make a humorous remark about the just departed propagandistic lady; like two mocking rascals her very pretty blue eyes flashed the returning Irene a greeting.

As Irene came in, she cast a somewhat astonished look into Ella's happy, excited face, and returned her gaze with such uncomprehending coolness that a rush of blood quickly turned Ella's face a bright crimson.

In a flash she felt ashamed and reprimanded by the fact that Irene's attitude was clearly more refined than hers and that with her reserved propriety Irene was instinctively shielding from frivolous witticisms the woman who had just been sitting here as her guest.

But it was not that alone; Ella would probably have gotten over that right away. For there was still the unchanged coldness in Irene's expression, just as if the young woman still standing there in her room, a relative by blood and her childhood playmate, were just as foreign, unwelcome, and indifferent as the other woman she barely knew. — —

Ella made an awkward move with her arms and tried to look as natural as possible, but she felt something choking her and her eyes blurring and burning. She stepped quickly to the window as though she were looking out.

Then, after a second's pause, she felt Irene's hand on the back of her neck— cool—cool fingers gliding with inexpressible gentleness over her neck and shoulders, but that with their gentle touching had something searching about them that gave Ella a secret shudder.

Irene said, her voice low: "—Overcome this. — — This bit of emotion—cast it off. It's not worth the moment you spend suffering with it. Forbid yourself from suffering because of me. — — You see, that's just the way I am."

And Ella felt rising up in herself the desire to hold her close instead of giving any answer—to hold her, whose coldness still hurt her yet whose sensitive understanding nevertheless pervaded all things. And in this moment Irene regained an old superiority that they both had long forgotten, but which she had already possessed when she still looked like a little old woman and Ella like a good, silly, dear child. —

Irene rang for the waiter and, as she and Ella stood side by side at the window, ordered a cold dinner with beer and wine to be served in the room. "Now you're to show me whether you still have the same appetite you used to have back when I would give you something nice, I, the one who never had an appetite for anything," she said, and sat down at the table.

"Oh, you still remember that, then?" Ella asked happily, "so you haven't forgotten everything from those days."

Irene nodded seriously, with a dismissive look, as though she wanted to say: "Ah, yes, I don't forget so easily at all, I keep all sorts of things—in my head." Then she changed the subject, saying: "So, tomorrow you'll come on time for the early train, won't you? Though I'm not at all sure that you'll like spending a whole month with Uncle Geyern. We live in such solitude, and of course you're not used to the country life."

"That's just why I'm looking forward to it," Ella claimed, enjoying her dinner, "you don't know how hard it is to sit out the summer in Berlin and teach at the lyceum—especially if, like me, you don't have any talent for teaching. I like to learn, I do a lot, I'm interested in everything, but teaching—"

"But it's grown-up girls, not children," Irene interrupted her, "that's more presentations than teaching."

"I'd prefer children," Ella murmured, "even if they should be more of a nuisance. — — Anyway: country life and lots of children around—ah—!" she broke off quickly and added: "But tell me about Uncle Geyern. I haven't seen him for a long time, either. About ten years ago I was visiting my parents. Even then he struck me as very old—at least over sixty for sure. So now he must be as old as the hills?"

"He is old, of course. Why do you ask that with such surprise, as if it were something remarkable?"

"Yes, because—I don't really understand it—a few years after he was with us you went to see him, and you were eighteen at most—so how can it be possible—" she stopped and became confused.

"—That he wanted to marry me then, you mean?" Irene finished her question calmly, "yes, that's the kind of whim that old men often have when they see really young girls and when these young girls are alone and without financial means. But why did that make you so red and embarrassed?"

"I was just afraid—I was anxious because I burst out with it," Ella confessed,

Irene's way still making her unsure whether she had done something tactless again.

Irene looked at her, thinking. "How lively you are!" she said, not with disapproval, just amazed, "how easily you blush. —— And we're the same age!"

"Wasn't that horrid for you?" Ella asked hesitantly, but with irrepressible curiosity; "and on top of that it must be so hard to be together day after day. ——— Isn't it really horrible that such an old man, actually old enough to be your grandfather—"

"His age was the only thing about it that wasn't horrid," Irene interrupted her, her voice calm, "and then I stayed with him—because there is something there that I love—." She hesitated as she said that, but did not go on to explain and fell to thinking.

Ella recalled how, after this marriage proposal and Irene's decision to stay with the old man, there had been nasty rumors about "fortune hunting," for quite rightly the old man finally did make her his beneficiary—but how many laughably contradictory views were to be heard about Irene, with the fewest of those who spread them knowing Irene personally. Some called her a fortune-hunting coquette skilled in all the gentle feline arts; others called her a woman with none of a woman's appealing charms, allures, and weaknesses; a third group saw her as a delicate, frail, fin-de-siècle creature, who, with her brother, a rather dissipated man of the world, constituted the last of an old family; yet a fourth group accused her of being brusquely mannish and aggressively rude, while a fifth faction driveled on after her brief visit at the estate about pathological sentimentality.

So there was surely nothing to be learned from what other people said, but in Ella there stirred a dark feeling that she herself would not learn much either and would perhaps soon indulge in uttering similar contradictions.

When Irene kept silent, she said after a while: "I'm supposed to greet you for your brother. He wants to spend next winter in Berlin, and it's not impossible that he'll come to see you."

Irene shook her head. "He won't do that. He finds me too disturbing. And why should he come? In the half year that I was with him so often before moving in with my uncle we had absolutely enough of each other," Irene remarked, suppressing a yawn.

"I can imagine that his loose way of life displeases you. But you are brother and sister, and in your family there has prevailed since times gone by such an unshakeable loyalty—"

"We last ones are ruined and shattered," Irene remarked with a smile, "and besides it's not just on account of what you call his loose way of life. But I have seen much. —To cite a few examples: he no sooner falls in love seriously—or at least he himself thinks it's serious—than right away he takes flight, showing all signs of fear; he flees seriousness, he flees any test of his strength, he flees life, its consequences, its responsibility. A second example: a mere infatuated dalliance that he ends for the sake of a new infatuated dalliance, which of course he has to do with a certain ruthlessness. And what happens then? He sits and laments, he even weeps; he feels sympathy with the poor girl, feels that his unfaithfulness is a weakness, and at night he dreams that she's torturing him to death with a curling iron. —If a man has no complete life left in him but keeps on pumping up the sorry bit that remains, then he looks like my brother. — — May his living ashes rest in peace."

Ella was silent, chilled by what she heard. She could not understand how Irene's sensitive tactfulness, which could not bear the slightest joke about one of her guests, could allow her to speak with such undisguised and indiscreet disgust about her own brother, without even according him the honor of raising his voice indignantly to defend himself—this voice with its profoundly indifferent tone.

Her brother, Udo, could not have brought himself to do that; for of course he never forgot that Irene was one of the von Geyerns, as he was, and thus one with him—one with the family itself, toward which blindly innate and habitual respect was the last and only respect.

A long pause ensued, during which Ella's thoughts wandered far afield from this coolness and toward what warmed her own heart.

"Well—and you? We should talk about you instead," Irene remarked at last—"good Lord, you, you're turning red again, for the third time today! What a dear thing you are, Ella."

Ella reached instinctively for a locket chain at her throat; she felt as though Irene's question had, as if by telepathy, penetrated right into what she had just been thinking about.

Irene saw her confusion and her gesture. "You're engaged?" she asked.

Ella stared at her, helpless. "How could you know that?" she cried out, closing her hand around her locket.

"You child! you don't speak with your words alone," Irene answered very gently and looked deep into her eyes; "are you wearing a picture of him around your neck?"

With a spontaneous move Ella took the delicate chain from her neck and handed it to Irene with profound seriousness. She did not understand it herself, but the person whom she had just found so objectionable had, with just the tone of her voice and a gaze, awakened her trust and opened her heart.

"He's a farmer? a forester? a landowner?" asked Irene as she struggled to open the locket.

"Yes! A farmer. But when did I mention that, then?" Ella said quietly, and it struck her that the most diverse bits of news and thoughts were coming out wordlessly, without her saying anything. Even now she was afraid again what Irene would ask next; what all would she know or want to know about her secret happiness—?

Irene looked for a long time at the man's picture in the locket. Then she leaned well back in her armchair, folded her arms behind her head, and stared silently at the ceiling. She did not ask a single thing. Her eyes were filled with a great pensive sadness, and for a moment she resembled again the little old woman of her childhood, who was so full of gloomy amazement about life.

The sight of her tore Ella from her chair, and before she even knew it herself she was already kneeling by Irene and embracing her in her ardent need to confess and confide. "—We have a long way to go yet—he and I—the two of us have so many material worries, and he has young brothers and sisters to care for, too," she whispered, "and still—Irene, we're so unspeakably happy! You should be so happy!"

Irene did not move. She merely said slowly, dragging out her words: "I don't believe that love saves us from our isolation—."

★ ★ ★

The entire morning after her arrival at the estate Ella had wandered with her old Uncle Geyern from the fields to the stalls. He had put her arm through his the whole time, doing the honors just as though they were paying a visit to a salon and he had to introduce her to the social circle. Ella forgave him in her heart for many a quiet prejudice, totally won over by the cheerful chivalry of the way he was treating her, and the old gentleman seemed completely delighted by the prospect of having this young, lively girl as a guest in his home for weeks.

And so, chatting and joking and on the best terms, they came arm in arm to the midday meal, which, as long as the season permitted, was taken on the large, glass-enclosed veranda of the manor. Irene, who had been out of sight the entire morning, gave them a brief and distracted greeting; clearly her thoughts were not with them, and Ella in this moment could not at all understand what had brought them so intimately close the evening before. The hotel room with its lamplight in any case provided a more beneficial frame for the strangely distant, isolated aspect of her character than did the open countryside with its bright, shining September sun shimmering above the autumnal crowns of the birch trees so that it looked as though their green leaves had hastened to turn yellowish gold for her sake so that all might radiantly proclaim its glory.

"Did you hear the milk cow bellowing, Irene?" the old uncle asked and moved his chair until the warm sun was shining directly on his back; "I just want to tell you, she's nursed that little calf too long, as I said from the start— six weeks is just too long. The little beast is refusing to take any other food for the third day in a row now. If you'd just listen to me for once."

"It will eat other food!" Irene answered, all seriousness, as if they were discussing the endangered life of a person dear to them, "if you'd finally just let me worry about that!"

The old man turned with a tone of suppressed bitterness to Ella: "You must know," he explained with irritation, "I always used to buy my milk cows from the farmers and use the calves that were born here only for draft or slaughter. The breeding of milk cows is clearly a calamity—senseless—"

"The farmers cheat you," Irene broke in quickly, "up to now they've always cheated you. You can't always spot a milk cow's problems when you buy it, they show up only later."

The old man rolled his eyes in lament toward the veranda's ceiling. His sunken cheeks showed more distinctly the light red that was always there and often made him look deceptively younger than he was. "You must know, Ella," he explained to his other niece, while with his slightly trembling hand he poured wine into his glass, "Irene's every third word is: you're being cheated. As if all people were villains and cheats. My God, these good, harmless people, the farmers! But Irene has such horrible fear of losing a few pennies."

"I'm miserly, you must know," Irene chimed in, ironically mocking his way of speaking.

"Yes, and you believe you're not?!" he went on angrily— "well, aren't you? With your miserliness you've totally ruined my nicest and most speculative plans. You go around focusing on the details, but I find that unworthy of the human spirit and try to ponder the big picture and its potential greatness."

"And all the while the individual 'small' things that make up the estate—the animals and plants—go to ruin," she interrupted him without emotion, "why don't you see it from this side? You speculate, perhaps very cleverly, but still in the end it's really just speculation with money, isn't it? Yet I don't care about the money, but rather about the growth of the things themselves. And that's why—"

"Well, why?" he asked excitedly.

"That's why the money flows from them willingly and abundantly right into my hand. I don't extort it from them, they give it to me in gratitude," she added calmly.

Ella wondered silently to herself if the two of them had such stimulating conversations every midday. Of course she could not judge the matter clearly, yet her heart was on the old man's side. She admired his almost youthful interest in everything, his liveliness; for what it was in him that rebelled against Irene's coldness was clearly life, while Irene struck her as more aged and bereft of emotion than the man, who was a good seventy years old.

After the midday meal he prevailed upon Ella to join him for a cup of coffee. "My actual quarters you haven't seen yet at all," and led her into a couple of old-fashioned and cozily furnished gentleman's rooms pervaded by the aroma of his tobacco smoke, "and if you want to do something particularly nice for me, then drop by here for a little while, be it after dinner or at twilight. Dear God, how I miss that, not a solitary soul comes to see me any more."

Ella wanted to fetch his pipe, which was already filled, and straighten out his tall grandfather's chair, but when he noticed what she was doing, he laughed with his beardless, wrinkled mouth, which still had his own well-preserved teeth, and, before she knew what was happening, he had pushed her into the depths of the big chair herself.

"You can have a footstool, too, a proper, embroidered footstool from the old days," he commented eagerly and made her as comfortable as he could. "God, of course I'm a pretty old fellow, but do I have to think about that all the time? always about that and only that? I feel spry, the sun's shining, and I'm still full of love of life, am I not? I can no longer travel very much, but if I had someone here—only now and then—who can offer a smiling face and a cheerful conversation."

He blew some smoke from his pipe, turning carefully to the window, and murmured: "But, you know, Irene, she's just waiting for me to die."

"But Uncle!" Ella cried out in horror, "how can you even say such a thing! You can't possibly be serious. Otherwise you wouldn't so trustingly give Irene a free hand in everything, the way you explained it to me this morning out on the estate."

He made a sorry face and shrugged his shoulders. "She just knows better—I have to give her a free hand," he said uneasily—"or what's now likely the case: everything works for her. Nothing works for me. Of course it's true, I never used to care much about farming but rather about philosophy, and so I dabbled in the arts and went out into the world—. But, really, she didn't bring any practical know-how into it either. And then consider the help: no one likes her, but not only do they all obey her; they all believe firmly in what she's doing—. She is virtually—and not just because it says so in my will—the proprietress of everything. So whether I die or not doesn't make much difference, does it? And still it always seems to me as if she's taking it away from me, piece by piece. — — And, you know, if I were young, I mean really young, then I'd fight with her and take it all back from her—piece by piece, until it was mine again, mine alone—."

He stood at the window, his long gaunt figure leaning slightly forward, and his clear intelligent eyes seemed fixed on something he was imagining. He was speaking almost in a whisper, with a tinge of hatred in his voice.

"But Uncle, you're dreaming!" Ella said, almost smiling, "everything does belong to you, piece by piece. What would be different here on the estate?"

"What would be different?" his eyes lit up cheerfully, "there would be a happy life and happy company here! People with lips and eyes like yours, and with your laugh, and the wine would sparkle in the glasses, and the greenhouse would offer up its flowers—so that we could still feel why we live in this beautiful world. — — Listen!" he added and put his long, slender, aristocratic finger to his lips, "do you hear? Irene's playing. On the piano in her living room. Do you play an instrument? Irene is a master at the piano. Mozart is her favorite. —You know, she's no idea what pleasure she gives me when she plays, which she does almost every day at this hour before I have my little after-dinner nap. It's so wonderful to nod off into a dream while she's playing."

Ella possessed little enough understanding or ear for music, but still, after she had left her uncle, she went, slow and listening, through the large fruit garden on the left side of the house where Irene's windows were.

The glass door that led from the living room directly out into the garden was wide open. Ella did not dare cross the threshold, but she could still see Irene's complete outline as she sat at the piano, and this was a very fascinating sight. She thought Irene looked completely different than usual—with her slender hips and the loose, dark clothing that she wore at home she hardly looked like a woman. Even her slightly raised head, with her half-length hair hanging free and falling so simply to her neck, was like a boy's. As she played she seemed lost in a pleasant dream and looked more charming than usual.

Without taking her hands from the keys, but just softly— softly trying a few chords, she suddenly called out: "I won't do anything to you, you can come closer if you like."

Ella stood embarrassed by the glass door. "So you saw me, then? I really didn't want to disturb you," she apologized.

"That doesn't disturb me—one person more or less." Irene dropped her hands and looked back over her shoulder at her; "and making music is not something so intimate for me as you seem to think."

"It isn't? Isn't it that way for everyone who is really devoted to it? Doesn't it lead you far—far away from everything? That's how it seemed to me, as a layman."

"Yes—far—but not deep; at least it doesn't take *me* anywhere deep," Irene answered and struck a note, "for me music is like reminiscing—do you know what I mean? not actual personal reminiscences, but still as when Grandmother tells the children stories, stories about her life and the lives of others—and the children listen, and in many ways it sounds like their little experiences—but far away and thus sweet. That's how it is."

Ella sat down on the edge of a chair by the glass door. She was happy at having found Irene so communicative. "Have you never done any composing?" she asked, full of interest.

"No." Irene furrowed her brow; she could not understand how Ella could not have known that herself, from what she had just said. "If I could compose, music would naturally be something completely different for me—and then you would have been disturbing me. It wouldn't be Grandmother's stories—but *my* stories that I would create, from the depths of my own life. — — I'm quite an unproductive person."

Irene stood up and then went on: "Don't sit there as if you were made of stone, you're really lively, don't hold back. Did I make you so timid yesterday? Or did the old man turn you against me?"

"Ah, Irene," Ella cried warmly, "old Uncle is good! I like him!"

"I think you like everybody. Did he really win you over with his courting?"

"Oh, rubbish, Irene, he's really not courting me. He's just so remarkably

lively for an old man. Because he's so absolutely healthy, mentally and physically. Think of what that says of his whole previous life. It's nice!"

Irene smiled. She said thoughtfully: "Now just you imagine, that strikes me
as so unnatural and monstrous that sometimes I can barely resist the temptation to tug at his sleeve and whisper in his ear: old man, it's time to die."

Ella almost cried out. She was unable to answer. All her sympathy for Irene
had suddenly vanished as quick as lightning, and all at once she struck her
as strange. To conceal her shock and indignation she rose from her chair and
went looking and checking through the bright room with its old baroque fur-
niture, its light floral wallpaper with no pictures hanging on it, and then she
stopped in front of a well-stocked book rack.

Ella's gaze scanned the neatly arranged works, first distractedly, then with
knowledgeable interest. "From here I shall borrow some things from you that
I should come to know better and more thoroughly," she remarked, "and these
old editions of Voltaire and Rousseau and the other French writers! And here
you have all the Encyclopedists."

"That's what we—the old man and I—read a lot of during our first time
together. We have similar literary tastes. He's still from the culture of the eigh-
teenth century, which was so precise and gracious," Irene said.

"And for the nineteenth century you haven't the least bit of space left on
these shelves?"

"No, as good as none. I find anything modern repellent," Irene answered
curtly.

"Every last bit of it?"

"Well, yes, in principle," Irene answered impatiently, finding it onerous for
the second time to have to explain something to Ella in detail. "I don't mean
this or that particular writer—I mean all art and science that, chronologically
speaking, lies so very close around us. I know perfectly well that it has to be
there—for the sake of you all— but it goes against my taste. The old man on
the other hand would probably like it, if he were of this age. But I must have at
arm's length what I would enjoy. Anything close disgusts me, and this negative
feeling doesn't make me exactly appealing to things and people."

Ella did not answer. "Is she human at all, then?" she thought, deeply astonished.

Irene had turned toward the door, which was just creaking open. One of
the girl servants, wearing a red kerchief that came down low over her eyes and
holding a bundle in her hand, was standing in the doorway with a tight grip on

the handle, in a state of embarrassed helplessness. She clearly wanted to make her presence noted in some way without being disturbing, yet this made her look as if she would much rather have pulled the red kerchief completely down over her face.

"It's you, Maleine," Irene remarked in a curt, businesslike tone. "You want to be on your way. Yes, here's your book." As she spoke, she went over to the desk and handed the girl all kinds of papers and documents from a drawer.

Maleine took them, turned them uncertainly about between her stiff, reddened fingers, struggling to say something that was weighing on her heart, and suddenly ran to Irene, reaching for her hands as she sobbed heavily. When Irene brusquely pulled her hand away, the girl fell to her knees.

Ella looked, her eyes filled with sympathy, at the clumsy, cumbersome figure that the large, patched shawl could not conceal and that, in this position and in the girl's condition, made an embarrassing impression.

"Stop your howling, Madeleine, I don't like it," Irene commanded, and her lips took on such a strong expression of disgust that they twitched.

The girl lay where she was and kept on with her heartbreaking weeping. "Never again!" she stammered, "only for this one time, never again—" and she lifted her pleading hands up to Irene.

"Again and again, more likely!" Irene interrupted her, full of disgust, with a sudden movement pulling her foot back from contact with Maleine, as if she had stepped in something horrid. The girl suddenly dropped her hands; Irene's gesture had had something so emphatic and destructive that even her weeping ceased.

Struggling to raise herself up by the nearest chair, she tried to stand again, reached for the bundle that had tumbled down beside her, and staggered out of the room.

There was a silence. Irene, the look of disgust still on her face, went to the door and closed it.

"What did she do?" Ella asked at last, her voice low.

"— Didn't you see?—"

"That?! —— But Irene, is that so bad that you almost have to kick a person for it—?! I mean, out in the country, that happens—"

"— Out in the country it is quite nice if people mate as do the beasts of the field," Irene completed her sentence, her tone ice-cold.

"Oh, no, I didn't mean that. But I still had to think that she was at least a thief or a totally impossible creature, judging from your behavior."

"A thief on an estate is very unpleasant. But there's no comparison at all. For ultimately, whether something belongs to one person or another is, aside from the slight advantage at stake, a matter of total indifference to me. It's impossible for me to become seriously stirred up for the sake of the laws or people's morality—"

"Not for morality?! Yes, but then—why all that indignation just now — —"

"My God! Out of disgust!! What difference does it make if it's made legitimate a thousand times over! In Maleine's case I can simply show the disgust that I must choke back a thousand other times. But with Frau von X or Y it's just as disgusting. I just can't bear it, this—this — —" her face was distorted, "a murderer who kills I prefer to this—this making of damned, filthy life—" She broke off, sat down, and covered her eyes with her hands.

Ella felt an inner storm and anger. A deep, glowing, gnawing outrage against Irene welled up in her and robbed her of words. What was going on in this excitement within her she herself was not able to analyze, but it was something that turned all her instincts in anger against Irene.

When after a long pause Irene took her hands from her eyes and looked up, Ella was sitting down, pale, her lips pressed together, and staring ahead.

Irene began to smile. "No, what a lively little rabbit you are!" she said, "how passionately you react to everything. I'm sure you'd most like to attack me in anger—well, don't hold your feelings in check, for the moment nothing can seriously fail to arouse my sympathy, after—after this—"

Ella raised her eyes with a gaze that silenced Irene. "I can't!" she blurted out, "don't talk to me—I really don't care—no, I no longer care for you at all, Irene—why should there be anger—we're too far apart for anger."

"Too far apart—yes we truly are," Irene acknowledged slowly, "and you don't feel that until now, and you can't like me any more, and that makes you suffer, you—you child, for liking comes naturally to you."

When Ella remained silent, Irene added after a pause: "Oh, you little people with your feelings! how dependent you are upon the moment! Yesterday you were just as badly motivated to be seized with a feeling of trust in me, and you showed me your heart and the locket you wear over your heart. And today the same kind of nullity—some kind of difference of opinion, some strange woman—causes such an immeasurable hurt—"

Here Ella sprang from her chair so suddenly that Irene fell silent. "Yes, immeasurable hurt!" Ella cried, beside herself, and her blue eyes blazed and flashed in a way that gave her simple, friendly appearance almost something of an unintended pathos; "— it hurts me because I am still closer to this woman than I am to you! It hurts me because what you curse so terribly is also mine— yes, also my highest and most sacred life's dream, do you understand? Because whoever casts aspersions upon it casts aspersions upon me as well, as truly as I am a bride, as truly as I hope to become a mother. And you, as you pull your foot back from our touch, keep your evil, inhuman thoughts quietly to yourself and step aside—step aside before us, for the way is ours—but not yours—no, not yours."

She broke off, almost trembling with emotion, and leaned back against the curtains of the glass door she was standing in front of. She had blushed deeply and tears were glistening in her eyes.

Irene kept perfectly still. She had folded her hands around her knees and inclined her head slightly in thought.

From outside came only the bright twittering of some blackbirds on the gravel path of the fruit garden, and from time to time the branch of a large pear tree, as it stirred in the soft wind, tapped gently against the windowpane.

Then, after a long, oppressive silence, Irene took a deep breath and said in her husky voice: "Yes, you're a person to whom life has given birth in its heartfelt joy. You have strength and heart and the courage of love in you. Just like you, young and unspoiled, is how we all should be."

Ella thought at first she was not understanding correctly. Slowly, with an expression of boundless amazement, she turned around.

No, Irene was not speaking ironically, but obviously in dead earnest. That she could speak ironically at all no one who saw her now would realize. Her whole bearing seemed totally transformed. In her eyes was the strange, vast sorrow of her childhood days; her facial features were somewhat slack, as if from hopeless weariness, and her whole bearing had something almost touching about it.

When she noticed Ella's astonishment and how in her eloquently expressive features—unable as they were to conceal anything—regret, confusion, and new love were struggling with each other, she gently shook her head and went on: "No, no, hold to your views, you grown child. Just don't think I was declaring my love to you. I don't find any of that appealing—what I just said to you and what sounds like praise. I merely grant those things their rights—and take to heart your words: that such monsters as I myself should step aside. — — It is small-minded and all too human not to praise something because one does not love it."

The last words she spoke more to herself than to Ella and seemed no longer to be paying attention to her but rather pondering her own thoughts. Ella stood staring at her and feeling the most contradictory emotions. She had an urge to take Irene in her arms and help her—she did not know how or even with what. She knew only that she felt inexpressibly sorry for her.

After a short pause Irene remarked in a friendly tone, as if she had suddenly just remembered an interesting fact: "Do you remember—the day before yesterday—Frau Doctor Fuhrberger? I spoke with her in Königsberg on numerous occasions. And she always reassured me of her sympathy. No matter what I did to make clear to her that I absolutely did not share her goals and aims, she still felt herself secretly drawn to me, as if she sensed in spite of everything: this woman is one of us. You see, that tells you something. It tells you that in the movement she represents, with its resolve to plunge into life and conquer— that a small seed of this movement has the smell of death upon it. Some kind of dying off of the full, feminine natural life, a waning of the full joy of feminine instincts — —. For those in whom those powers are at full strength — — do not have such a disastrous liking for me. They 'no longer care for me at all' — — like you."

With these words she stood up slowly, walked over to the confused girl, and did what that girl had just now wanted to do herself: she took her gently in her arms and stroked her blond hair. "—Now you two should marry and build your nest," she said suddenly, "—now as long as so much sun is shining so warmly from you. Can't you do it with modest demands and some effort?"

Ella gave her head a vigorous shake; her own cares with life and love, which she had totally forgotten, now, when she heard these words, weighed so heavily upon her heart that she forgot all her sympathy with Irene; now as if by the stroke of a magic wand her trust in Irene as a superior, advising power came over her.

"—We are working—and working—the two of us; we live frugally and devote all our strength to coming together at last— we struggle—and we struggle, day by day—and from all life we want nothing—nothing other than our love and happiness. But we can't do it, and probably won't be able to do it for some time, and the dismal little cares take all the joy out of it," she said, and hot tears ran down her cheeks.

Irene's gaze fixed with an indefinable expression on these streaming tears. She fell silent and looked at her with astonished interest.

★ ★ ★

The morning fog was still steaming and rising so thick over the fields that it concealed all shapes and forms; and far off, at the eastern edge of the forest, the first rays of the sun came shooting out, reddish-yellow and fan-shaped, above the fog-shrouded horizon. With her skirt gathered up, Ella was walking through the estate park to the stalls to fetch a glass of fresh cow's milk from the first milking. She was still too early for that; over in the yard a couple of maids were just loading the big cans for straining the milk onto a cart and did not seem to be in any special hurry to drive over to the stalls. But after the previous evening Ella had had only a brief and restless sleep and had stolen out before dawn, for that was one of the country pleasures for which she was glad to sacrifice any long sleep.

From the cow stall came a variety of noises, the rattling of a chain, a sleepy lowing; the low door had already been unlocked and was standing half open, and Ella was just about to step in and set her glass on the bench by the small stall window when to her utter amazement she heard Irene's voice coming from the depths of the room.

When she first stepped into the big, wide stall she could not make anything out clearly. In the dense twilight there was only the occasional glimmer of a soft, round cow's eye, or the shimmer of the shiny polished edge of a crib when a little gray brightness fell upon it through the opening of the door. The air was so sultry it choked in here, and mixed in with the warm stall air was a bitingly sharp sour smell given off by a yellow-brown fluid in one of the troughs.

When Ella came in, Irene noticed her at once and rose up off her knees behind the trough, where she had been kneeling beside a small, thin little calf. Over her dark woolen dress she was wearing a soaking wet apron; she had rolled up her sleeves, and she was holding a milk pail in her left hand.

When Ella, full of amazement, came closer, Irene set the pail on the edge of the trough and simply said, in a deeply satisfied tone: "It's taken food. For the first time. But now the danger is past. I knew for sure that I would do it."

"Did you feed the little calf that Uncle was talking about yesterday noon and that was calling so for its mother?" Ella asked curiously.

"Yes—it's working, slowly—slowly. I imitated the udder with my hand and let it suck," Irene answered and raised her milk-soaked right hand, giving it a strange form, "you have to clip your nails as short as possible, of course. The mother is kept totally apart now, a magnificent cow! But she's still grieving and longing a lot, you can't watch without feeling sad, but unfortunately she can't be spared this pain."

She was speaking in all seriousness and totally consumed by the topic she was describing to Ella. Then she took off her apron, stepped outside the door, which she threw open wide, and shielded her eyes with her hand as she looked out for the milk can and the maids, who were just arriving.

"It's good that you didn't come until now," she remarked to Ella, "yesterday I told you that music wasn't an intimate concern for me and one person more or less listening didn't bother me at all—but with this it's different. With my animals and plants I'd like to be alone. That's why I avoided you yesterday morning, you and Uncle, when for hours on end you were making every little place on the whole estate unsafe."

The arrival of the cart absolved Ella from making any answer to these charming words; Irene called out a few orders to the girls; and much as her voice sounded frosty as she did so, so her face seemed almost grim with its total lack of goodwill and cheer. With their eyes lowered, shy and awkward, the powerful country girls marched past Irene with their milk cans, one after the other, into the stall, while Irene, like a slim dark shadow, leaned against the wooden door in the dawn's light.

Outside in the meantime the morning light had colored the sky pink across its entire breadth. The fog was beginning to break up, weaving along in flat strips over the stubble fields and meadows, while up in the sky it was tending to ball up into harmless little clouds that went sailing quite quickly over the landscape as if they had to reach another destination by the breakfast hour, while those down on the ground could barely feel anything of the wind that was driving them along high above.

Irene stepped in front of the stall door and turned a searching look toward the pink sky. "It will be another wonderful day, a perfect summer's day— and, I believe, the first of a series of similar days," she said, almost happily; "I am happy for our fruit. The fruit garden you haven't really had a proper look at, for what Uncle shows — — ! I'll take you there later; as a future farmer's wife you have to be interested in that."

Ella nodded and replied: "Yes, indeed, especially after everything I've already heard about it. Do you know, I recently heard that several of our mutual acquaintances are making the most adventurous speculations about how you, for example—you alone—get those giant hazelnuts that grow in bundles."

"With duck droppings," said Irene.

"With—?"

"Duck droppings. You have to let the ducks stay close to the hazel bushes; between hazelnuts and ducks there's a secret sympathetic relationship."

Ella began to laugh.

"You see, that's it: humans laugh when something goes a hair's breadth past their understanding," Irene went on, quite without any sharpness but with an enthusiasm she rarely showed, "people are beginning only now to consider these important and mysterious relationships in nature—can you believe that?! Where did people have their noses and eyes and ears before? — — I'm spending hours, days, months to figure out such things. — — But I can still hear Uncle's laugh, for example, when I advised him against using the chicken incubator. The whole operation with that was veritable nonsense! Just like one of his ideas!"

"But why? why did you advise him against it?" Ella asked with lively interest.

"Why? Because the little chicks from the incubator lose their most useful instincts. They no longer know the signals that the rooster gives when looking for food, they lose the blind certainty of their young lives."

Ella seemed about to say something that she had to struggle to suppress. For a few minutes the two were quiet and listened silently to the tireless jubilation of a lark flying over the stubble field at the side of the stalls. Then suddenly Ella burst out with it: "—Explain to me now—no, now that really is something that I cannot understand at all: you live in these things this way with your whole soul—pursue them with absolute devotion—and just yesterday you claimed so abruptly that you don't care to tolerate a thing that becomes too close to you, and that you can enjoy something only from a great distance."

Irene interrupted her brusquely: "—Who's talking about enjoying, then? Who's telling you that that's something I enjoy? How can you know that this doesn't require a great, a very great self-sacrifice on my part? Do you think I have the body, or the habits, or the nerves for farmwork—?"

"That's just what I can't understand, Irene," Ella said meekly, "why would you force yourself to do that and endure all this—even the pregnant mother animal and the hungry calf, while—while for example Maleine found you so unmerciful."

"Ah, Maleine!" Irene repeated, furrowing her brow in disdain, "well, that's the limit for me, then my disgust becomes gigantic. Among plants and animals it doesn't come up. You humans, you isolate and oppress me with one-hundredfold disgust— but among these much more primitive forms of existence, among those that still grow so very directly out of the natural soil, then my disgust eases a bit—and I release myself a bit from my self—and then perhaps in fact I do a little of what you all try to do in such generous and manifold fashion and with ever new sensations and passions and love affairs, but still try to do in vain: I fuse with what is around me—" Her face had become very serious, and in its seriousness almost reverent.

Ella stopped asking. She was suddenly ashamed of her questioning and of all the clumsy, heavy-handed, and awkward things that people said to people. Irene's way, when she spoke with this husky voice, which could be like distant music, had such suggestive power that for a moment Ella could feel how a person might prefer to let a cool flower glide through one's fingers rather than embrace someone—.

One of the maids came with the first bucket of milk, still steaming from the stall, and Ella went to fetch her glass to have it filled. When she came out again, Irene was no longer by the door. The morning went by without their encountering each other again. But when midday approached without sight of Irene and when she finally sent word to the servant not to set a place for her for dinner, Ella became uneasy and wanted to go find her.

"For God's sake, don't," said the uncle, who was just coming to the table with two wonderful La France roses and asked Ella to put one in her hair and one at her breast, "you don't have to worry about Irene. Sometimes she doesn't even eat at all, sometimes she has something quite funny, alone in her room, for example, some kind of cereal or simple soup, then again at other times nothing but little delicacies. Why bother her?"

He grinned, quite pleased at the sight of the small table set for two, and took pains to play the most pleasant and entertaining tablemate for Ella. Soon the both of them were in the most cheerful mood. Here Ella no longer felt clumsy, heavy-handed, and awkward; here she was not afraid to offend, hurt, or misunderstand. She needed only be her fresh and lively self, as she was, to get on in perfect harmony with the old uncle and quite simply rejuvenate him.

When it was time for dessert, the old man, out of the joy of his heart, had champagne brought from the wine cellar. The seldom-used silver bucket was brought to the table, the cork flew from the thick-necked bottle, the old-fashioned, long, fluted glasses clinked, and the old man's rosy cheeks went a darker pink, like a child's when it skips school. "Life with you is good!" he said to Ella and filled her glass anew, "yes, if you knew how it was when I first drank champagne with Irene—. Since then it's tasted just plain bitter to me, you must know."

Ella was cautiously silent, because it occurred to her only now that the old uncle's feelings toward Irene were considerably different then than they were now, and that now perhaps a good deal of the rancor of the rejected man might still be at work within him. She herself liked him with his chivalric charm, but she could well imagine that a decade ago that same charm might have been going through a dangerous phase of transition.

After a few additional glasses of very cold French champagne the increasing loquacity of the old man took on a tinge of the elegiac. He began to talk to her about the necessity of not being buried when he died but rather burned in a crematorium. "Just not back to the earth!" he declared, all afire, "it's best for the mortal shell to go up in smoke and flames! One less ugly image would then cling to death, and that's the important thing. If we could only imagine death to ourselves as something indestructibly beautiful, then perhaps dying would be more festive, even more cheerful."

"I find the one as unpleasant as the other," Ella admitted frankly, "and I think the loveliest thing about death would still be if, at the end of a long and beautiful life—it were a death for two."

The old man nodded approvingly. "Just make sure that they really burn me, for Irene favors burial," he said, and his thoughts kept coming back to Irene; "she claims that such a burial plot, with green grass and flowers, is something precious. She thinks right away of fertilizer—you see, that's really her specialty—duck droppings and graves," he asserted glumly.

Ella, who was beginning to worry about her uncle's condition, encouraged him to adjourn their festive table for two so that he could go lay his head down in his room for a while.

"Very well, my dearest, my fairest," he replied obediently and, rising, raised his champagne glass to her, "then let us drink one more toast: to two kindred spirits, shall we say? For I get along much better with you than with Irene, wouldn't you say? You will prefer me to her, because I am more content — — because the two of us are more content—"

Ella nodded, clinked glasses with him, and emptied hers. "Youth seeks out youth!" she proclaimed in high spirits and was a bit unclear whether she herself was far removed from being as tipsy as he was from the champagne.

After she had carefully accompanied the old man to his room and made him comfortable on the divan with all kinds of cushions and blankets, he sat up again and listened toward the window. "Irene's not playing," he murmured, "if only she'd play a little—lull me to sleep. —— Dinner music —— sleep music; ah, I beg you, go find her and tell her that she should do an old man like me the favor," he added, almost miserably, and his deep weariness lamed his tongue.

Ella went out quietly. To go to Irene uninvited she preferred not to do, and so she cut through the fruit garden as she had yesterday and once again found the glass door wide open, but today the room was empty.

Ella turned around and went out the gate of the garden's fence into the open field. There, in the middle of a meadow, its high grass untouched by any scythe, stood Irene. Around about her a very young foal was making grotesque jumps, its long clumsy legs and disproportionately heavy head kept on making it stumble. Irene was teasing the foal and playing with it, with one moment its loud whinny, the next moment her bright laughter resounding across the meadow's fragrant, waving grass, and, with every move she made, Irene's loose hair fell over her brow and eyes. The foal's mother stood lethargically nearby, munching clover and watching with sleepy eyes.

Someone seeing Irene from this distance could take her by her size and gestures to be a half-grown girl playing in the meadow.

"And so that's what has made you forget your music!" thought Ella and stared at her as if she were an enigma. She felt it had to be embarrassing for Irene to be caught doing this, and she was ready to leave quietly.

Then Irene called over the meadow: "Just wait, I'll be right along, I wanted to speak to you anyway!" And she was already on her way, while the foal, wagging its thin tail, watched in amazement.

"You surely must find the animal immensely ugly, don't you?" she asked and brushed the hair away from her hot face, "but you just have to feel its silky-soft little hide, and in a twinkling it becomes beautiful—wonderfully beautiful."

With her hand she was shielding her eyes, which were weakened and could bear little light, and looking back to the meadow as it lay in the shimmering, trembling afternoon sun. "Isn't that a kind of paradise, the life of this little foal, which was born in this meadow and thinks it the grand garden of the world?" she remarked, "which really knows about nothing but this tall grass and red clover at its feet, this bright blue sky full of sun over its head, and the warm, breathing body of its mother, which provides it with nourishment, a haven, and a bed at night? Yes, that surely is a paradise. And it's good that the animal can't talk out loud and describe the paradise of its life to us, because otherwise all the longing would leave us empty and ill."

"How cheerful you are, and how bright you look," Ella said happily, "and I was worrying about you because you didn't come for dinner."

Irene gave her head a slight shake and headed back toward the house. "If I seem happy, then you are to thank for it," she answered, "I want to explain it to you right away. Were you just going to your room? May I go with you?"

"Yes, of course, if you want to make me happy." Ella took the shortest way diagonally across the park to her room, which was located on the ground floor beside the main living quarters. "Uncle will probably have long since fallen asleep by now and no longer miss your music."

"He'll become accustomed to that easily enough, or think of another lullaby. For soon now there'll be a different kind of life in this house, when you marry your farmer and move here and also bring along your two little brothers, whom you still have to look after," said Irene.

Ella suddenly stopped in the doorway of her room as she was entering. "How do you mean that?" she asked, uncomprehending.

Irene sat down in the middle of the divan, raised her head, and went calmly on: "The old man will simply come to life again! And you will all live, happy and at work, around him. He is sure to leave the properties to you and your family once and for all in his will."

"My God, you're talking nonsense!" Ella cried out in alarm and went over to her, "I was just with Uncle Geyern. He doesn't know anything about it."

"He'll know about it tomorrow," Irene answered, "for that is the right and sensible thing to do, and I shall take care of arranging everything. Just leave that completely to me. The old man will be giving himself the most heartfelt joy by doing that, and he always obeys my will, in spite of all his grumbling—for in fact he feels all too well how practical my decisions are, how little subjectivity plays a role—"

Ella had fallen at her feet and buried her face in Irene's lap. She was weeping.

Irene's features took on an expression of suffering. "Pull yourself together!" she said curtly, "take it as a self-evident given, and act accordingly as well. It's not the end of a world here. I don't see how you can become so excited about something like that."

"—I still can't believe it at all!" exclaimed Ella blissfully through her tears, looking up out of moist, radiant eyes that were like the eyes of a child being showered with presents, "—just imagining that we are now finally—finally— and so suddenly—and that in all our happiness we'll be living with you—Oh, Irene, and we shall all be living for you, too—"

"I think you're dreaming," Irene remarked coolly, rejecting the idea, "I won't be around at all. I'll be leaving here straightaway."

"You'll be leaving?!" Ella looked at her, surprised, and reached for her hands, "— right now? But where are you going, why? Oh, Irene, I truly believed you actually liked me and that's why you wanted to have me here—rather than living alone with Uncle."

Irene smiled imperceptibly, a smile peculiar only to her, which merely flitted around the corners of her mouth without enlivening her gaze. "If the old man weren't here with me I would like it better, of course. But if I simply must endure the proximity of a person, then I really would most prefer that of the elderly. On the other hand, with you young people—" here she cast a strange glance past Ella and added more quietly: "— when you come to be— like Maleine—"

Ella fought back the embarrassed feeling that came over her with Irene's words; the strong, warm feeling of gratitude in her and an almost jubilant feeling of happiness had engulfed everything. Nevertheless it only just now occurred to her again how far—how infinitely far they were from each other, just now, where Irene's actions made them seem so close.

She remarked timidly: "But dear Irene, then for you all this is only a loss! You do belong here so completely. You're devoted to every little plant, to every animal, to every stone here—more than to anything else!"

"Plants, animals, stones, and the like can be found just about everywhere, after all, they're not confined to Uncle Geyern's estate," Irene answered, shrugging her shoulders, "that's how they're so pleasantly different from the human objects you love to cling to, each acting as if it were so terribly original. To me it's all the same. I'll find in every blade of grass and every cloud what I need. Mine is not the old man's estate, for mine is the entire world."

"No! In spite of that, I'll not bear it! The idea that we're chasing you out of here, I can't bear it!" Ella called out excitedly and sprang to her feet, "you can put as pretty a face on it now as you like, but even then it still remains an immense sacrifice of love, a renunciation of such selflessness—"

Irene became impatient. "Sacrifice! Renunciation! I want to tell you something, Ella, it is tedious to have to explain everything to you in such elaborate clarity so that you don't judge it according to convention. You see, you may have learned much and even pondered all kinds of things, as people say, but you're not especially clever, my dear."

"You're a noble person, Irene, and you're saying all that just to cover it up," Ella persisted, without showing emotion.

Irene sighed. "Did you really not see, before, in the meadow, how happy I looked? And didn't I explain to you that you were the reason? Well, then. You caused me to have a thought that made me happy—just how am I to make that clear to your homespun reason? In me your comment of the evening before left its mark, when you said people like me should step aside—no, just don't become excited right away now!—so then I somehow understood that perhaps I could bring myself into a better, more pure harmony with all things if I really did that once. —In my feelings I cannot be one with you, I am not able to— but through such an act I can be, to a certain degree: I won't stay on here to be disruptive in the midst of your differentness, but instead I'll give you all room— and in that way take part in it a little."

She was unable to keep on talking because Ella had her arms around her neck and was covering her cool, pale mouth with kisses, but she put up a struggle.

"Don't talk that way—I can't bear to hear you talk that way—you have a better heart than all of us," Ella begged passionately, "and that's why it can't stay that way! No, surely not! While it may be the first step that you build selflessly upon the happiness of others—the last step will be your own happiness, and you really will live and love and rejoice as I do!"

"Never will a delicate blade of meadow grass grow into a fruit tree," answered Irene in a superior tone, trying to calm the excited girl, "let it be. Only in the smallest, most modest role can I serve life and its goals—I cannot take part. When in the warm egoism of your love you lean upon your husband, or when you will feel the pleasure of nursing your child, then in all that there resides an infinitely greater outpouring of feeling than in my 'renunciation' for you all."

She freed herself from Ella's arms as though she could no longer bear the caresses that she had put up with reluctantly and that she had absolutely not returned. Then, silent and thinking to herself, she paced the room.

The sun was already shining at a rather low angle through the large crowns of the beeches and birches of the park, its slanted rays filling the whole room with a peaceful gold light that bestowed a transformed brightness on every object.

Irene may have felt herself reminded by that of the late afternoon hour: she stopped pacing back and forth. "They're waiting for me in the servants' house," she commented, "we've certainly just had a long, long discussion here, too!

You, stay and write the letter that's probably already burning in your heart, Frau Farmer."

And approaching Ella and gazing into her rosy, girlish face, she went on slowly: "I wish you happiness. You will feel all manner of happiness—there are, of course, several sorts of happiness—but there is one—mine—that none of you shall ever feel. You may like to live here on the estate, and you may come to love every bit of it, as farmers and as people. But still, be like me and do not take it for granted. Do not take it all at equal value, the most grand along with the most minor thing, as if it were all one and the same! as if, for example, it were all there just for us people. See it instead as prevailing in its own beauty, from eternity to eternity—and we ourselves only a small part, a tiny part of it that also flows humbly into the mighty whole."

Suddenly, she said in a different tone—with an almost tormented tone in her voice: "You know, artists feel about things in a similar way. Artists still do, more than others. Likely for that reason I have felt in many a moment—and hoped arrogantly—that I could find salvation in doing that. But I am no artist ——I am unfruitful," she ended very quietly, the way people admit something shameful. She had gone pale as she spoke these last words. Slowly she turned toward the door.

Ella had stood there the whole time with her arms at her sides, looking at her wide-eyed. Now she said, pleading urgently: "Irene!—don't leave like this! You see, how am I to thank you—even if I embrace you, it's unpleasant for you. Not once have you kissed me or given me a loving touch. Irene—release me from this burden—let me be close to you—I am longing to be!"

Irene raised her hand, strangely, almost with solemnity, like someone who is about to give a blessing. But her hand reached out, glided with open fingers from Ella's hair down to her soft neck, as a hesitant, almost shy caress. And again Ella felt secretly, as she had on the first evening of her reunion with Irene, the searching and trembling in these groping figures—something like a longing, or a question, or even only an anxiety that she did not understand; and then when Irene took her face in her cool hands to kiss her lips, then she felt a shudder and suddenly closed her eyes ——

Yet no sooner had Irene quietly left the room than Ella dashed to the window, opened it wide, and leaned out. —If she really was going to the servants' house, then she had to go along the alley of beeches here not far away.

The sky was aglow. As if, from the sinking sun along the whole western horizon, the landscape had been ignited in smoldering flames, a deep crimson red colored the entire background, against which the trees of the old park stood out in almost solemn stillness. A strange coal black, they stood there against this wall of fire.

Now Irene was coming. She was walking slowly, the hem of her skirt brushing the ground. A few times she stopped and reached out toward the autumn branches, as though she were about to pluck the colorful leaves—they, too, coal black against the crimson red—and branches and twigs and all lines all around seemed behind the sun's back to be joining into fantastic new forms, in which Irene's outstretched arm and the fine line of her back merely formed a few more dark lines.

Ella folded her hands and watched her, her eyes burning. Before her eyes there was a whirling and fluttering of nothing but impetuous happiness, almost painful in its impetuousness; it simply came upon her with all its sudden images of the future, each chasing upon and replacing the next. She had Irene to thank for all that; Irene had brought her life's happiness into the room just as someone can break off a rose and throw it in through the window. But only in that moment when Irene herself left her did Ella feel it completely, and she was released from one last spell.

She wanted to thank her, so much, so much! But she was able to think of nothing, to feel nothing but happiness—and from this warm happiness Irene was so far—so far—removed! There she was now, walking away between the grand old birch trees, delicate and slender, her head slightly inclined as if from a weary, weighing sorrow—and Ella felt her heart suddenly contract, and she felt as though she had to call out something after her—loud, loud— and as though Irene were going slowly from her, ever farther and farther away from her, not merely with the few steps she was taking, but ever farther from her gratitude and her understanding. ——

Ella pressed both hands to her dazzled eyes.

No, she would always remember Irene for what she had done, for the rest of her life until she died. But just for now, only in this first euphoria and joy, it was as though Irene were eluding her. —Was even that ingratitude? Again and again Irene was sure to stand before her, like a light in the darkness, like a grand, sorrowful gesture. — Only now—just not now! First of all something of the full happiness, something of the magnificent plenitude of life—but after that, yes, then it would be Irene who would lay claim to a good portion of her and be ever present—but later —— — later —— yes, perhaps really only much, much later —— — when she was old—not until she was old — — —— — in death —.